Reviewers Love Meliss

"Melissa Brayden has become one of the mo genre, writing hit after hit of funny, relatable, and very sexy stories for women who love women."—*Afterellen.com*

You Had Me at Merlot

"Sweet and delicious…Melissa has packed this story full of quirky characters who are all unforgettable and contributing in their own way to making the story memorable."—*LESBIReviewed*

The Forever Factor

"Melissa Brayden never fails to impress. I read this in one day and had a smile on my face throughout. An easy read filled with the snappy banter and heartfelt longing that Melissa writes so effortlessly." —*Sapphic Book Review*

The Last Lavender Sister

"It's also a slow burn, with some gorgeous writing. I've had to take some breaks while reading to delight in a turn of phrase here and there, and that's the best feeling."—*Jude in the Stars*

Exclusive

"Melissa Brayden's books have always been a source of comfort, like seeing a friend you've lost touch with but can pick right up where you left off. They have always made my heart happy, and this one does the same."—*Sapphic Book Review*

Marry Me

"A bride-to-be falls for her wedding planner in this smoking hot, emotionally mature romance from Brayden…Brayden is remarkably generous to her characters, allowing them space for self-exploration and growth."—*Publishers Weekly*

To the Moon and Back

"*To the Moon and Back* is all about Brayden's love of theatre, onstage and backstage, and she does a delightful job of sharing that love… Brayden set the scene so well I knew what was coming, not because it's unimaginative but because she made it obvious it was the only way things could go. She leads the reader exactly where she wants to take them, with brilliant writing as usual. Also, not everyone can make office supplies sound sexy."—*Jude in the Stars*

Back to September

"You can't go wrong with a Melissa Brayden romance. Seriously, you can't. Buy all of her books. Brayden sure has a way of creating an emotional type of compatibility between her leads, making you root for them against all odds. Great settings, cute interactions, and realistic dialogue."—*Bookvark*

What a Tangled Web

"[T]he happiest ending to the most amazing trilogy. Melissa Brayden pulled all of the elements together, wrapped them up in a bow, and presented the reader with Happily Ever After to the max!"—*Kitty Kat's Book Review Blog*

Beautiful Dreamer

"I love this book. I want to kiss it on its face…I'm going to stick *Beautiful Dreamer* on my to-reread-when-everything-sucks pile, because it's sure to make me happy again and again."—*Smart Bitches Trashy Books*

Two to Tangle

"Melissa Brayden does it again with a sweet and sexy romance that leaves you feeling content and full of happiness. As always, the book is full of smiles, fabulous dialogue, and characters you wish were your best friends."—*The Romantic Reader*

Entangled

"Ms. Brayden has a definite winner with this first book of the new series, and I can't wait to read the next one. If you love a great enemies-to-lovers, feel-good romance, then this is the book for you."—*Rainbow Reflections*

"*Entangled* is a simmering slow burn romance, but I also fully believe it would be appealing for lovers of women's fiction. The friendships between Joey, Maddie, and Gabriella are well developed and engaging as well as incredibly entertaining…All that topped off with a deeply fulfilling happily ever after that gives all the happy sighs long after you flip the final page."—*Lily Michaels: Sassy Characters, Sizzling Romance, Sweet Endings*

Love Like This

"Brayden upped her game. The characters are remarkably distinct from one another. The secondary characters are rich and wonderfully integrated into the story. The dialogue is crisp and witty."—*Frivolous Reviews*

Sparks Like Ours

"Brayden sets up a flirtatious tit-for-tat that's honest, relatable, and passionate. The women's fears are real, but the loving support from the supporting cast helps them find their way to a happy future. This enjoyable romance is sure to interest readers in the other stories from Seven Shores."—*Publishers Weekly*

Hearts Like Hers

"Once again Melissa Brayden stands at the top. She unequivocally is the queen of romance."—*Front Porch Romance*

Eyes Like Those

"Brayden's story of blossoming love behind the Hollywood scenes provides the right amount of warmth, camaraderie, and drama." —*RT Book Reviews*

Strawberry Summer

"This small-town second-chance romance is full of tenderness and heart. The 10 Best Romance Books of 2017."—*Vulture*

"*Strawberry Summer* is a tribute to first love and soulmates and growing into the person you're meant to be. I feel like I say this each time I read a new Melissa Brayden offering, but I loved this book so much that I cannot wait to see what she delivers next."—*Smart Bitches, Trashy Books*

First Position

"Brayden aptly develops the growing relationship between Ana and Natalie, making the emotional payoff that much sweeter. This ably plotted, moving offering will earn its place deep in readers' hearts." —*Publishers Weekly*

By the Author

Romances

Waiting in the Wings

Marry Me

Heart Block

Exclusive

How Sweet It Is

The Last Lavender Sister

First Position

The Forever Factor

Strawberry Summer

Lucky in Lace

Beautiful Dreamer

Marigold

Back to September

You Had Me at Merlot

To the Moon and Back

When You Smile

Soho Loft Romances:

Kiss the Girl

Ready or Not

Just Three Words

Seven Shores Romances:

Eyes Like Those

Sparks Like Ours

Hearts Like Hers

Love Like This

Tangle Valley Romances:

Entangled

What a Tangled Web

Two to Tangle

Visit us at www.boldstrokesbooks.com

When You Smile

by

Melissa Brayden

2024

WHEN YOU SMILE

ISBN 13: 978-1-63679-671-0

This Trade Paperback Original Is Published By
Bold Strokes Books, Inc.
P.O. Box 249
Valley Falls, NY 12185

First Edition: June 2024

Credits
Editor: Ruth Sternglantz
Production Design: Stacia Seaman
Cover Design by Inkspiral Design

Acknowledgments

When looking back over my life, the most formative period, by far, was my time spent on a college campus during my undergraduate years. The second most formative time was the pursuit of my MFA. Put the two together and you have the setting for this little romance that took off in my brain and never looked back. Taryn and Charlie are special characters, chasing dreams and negotiating their feelings, outlooks, and who it is they truly want to be in this world. There's something incredibly pure and important about their journey that I wanted to explore in more depth. I hope you enjoy the ride.

If I were giving out donuts, there are so many people I would need to send boxes and boxes to in repayment for their help with this novel. First box goes to my kind, patient, and very smart editor, Ruth Sternglantz, who helps me see what I cannot on my own. Another dozen thanks to Sandy Lowe for guidance, a sounding board, and help to get the best books written. Radclyffe gets so many donuts for steering the ship and allowing me to stay on board for all the fun stories. Stacia Seaman, Toni Whitaker, Cindy Cresap are all invited to my donut party for the excellent and complicated work they do behind the scenes. I hope all the proofreaders are hungry because without them, I'm sunk. Inkspiral Designs crafted another great cover for me, so I'm sending out the baked goods. I don't have to send the people in my home donuts, because we have them so often as it is, but Alan, Everett, and Camryn are certainly worthy and supply me with the perfect amount of love, cheerleading, and space (when I need it) to create.

Readers, I'd send you all tons of donuts if I could because you make all of this possible. Thank you for discovering my work, hanging around, and going on these little journeys along with me. Let's keep it going! Donut Cheers!

For all the creators

Prologue

There were so many things that eleven-year-old Taryn Ross loved about summer. The manner in which the sunset mixed its colors and sent them out for all to admire. A thick, cold milkshake just out of the blender. The way her skin felt when it touched the cool water from the pool for the first time. But the best thing by far about this particular summer was her babysitter, Charlotte Adler. There was simply no human half as beautiful, cool, or kind. Taryn more than looked up to Charlie, as her friends called her, but actually sat in amazement of her. She was five years older than Taryn with amazing curves, red sunglasses, and the blond hair everyone else seemed to buy but came naturally to Charlie. She also carried raspberry gum in her bag at all times and laughed genuinely at Taryn's attempts to make her smile.

"I get it. You're adorable, but don't fall on your head," Charlie had called in response to Taryn's silly handstand that afternoon. "I think your parents would prefer I return you to them alive." She then checked her phone for incoming texts from her wide array of teenage friends. She probably had a million offers that weekend for who knew what, and Taryn wanted to. From the table on the deck beneath the sun umbrella, Charlie smiled and shook her head at something on her screen. How was she so effortlessly cool but also intelligent and softhearted? Taryn wanted to be every bit like Charlie, but also be her best friend. Complicated. She'd have to settle for Charlie's once or twice a week charge while Taryn concocted new reasons for her parents to have to leave the house more often.

The summer was coming to a close, and the school year would be starting soon. There had been moments during their summer together that were seared into Taryn's memory like a stamp on a passport, the details too important to fade. Today felt like it might become one of them, her senses heightened, the afternoon in full blaze beneath the unforgiving sun. The Popsicle she'd been savoring had melted, leaving a red and blue sticky stream down her wrist. Who even cared when they were having so much fun? The day had been entirely worry free and carried them on its winds. Once she and Charlie bounced happily from the pool in her backyard to the deck, they let the warm air dry the drops of water from their sun-kissed skin. There was laughter, music from the portable speaker Charlie always seemed to carry in her oversized babysitter tote, and snacks like the Popsicles her mother had left them with a note to *Enjoy yourselves!* It was shaping up to be the best day Taryn had experienced in a long time.

"You might want to take that bracelet off," Charlie said, nodding her head in the direction of Taryn's silver charm bracelet, now under assault from the dripping Popsicle. The bracelet had been a gift from her father on her ninth birthday, and whether or not it was juvenile, she loved it completely because he'd taken the time to pick it out for her. She'd been blessed with wonderful parents who were both funny and warm. Their three-person family was small but tight. So far, Taryn had collected a total of seven charms for her bracelet but had her eye on a four-leaf clover she hadn't quite saved up enough to purchase. She'd been born in March, after all, and claimed anything Irish as her own.

"Oh, man. Thanks," Taryn said, catching the clasp and releasing the bracelet. It slipped easily from her wrist and landed silently on the woven outdoor table. She wasn't much of a jewelry person, but the bracelet was different. It was a way for her to feel like herself, express the parts of what made her unique. She slid a strand of her hair behind her ear. Generally boring and brown, it was currently sun-streaked from three months of pool time, making it one step closer to Charlie's blond.

"Anytime. Want another soda?" Charlie stood between her and the glistening blue water, the towel on her shoulder partially covering the top of her red bikini. She had boobs already. Good ones. Taryn blinked up at the striking image, the way the light offered both highlight and contrast, terms she'd learned in the art course her mother had signed her up for on Wednesdays. Taryn blinked, lost in the captivating sum of all the elements combined. The sky was a swirl of orange, pink, and purple—almost too beautiful to look at, as was Charlie. So much so that she'd forgotten the question. Charlie took a step forward, and the composition dissolved, the blue water appearing again, her silhouette gone. "Taryn, you in there? Do you want something to drink? I could write out the question."

"Water," she said quickly, eyes on the pool, trying to disguise her momentary fixation. Intriguing images had always been fascinating to Taryn. She was drawn in to the mystery, lost in what made things beautiful, even if she wasn't sure how to be a part of the beauty just yet. That was okay. An outsider looking in.

"Are you pool drunk?" Charlotte asked, her lips curling into a grin. As she passed, she placed a hand on Taryn's head affectionately.

"No. Just tired, I think." They'd been swimming for the past two hours, so the response made sense, even if it wasn't the true reason for her distraction.

"We can have dinner on the couch if you want. Frozen pizza."

"And lemonade slushes?" That had her sitting up straight. Charlie had made them slushes the last time she'd been over, and Taryn had never tasted anything so refreshing in her entire life. She'd tried to duplicate the treat on her own but had failed miserably because, well, she wasn't Charlie.

"You're on." Charlie stepped out onto the deck with one foot, mimicked shooting a basket and scoring, and then went back inside. The whole thing left Taryn grinning.

"Best day ever," she called after Charlie. Actually, the *day* was minutes from slipping into evening, which meant her parents would be home soon along with Charlie's, Ronnie and Deirdre. Ronnie and Taryn's father worked for the same luxury car dealership and had apparently hit it off while shooting the breeze one slow day in the showroom. Until she'd met Charlie, Taryn had argued vehemently that she didn't need a sitter anymore. She'd be going into the sixth grade soon, an age when kids took babysitting jobs *themselves*. It was frustrating to still be hanging out in the kid section when she was much more mature than her family gave her credit for. Her mother, however, was adamant that Taryn couldn't stay on her own until her twelfth birthday, still seven ridiculously long months away.

"You realize I'm not going to burn the house down, right? I'll watch TV on the couch. Maybe I'll get wild and read a book, which you always encourage me to do. I don't need someone looking over my shoulder."

"Uh-uh." Her mom was not convinced. "None of that matters. It's about my peace of mind. Next year, things will be different. Until then, you're out of luck."

Taryn's whole opinion changed once she'd gotten to know Charlotte Adler. Those protests had died easily on her lips. They had a good time together, and with Charlie, Taryn learned more about the world than she ever had in school. In addition to babysitting, Charlie also lifeguarded at the YMCA, and that pool had always offered Taryn and her friends a front-row view to the older kids' lives and interactions. The teenage boys showed up beneath Charlie's tall chair anytime she was on duty, looking like they'd done about fifty push-ups before walking over. Taryn and her friends would bet on which of the boys Charlie would acknowledge first. As the guys strutted past her chair, Charlie would offer an occasional four-fingered wave without so much as turning her head in their direction. This was a move Taryn had decided to adopt, practicing the still-chin, four-fingered hello in the mirror multiple times a week. Eventually, she'd given up, conceding that she couldn't pull it off. She was no Charlie. But then, who was?

"Come talk to me while I make the pizza," Charlie called from inside. "We can toss a few extra pepperoni on for a hell of a good time."

Taryn didn't have to be asked twice. She quickly gathered her towel and bracelet and scurried inside. Perched on the bar stool across the counter, she tossed the extra pepperoni onto the pizza like tiny frisbees and told Charlie all about her friends, Lara and Alyssa, and how she hoped they'd have lunch together this year, the first time their group would encounter multiple lunch periods.

"I'm going to give you the best piece of advice I've ever received," Charlie said, gesturing with her spatula. "Are you ready?"

"So ready," Taryn said, unable to stop smiling or take her eyes away from Charlie. She was captivated by the way the part in Charlie's blond hair seemed to change effortlessly whichever direction she happened to flip it.

"Don't worry about what might happen until it does. You just wind up wasting a lot of energy that you could have spent"—she gestured to the pie in front of her—"eating a lot of pizza or running with your dog in the backyard once the sun goes down." Both things sounded amazing to Taryn. "Does that make sense?" Charlie asked. She met Taryn's eyes with her shimmering blue ones.

"Totally. I'll try not to stress. You know, or whatever." She had to look away. The sincerity of the conversation made her inexplicably nervous. She did better with Charlie when she played the role of mischievous kid.

"There you go. You got this. Sixth grade will be a breeze, and I can't wait to hear all about it."

That part made Taryn's heart swell because Charlie really did seem to care about her. They were friends in their own unique way, even if Charlie was paid to be there. She was always friendly to Taryn when they saw each other in the real world, going out of her way to stop and chat, making Taryn look like a social rock star in front of her eleven-year-old friends.

They spent the next two hours chilling on the couch watching a PG-13 movie about the last night of high school that made Taryn feel mature and educated on all things teenager.

"Asking for a friend. Are high school parties really this dramatic?" Taryn asked after a girl ran out the door crying while her best friend grabbed another beer and glared after her. Intimidation tapped her on the shoulder. How was she going to survive in that world?

Charlie shrugged and stole a handful of buttery popcorn from the large silver bowl between them. "Depends on the party."

"Then I might be in big trouble. I'm going to be that lonely girl on the side of the screen looking for adults to make conversation with."

Charlie frowned. "No, you're not. But I think everyone feels that way before you figure out who you're gonna be."

"Cool to know, I guess." The truth was Taryn didn't have a clue who she was going to be, but it was clear that Charlie's calm confidence meant she already had. It made Taryn want to try harder to put her stamp on the world—as her dad often said—and go out there and take on the hard stuff. Maybe she should learn to play an instrument or run for class office. Charlotte Adler status was something to strive for.

"And do you want to know what I already know?"

Taryn nodded, eager for that information.

"You're gonna go out there and knock this world over with all the things you're going to accomplish, and one day I'm going to get to say I told you so."

Taryn could hardly speak after that. Charlie was probably just trying to be a good role model or whatever, but the words left Taryn on a high for the rest of the movie. She happily ate popcorn, laughed along with Charlie, and secretly wondered about all that was ahead of her that year. Sadly, her fantastic evening was interrupted when the four parents arrived home with grins on their faces, smelling like wine and garlic bread and gushing about their night.

"Tare-Bear," her mother said loudly, encircling her neck from behind. "Charlotte's parents took us to the neatest little pizza place. I'm going to take you there one day soon so you can soak up the culture. So authentic! So chaotic! Your little heart will sing a song."

"Mom, did you have a glass of wine?" That pulled a laugh from the other three adults.

"Vino? Do you mean vino? I did have one. Yes." She gave Taryn's cheek a loud smack. Her mother's excitement at pretty much everything was not at all new. She grabbed hold of life and leapt. Loudly. Taryn didn't. Well, *yet*.

Off to the side, she watched as her father slipped a folded-up wad of cash into Charlie's hand, and she thanked him. While her mom sang something that sounded close to Italian in the kitchen, Charlie took three steps and pulled Taryn into a dedicated hug. "You have a good first week at school, okay? And less worrying, Taryn. You're gonna be great out there. The next time I'm over, I want every detail. I mean it."

Taryn smiled, nodded, and hugged her back, savoring the warmth that came over her but also feeling a little bit shy all of a sudden. Plus, being close to Charlie physically brought on an overwhelming wash of feelings she didn't know how to name. "Yeah, okay. You got it."

Four weeks later, Ronnie, Deirdre, and Charlotte moved from Dyer, Indiana, to sunny California without much notice at all. Ronnie announced plans to open up his own dealership and apparently didn't want to wait. Her dad was sad about that. He popped open a beer in the kitchen and shook his head. "Lost a good salesman and a buddy."

"Wait. The Adlers are moving?" Her heart dropped. She couldn't imagine not having Charlie-nights to look forward to anymore.

"Afraid so, kiddo. Good thing you don't need a babysitter much longer, right?"

"Yeah," she said flatly, her words echoing in her head, hollow and weird. Her chest ached, and all sorts of plans she'd made evaporated. Life without Charlie Adler in it sounded dull and unexciting. The little spark of excitement she'd come to cherish was extinguished in an unceremonious whoosh. "Good thing."

Chapter One

From its historic red and white brick buildings to the sprawling green lawns and colorful trees, Hillspoint University knew how to make an impression. The kaleidoscope of autumn hues grabbed Taryn by the throat the minute she stepped out of the car and into her new life on her own. She swallowed as a rush of intimidation hit. Luckily, she'd been prepared and took a long, slow breath in, reminding herself that everyone was nervous on the first day of anything important. She'd made a mental plan to keep her anxiety in check, and part of that meant physical check-ins with herself, deep breaths, and staying out of her own head.

She'd been impressed when she'd visited the university three years ago, imagining she'd attend as a freshman and take the world by storm. She'd had goals and aspirations and confidence for days on that visit, which felt like almost another lifetime now. She remembered being gobsmacked by the campus that looked like something out of a beautiful film, proud that her grades had all but guaranteed her admission. Unfortunately, she'd made the decision to defer.

She took a deep breath and, as anxious as she was, just let the moment wash over her. The grounds, the buildings, the meticulously maintained walkways were nothing like the community college she'd studied at for the last two years. Hillspoint felt vast and important by comparison and steeped in traditions she'd only just begun to study. She felt smarter just standing there and like her life was about to begin. The world suddenly felt full and limitless.

"You okay?" her mother asked quietly, giving her elbow a squeeze.

"It's now or never, right?"

"Tare-Bear. You're gonna knock 'em on their asses. Remember who you are."

She nodded as her mom scooted around the other side of the car to gather a box to carry up.

"They said you're on the fourth floor?" her dad asked, loading her belongings onto the portable cart he was so proud to own. She had to admit, he looked good, stronger lately and with more stamina. At the same time, she didn't want him to overdo. He kept a smile on his face, but each small movement caused a weakening behind his eyes signaling his supreme effort. Taryn hated everything about the new normal. *Fuck fate*. Thank God his prognosis was good. The unexpected stroke and her father's slow recovery struggles had been devastating. But at least the damage hadn't been as extreme as they'd once feared. He'd had to adjust his life and manage his own expectations about what he was capable of, but he was still here. He even managed to smile more now than he ever had before, appreciating the life he'd almost lost.

"Yes, but I can get that stuff." He wasn't listening. Just as stubborn as he was generous. She turned, seeking backup. "Mom, heads-up. He's trying to—"

"Tad, stop that immediately," her mother said, stalking around the car. "Halt in the name of Willie Nelson." She was a tall and strong woman, who had no trouble asserting herself.

"What?" her father asked, annoyance lacing his delivery.

"Kindly drop the bags, sir." With a pointedly placed hand on her hip, the world knew Martie Ross meant business. Her father deflated and placed the box he held on the cart before stepping back.

"I was just fine. I know my limits," he said in defense. But his right side didn't work the way that it used to, weaker and less coordinated now. Excess exertion overwhelmed his system and knocked him out for the entire next day. He was back to work part-time after a good portion of a year at home, building himself back up again through rigorous rehab. He still lost words sometimes, and the doctors thought he likely forever would, but it didn't matter. Taryn always knew what he meant.

"I'm sure you do, you handsome man," her mother said. "But I love you so much that I can't let you get near those limits. We got this, right, Taryn my girl?"

"For sure."

She had to admit, it felt awkward to have both her parents escort her to her on-campus apartment as an incoming junior. She wasn't eighteen and appropriately wide-eyed. Her wide eyes were late to the party, partially her own doing, which accounted for the embarrassment. Her own failure to launch was still a sore subject and a part of her history she didn't look at too closely. The realization about where she *could be* right now versus where she *was* still shocked and shamed her. She had to find a way to set it aside, and maybe that's what this new leaf would do for her.

"I'll lead the way!" her mom bellowed.

"Maybe less yelling, though?"

"As you wish," her mom whispered.

Her parents had quickly voted themselves onto the move-in committee, reorganizing her belongings after she'd already packed them, tossing in various goody boxes in case she got hungry and couldn't figure out where food was sold, and—her personal favorite—supplying handwritten notes to be opened whenever she felt tested or low. Her parents were well intended, if not aggressive in their mission to protect her from the world. Either way, they both warmed her heart and also made her want to army-crawl under a table and hope no one noticed their attention.

But today was a noteworthy day. Embarrassment be damned. She'd swallow it down and concentrate on all that was ahead of her. Taryn was ready to spread her wings after working so hard her first few semesters in a combination of online and in-person courses. This would be the first time she lived on her own. But rather than allowing fear to overwhelm, she'd embraced the excitement and curiosity that came with this new chapter. In all honesty, it felt like she was finally hitting unpause on her frozen life. There were things she wanted to do in the coming years, relationships she hoped to build, a career she planned to prepare for. She reveled in the idea of finally being a part of something as academic and historical as Hillspoint University. "The first minute of my new existence," she murmured, following her parents up the sidewalk.

They wheeled her mass of belongings up the ramp in front of Alexander Village, a six-story building of red brick, white trim, and six towering white columns. They'd turned it into a series of small apartments geared to upperclassmen with a qualifying GPA. The building itself had to be over sixty years old at least, partially covered in ivy and surely harboring a few echoes of the past.

"Look at my daughter's fancy new home." Her mother pointed at the words *Honors College* next to the door and ran her fingers across them reverently. Taryn had always succeeded academically but didn't need it glorified. Especially *now*.

"Mom, stop. We're all good here," Taryn said, as a group of

students moved past them in midconversation. Slightly mortifying. She prayed they hadn't noticed the parental gushing as they pressed on. Within Alexander's walls, she'd be living in a two-person apartment, sharing a common living room with a roommate, but with her own small room as well. Since she didn't know a soul at Hillspoint, she'd requested to be paired up. She blinked against the wave of anxiety that nearly made her turn around and head to the car. *Stay strong and ride it out. Stay strong and ride it out.* Mantras tended to help give her something to hold her focus. When the fear crept in, distraction was key. Somehow in the past two years, she'd watched her confidence wane as she sat by and watched. Now it was time to dig herself out. Somehow.

And here we go. They arrived in front of a tall wooden door and knocked. When there was no answer, she shifted her weight before entering with the key she'd been provided at the front desk. The door opened to what would be her home for the academic year. *Wow. Big moment.* She was standing in a small living room that felt larger than it should, due to the high ceiling, with a couch and a chair.

"Now this is nice, Tare," her father said, taking an admiring stroll. "This is really great. You're gonna like this, Bear." A nickname from her newborn years she hadn't managed to shake.

"Yeah, pretty cool," Taryn said, holding still and taking in the details of the room, wanting to memorize everything. Hers. At least for the year. Green curtains and smoky-white and gray carpet. Definitely some wear showing, but she didn't care in the slightest. A bolt of exhilaration hit because this was really all happening. Even the couch was identical to the one in the brochure, complete with the same beige and darker beige striped throw pillows. She loved it already.

"The fridge is so spacious," her mother crowed, examining the interior of the small refrigerator nestled in the corner. "It has a pullout shelf for the milk. You just pull, look, then—milk. Voilà."

Taryn laughed. "Genius. A moving milk shelf." That's when she heard movement coming from behind an open door on the right side of the living room. Her roommate must have already arrived. "I think she's here," Taryn said quietly. Had she heard their fascination with the mobile milk shelf? *God.* Her parents looked at each other in delight, giddy and wide-eyed. This was such a big day for them, so she tried to be patient. She knocked quietly on the connecting door. "Hey," she said to absolutely no answer. She rolled her lips in, shifted her weight, and banished the stress that arrived on schedule.

No answer.

She paused, unsure what to do. More noise. Finally, she eased the door open the tiniest bit to see a brunette wearing large headphones and standing on her head against the wall. New. Couldn't say she'd encountered that one before. Taryn stepped halfway into the room. "Hi. Excuse me. So sorry to intrude, um, on the headstand." She added a back-and-forth wave. The motion seemed to do the trick, and the girl's brown eyes snapped into focus. "Hi. I'm Tar—"

"Oh shit." The girl cascaded her feet forward one at a time and righted herself like a proper acrobat. "You're here." The headphones hit the floor with a bang. The girl didn't care. "And I'm hanging upside down like a bat. Great first visual, Caz."

"Nah, I don't mind." Taryn gestured to the wall. "But can I ask about the headstand?"

"Centers me. I'm a weirdo who wears cat ears and stands upside down while listening to some relaxation podcast, but I promise it's bullshit. The harmless kind. I'm Caz Lee. Did I say that other than to myself?"

"I picked up on it. I'm Taryn Ross. We're roommates."

"Super cool. I got your name in the email. This is my third year at Hillspoint, though I have a few hours before official junior status. I like a light load."

"I get it. I tend to take too many hours. From Indiana?" Her heart was beating way too fast, but she was doing just fine. The smile was real. *Keep going.*

"Originally from this town an hour from Tokyo, but I've been in the States since I was four."

Taryn was impressed, having not traveled much herself just yet. One day she hoped to grab a backpack, some good shoes, and see it all. If she could just conquer this one small task of college first. "Oh wow."

Caz tilted her head. "You must be a transfer. I've never seen you, and I would definitely remember. That's a compliment. I like to signpost."

"Thank you. For both. And, yeah, I'm transferring from Belmont Community, which is just outside Dyer."

"And do they go with you?" She gestured with her chin to the doorway where Taryn's parents stood gaping with glee, clutching each other like she'd just won Miss America.

Taryn rocked on her heels and slid her hands into her pockets. "Those enraptured people are my parents, just dying to meet you."

They took their cue. Her mother stepped forward, dripping with mildly controlled enthusiasm. "What do you study, Caz? I'm Martie Ross, and this is Ted. We're from Dyer, a few hours away."

"Pleased make your acquaintance. Stoked, actually." Caz touched the back of her dark hair, currently in two low-sitting ponytails. "The question you asked is complicated. My dad wants me to stick with academia so I can grow up and be a school principal like he is, but I'm more of a creative free spirit."

"Amazing," Taryn said, aiming for rapport, hoping her parents would follow in her very validating footsteps.

"My major is undecided, but I am aware that the clock is ticking." Caz nodded.

"Just keeping your options open. What do you, uh…create?" her father asked. He'd had to search for the word *create*. Taryn knew that look, loving but also very practical.

"Currently working with pebbles."

"I love it," Taryn said, not fully getting it at all.

"What do you do with them?" her mom asked. "So many options, really."

"I don't know just yet, but I'm getting to know them. Soon, I'm hoping to have the direction of my pebble art figured out. It's still early."

Her mom nodded like it was the most obvious ever. Bless her. "Caz, I wish you all the luck on your journey. Find all the good pebbles."

"I'm gonna try," Caz said very seriously. She turned to Taryn. "I could totally chill with these two. You lucked out." She was quirky and earnest. Taryn could definitely work with those qualities. "Do you all want to sit down, order some food?"

"No. No. That's okay. They said they're gonna stop somewhere on the way home. Gives them a break from driving." She turned to her parents expectantly, dread gathering in her stomach. It was now or never.

Her mother ignored her. "Should we unpack?"

"No, I got it." Taryn added a smile. Delaying the good-bye would drag this whole thing out. A second flutter hit as she realized that this was the moment she'd looked forward to and avoided in tandem.

Her parents stared back, not fully understanding that this was the part where they probably needed to say good-bye or risk making her look like a coddled child. She wasn't. Plus, her goal was to project swagger, independence, and the ultrachill attitude she didn't quite have on the inside. Yet. The new *university her* depended on these impressions. Plus, they'd all agreed that her folks would load Taryn in and head home, which would put them back in Dyer before dark, a time neither of them enjoyed driving.

"Oh," her father said. He tapped her mom's arm. "We better let these two handle all this."

"Already?" her mom asked in a semipout. "Okay, okay. I'm stalling because I'm feeling misty. I'm gonna wake up tomorrow, and your bed won't have been slept in." A kiss to Taryn's forehead. "I won't leave half my bagel in case you want it because you won't be there." Another kiss. "You're not going to join a cult, are you?" A concerned stare with Mom-eyes was cast her way.

"Nope. No plans to. I'll see you in a few weeks for fall break, remember?" Taryn said. "And I'll expect that bagel half."

Her dad placed his good hand on her head and gave it a slow, affectionate shake. She couldn't crumple here. Not now. She fought the emotion it kindled because it didn't fit the persona she was shooting for in Caz's presence. Fuck it. This was her dad. She fell gently into his chest and offered a long squeeze before finally releasing him, tears filling her eyes. He was going to be okay without her. She hoped she would be, too. A deep breath. Her father, specifically, was a quiet, kind support in her life. He was a friend to all, even the insects he escorted politely out of the house, which was why he was so effortlessly good at sales. People trusted the guy, and he did right by them.

"Oh no. I'm not ready for this," her more dramatic mother proclaimed, opening her arms like they were about to be separated by war. She was the say-whatever-thing-popped-into-her-head kind of parent, which made for some very heartfelt—but tricky—public exchanges. Taryn moved slowly into the hug and allowed her mother to hold on as long as she needed, which, it turned out, was an extraordinarily long amount of time. With a final, final wave, her parents slipped out of the room, leaving her with Caz and an uncomfortable lump in her throat.

"They are so into you," Caz said, after a long beat of silence. "Like, *really*. Your mom and the waterworks were battling hard, and she didn't win."

"I know," Taryn replied seriously. "Her emotions brim right beneath the surface until they leap forth. Just her thing."

"Hey, it's okay." A pause. "You're really lucky. I don't think I've ever misted up over my parents. Or them over me, for that matter."

"Yeah." Taryn exhaled, settling in, relieved that Caz saw the value in her family dynamic. "I know I am."

"Want to go eat? Food always helps me feel better. Baked goods especially. Your bagel thing got me in the mood to carb load."

She blinked, the non-sequitur rescuing her from her thoughts in a stroke of good timing. "Hell yeah." She dabbed her cheeks, clearing them of tears, well aware of the wide grin that spread across her face. "I'm actually starving. Carbs would be great."

"Follow me down four floors." Caz, a Hillspoint veteran, supplied helpful information as they walked the exteriors. The day was nice and so was the picturesque route to the dining hall. "Fire ants lurk over there in small mounds. Don't sit in that grass no matter how beautiful it may look. Across the street is better."

"Noted. Awful ants."

"Best coffee spot is next to the volleyball gym. Avoid the kiosk in the student center. The baristas suck and own it like bitches. They won't even try and will laugh about it later."

"Lazy bitch baristas. Got it."

"Our RA is named Gray, and he's more fun than he is helpful. But definitely hit him up to move heavy shit because why not? Free labor and he loves the attention from anything female."

"Gray the guy who moves heavy shit."

Caz pointed to what looked to be a dormant intramural field in the distance. "Hot guys congregate over there around four p.m. when most of the classes for the day conclude. Hot girls can be found in front of Avery Hall over there. Not sure yet where your interest lies, so I'm covering my bases."

"Um. Girls." *Wow*. She blinked in shock at the ease with which the words had left her lips. She'd known she was gay for three years now, but Caz was the first person outside of her home that she'd ever informed with words. "I've never said that out loud to anyone besides my parents, so I'm taking a moment here."

"Wait." Caz stopped walking and turned, a frown on her face. "Never?"

"Nope. Not even a hint until, well, this very moment. It feels… surreal." She was smiling. The moment was still in progress, but all signs were pointing to it being a good one.

Caz nodded and grinned, as if letting herself record the importance. "I'm more than honored." She walked on. "So you'll want to hang over there," she said, indicating the hot girls gathering spot across the big lawn. The casualness with which she'd moved forward was the best gift Caz could have given her. Something she'd struggled with for a long time had just been noted as just another cool part of her to add to the collection.

Taryn couldn't stop smiling. Did this mean she was officially out? Everything in her said yes. And in that very instant, the weight of the world was casually shifted right off her shoulders, just like that. The day was sunny, the prospects good.

Admittedly, she'd lived a pretty solitary existence the past two years. Most of her high school friends had headed off to colleges spread out across the country as she sat on the steps in front of the house in Dyer, Indiana, that she'd lived in since birth. A total failure to launch, and feeling every moment of it. While her peers were away, she'd quietly gone to classes, helped with dinner, driven her father to appointments, and ended each night studying alone in her room, sometimes falling asleep at her laptop. Her grades, as a result of her less than full social scene, had skyrocketed. Any kind of romantic prospects, however, had withered a slow death.

Everything at Hillspoint felt noticeably different. This place, this blossoming campus with intelligent people around every corner, made her want to crawl right out of her shell and introduce herself, something her second-guessing would have shut down immediately just months ago.

Taryn shimmied as a tingle slid up her spine. Flurries of anticipation floated over every inch of her. She had a distinct feeling this year was about to change absolutely everything, and in many ways, she wished she could fast-forward her own story just to see how it all turned out. She hoped her ending was a happy one.

❖

The semester hadn't started yet, but Charlotte Adler could already anticipate the size of the workload about to rain down on her. Within two weeks, she'd likely be saddled with over a hundred pages of reading, a research project, and forty intro essays to grade as a grad instructor. In her third and final year in pursuit of her MFA, she'd come to know what to expect from a Hillspoint semester.

And this was easily the calm before the storm.

It was nice to be back, though, inhaling the cool autumn air and seeing the friends she loved. Given that this was her last year, she planned to soak up every minute of academic life, even though the rigorous program would have her regretting that plan soon enough. She was certainly writing more than ever, thanks to the summer stipend the program provided, which had given her space to buckle down and focus on her work for three months, rather than having to take a full-time job. Having a strong work ethic, she'd still picked up the occasional nanny gig through the high end agency that made it well worth her time.

As Charlie crossed the quad in front of Old Main, she spotted Danny McHenry, her boyfriend of the past three years, with one sneaker-clad foot on a bench, standing with his best friend, Lawson, and another mutual classmate, Emerson, who screamed her name and beckoned her over like a cheerleader at a Saturday night game.

"Charlie! Whoop! Get over here right now!" Emerson was sweet as could be but definitely grated when she leaned into hyperbolic affirmations, and when did she not? She also tended to glorify Danny and his famous mom on a regular basis. Perhaps a crush? Not that Charlie minded. She was secure in their relationship, which she would describe as mature and comfortable, given that they'd known each other since childhood. Danny's mom and hers had been best friends for decades before Charlie's mom had sadly passed, three and a half years prior. Sadness still nestled in her chest over the loss. It still felt like yesterday and hurt just as potently.

"Well, look who finally decided to grace us with her presence," Danny said playfully. His sandy brown hair fell across his forehead in that I-didn't-do-my-hair-but-it-looks-good kind of way. In that moment, she smiled and they locked eyes. She'd been nervous about this part, having anticipated their reunion all day. They'd spent most of the summer apart because Danny had been accepted into a prestigious writing colony in Tennessee that he simply couldn't pass up. This was actually the first time she'd seen him in six weeks, and she wondered how reentry might feel. He broke into a huge smile as she approached, and that little gesture made everything in her exhale. It meant they were okay, still them, in their warm, compatible way.

"Hi," she said and easily moved into his open arms. She relaxed into comfort and familiarity. Danny was not just her boyfriend but family, and always had been.

"My girl." They shared a sweet kiss as their friends looked on. It was good to see Danny, like her favorite blanket back around her shoulders. They'd texted daily, and she'd listened to him rave on about his experience at the writing retreat and the prestige associated with it, while wishing desperately she'd been accepted as well. Danny was at the top of the ladder at Hillspoint, so he'd received their department's top recommendation to the summer program. He'd been the only one of their group to receive admittance, which left Charlie disappointed but happy for Danny. Having a best-selling author for a mother certainly added wattage to his spotlight, but that was just part of life. "Weird being back here, huh?"

She shrugged. "I'm kind of excited, myself. But then again, I didn't have to give up a fancy writing existence."

"The scenery alone was immensely inspiring. I don't know how I'm going to manage back in a classroom environment after that." He probably didn't mean to elevate himself and make the rest of them look basic, but he certainly had the tendency, a fault she'd excused many times. Daniel McHenry wasn't a pompous human, but sometimes he didn't hear how he sounded. Though they'd known each other for years, here at school, he was also a fellow MFA candidate in Charlie's creative writing program, meaning they would have at least two of three sections together. That meant that soon they'd be elbows deep critiquing each other's work, debating the week's reading assignment, and generally up close and personal in each other's faces. The arrangement could definitely strain even the strongest of relationships, but so far, they'd done their best to navigate the stresses. Maintaining their own apartments had been a purposeful decision to give them time apart when they needed it.

This year was going to be an important one. They'd be planning for life after grad school and not just professionally. Would there be a proposal, or would they simply get a place together after graduation? She harnessed the hope as fuel, and with a deep fortifying breath made the choice to relish every moment of her last year on the campus she'd grown to love.

Emerson, who'd become a necessary annoyance after years in the trenches together, hopped like a happy chick about to be fed. "Getting the band back together now." She brought her shoulders to her ears and beamed. "Our resident couple reunited. Goals, man. Wistful sigh in action." She demonstrated.

Danny kissed Charlie's head. "Missed you."

"Same," she said with a smile. Their time together was laced with laughter, interesting conversation, and a lot of her feeling like she sometimes let him down. Their passion meter was a little on the average side, but that didn't mean there wasn't tons of time to work on that aspect of the relationship. They had bigger things to focus on in the here and now. Sex, passion, and fun in the bedroom were fairly low on her list, but they were capable adults who'd get there in time. Their plates were full. That was all.

Charlie turned to Emerson with a grin and opened her arms. The petite redhead had always reminded Charlie of a yappy Yorkshire terrier, adorable yet tiring, prone to mischief and unwarranted positivity. She practically leapt into Charlie's arms. "And here I come, ready to strum bass."

"Totally not the bass player," Lawson said, his dark eyebrows drawn into a V. He was Danny's best friend and biggest cheerleader, always there to hype him up in class. A mediocre writer himself, but his confidence seemed to get him places. "You're on vocals, Em. I'm bass. Danny's guitar, and Charlie's drums." He stared at them in shocked judgment like there would be little question as to those assignments.

They collectively paused and regarded him.

"You've really put some time into that," Charlie said.

He shrugged and slung an arm around her shoulder. "Start warming up those hands. I'm guessing you're with us in Rhetoric and Comp in five."

"That's my understanding."

"Third year. Let's go!" Emerson cheered, striking an actual cheerleader pose. There was no universe in which she wasn't on the squad in high school.

The four of them, along with a small handful of other classmates, moved through the program together, withering beneath the brutal workload and leaning on each other for support. They each brought their unique personalities and writing styles to the table, which made for an interesting time. Their ninety-minute classes were often tense and ended on a less than comfortable note. When viewpoints were expressed, feelings were sometimes hurt. But in the end, when all was said and the writing shelved, they respected and admired each other. Gathering at Toby the Tiger's after an especially trying day was not uncommon. Beer was on whoever had been the biggest asshole during critiques.

"Why do you call your place Toby the Tiger?" Charlie had once asked the owner, regularly referred to as He-Man, one night from across the bar. "Isn't the common reference *Tony*?"

"Tony serves people cereal. Toby serves bourbon," he'd stated gruffly. She'd spotted a mermaid tattoo next to an anchor and wondered if he'd served in the Navy.

"Is that your real name? Toby," she'd asked, basking in her buzz.

"Hell no. I'm Brett, Crusher of Beers, Breaker of Hearts. Cheers to the revolution."

"Cheers," she said obediently. Brett was a force. Toby remained a phantom.

Regardless of the naming mystery, Charlie had grown to love the small college dive bar comprising dim lighting and too much wood to be fashionable. Maybe they'd even hit it up this week where they could haunt the dartboard and discuss why their instructors lived to torture them.

"Are we walking?" Emerson asked the group, indicating the Saunders Building, fifty yards away. They turned and stared up at the familiar structure in silence, probably all realizing that this was the last carefree moment they'd have before the brutality of third year hit them like a wrecking ball to the chest.

"Now or never," Charlie said, leading the way up the eight steps they'd all trod many times in the past. She'd logged more time in this building than she cared to count, but she'd also written some very important words that she was proud of. It evened out.

"Hey," she said to Danny once they were settled across from each other around the small conference room table that would serve as their classroom. It was something they often said to each other, a shorthand and way of semiflirting.

"Hey back," he said, glancing at the table and back up. It felt like a stumble, their rhythm off. They just needed time to find their footing. That was all.

"Here goes everything," Lawson said and stuffed his backward ball cap into his satchel.

Emerson tapped the table. "I have a feeling that this year is going to be the best one yet," she said.

"It better be," Charlie countered. "It's all we have left."

"Onward literary soldiers!" Lawson said too loudly for the small room. "Grab thy pen and use it as a sword."

Emerson seemed to like the battle cry and tossed a fist in the air. Charlie and Danny exchanged an amused look. The year held promise, and Charlie was ready to explore exactly what that might mean. She had a future looming after grad school, and she wanted to take every opportunity to prepare for a career as a successful writer, someone who made a difference in this world with her words.

"You ready?" Danny asked her quietly.

"I think I actually am."

CHAPTER TWO

Tonight was an important night, and Taryn didn't want to blow it. Her skin tingled in anticipation, her stomach jittery with nerves. After Spanish class, the ruiner of her existence, let out for the day, her thoughts turned to the night ahead. The marvel was that she actually had plans, which meant she had a social life again. *Her.*

After a month at Hillspoint, Taryn had slowly started to establish a circle of friends she actually liked. Caz had introduced her around, coming in clutch to make those connections happen. Those people had introduced her to a few others, and now her existence at Hillspoint was dotted with *Hey, Taryn*s, which felt better than she could have imagined. She lit up after a good *Hey, Taryn* and felt more and more comfortable as the days pressed on. She was finding her social footing and allowing herself to embrace it. But she'd been on campus for close to five weeks before she scored an invite to an actual college party, leaving her eager, underprepared, and questioning her social skills. Never helpful. Having hidden away her first and second years, she'd missed out on what the actual party experience was like. Her indoctrination would happen in just six short hours, and now that it was upon her, she wasn't so sure she wanted to go.

"This is the problem. I suck at small talk," Taryn told Caz and their next-door neighbor Sasha, who had the prettiest chestnut hair and held the firm belief that if people ate more ice cream, most everything would be sweeter, if not colder.

"No, you don't. I can vouch for your conversational prowess," Sasha said, lying on her back in the middle of their couch. She tended to make herself at home, which was actually a relief. No need to host Sasha, ever.

Taryn held up a finger. "Let me rephrase. I hate small talk. It takes work, and I run out of polite things to say after ten minutes—and then, dead air."

"No one small-talks at these things. You can barely hear." Caz turned around in her desk chair. "And also? Get out of your head and get into mine because I think you're awesome and would kiss your face off if we weren't so platonic it hurts."

Caz, she'd learned, was the kind of friend who pumped you up when you needed it most. "Oh, well in that case I'm flattered and would top you in a second." She offered a playful wink and Caz winked back. Friendship rhythm was intact and thriving.

"What are we going to wear, though?" Caz pondered, strolling to her closet door on a perplexing mission. "I never like to choose too early because moods are like the weather, ever-changing, but now we're sorely pushing it. The clock is not our friend. We need to be sexy."

Taryn chewed her lip, attempting to assemble the meaning. "Just in general, or…"

"For the events of this evening, kind madam." The party at Tau Kappa Epsilon was saints and sinners themed, which left a lot to interpretation. "We need to impress, stand out, show off our tits." She emphasized by pushing hers forward.

Taryn held up a finger. "Hmm. No. Not planning on that last part. Mine are shy. We shouldn't ask much of them."

"Well, tonight's their debut." Caz shut the closet door, clearly deciding nothing inside would do, and stalked back into the living room. "These parties are always half-naked parties. It's the collegiate way."

"That's why I love them," Sasha sighed.

Taryn squinted. "But should it be? Really?" Taryn wasn't sure she was ready to put it all out there, college party or not. Yes, there would likely be hot girls there to get to know, but her dignity did have a say.

"I don't know why you're worried about it. If I had your body, I'd be naked right now," Sasha said. "I'm thinking of wearing my hair up to show off my neck. I'm told it's stunning."

Taryn didn't hesitate. "And it is. You have a killer neck. No question."

"Sure, agreed about the neck, but we need to focus," Caz said. She'd suddenly turned loud, which Taryn understood was Caz's way. Her volume fluctuated with any slight shift of topic or emotion.

"I'm listening," Taryn said.

"The shouting is a choice," Sasha said. "Try nonchalance, like me." She ran a finger down her neck, still preoccupied with it.

"Idea forthcoming."

"Hit me," Taryn said.

Caz offered a nod and stepped forward. "There's a vintage store on Fourth. We can score cheap—and hopefully downright sexy—outfits. I'm willing to give up my parking space and drive, which we can all admit is a mighty sacrifice for the success of our merry band. Are you in?"

"I've got nothing better to do," Sasha said.

Taryn laughed. "How can I say no to such a huge parking gesture?"

Caz went very serious. "I thought you'd see it that way."

The vintage shop, aptly named Witches of Wayback, was crowded with so many miscellaneous objects that it was difficult to shop in any effective manner. The two-room space overflowed with circular clothing racks and shelves up to the ceiling crowded with pots and pans, cookie jars, old telephones, and knickknacks of many enviable shapes and sizes. In the center of the room, several mannequins seemed to be conducting a meeting in their 1920s finery, one wearing a witch's hat. That was all well and good, but Taryn was quickly seduced to the real show a few feet to the right in a lonely corner. The unremarkable gray shelf sang to her like a siren.

"Oh wow," she murmured, moving to the display of used cameras sitting together in a jumble of straps and lenses. "Well, look at you." Taryn picked up an older Nikon model and fiddled with the focus ring. Caz was lost in corsets and leather, and Sasha was holding a conversation with a blow-up Snoopy doll, giving Taryn space to explore her find.

"I could totally work with these kitten ears," Caz said absently. "Ever have sex in kitten ears?"

"Can't say I have," Taryn called back.

"Missing out. Oh! And the purple fur matches the lining of this corset. They need to be together. They're going to be. Mine, mine, mine."

"Matchmaking like a pro over there," Taryn said absently, clicking the shutter and resetting. She might have just fallen in love.

While Caz whipped through hangers in the sexy section, Taryn explored a couple more of the truly impressive-looking cameras, but none really compared to that first Nikon. She'd begun to find her footing in her photography courses, sinking deeper and deeper into the art and technique. She'd taught herself about shadow and contrast, using the light to create a mood, but before coming to Hillspoint, she'd always just used the camera on her phone. Now that she was learning her craft more formally, she'd considered purchasing a camera, which would free her up from renting from the department, but the newer models were out of her price range. She checked the tags on a few of these older guys and was shocked at how affordable they were. Why hadn't she considered going used before?

"Tare. This would look unbelievable on you. Your boobs would act as the Bat-Signal to all females in the vicinity. Lesbian achievement level unlocked." Caz held up a white vest and pants set as if she'd just made the sapphic discovery of the decade. "No one will breathe if you wear this."

Taryn raised a brow. "Um, maybe I should start with fewer females. Plus, I don't have a shirt that would work underneath."

"A shirt? Who needs a shirt?"

Taryn blinked. "This is a scandal in the making."

"I vote yes." Sasha whirled around and landed next to Caz. "That's for Taryn, right? That has to be for Taryn, her flawless skin and boobs."

"See?" Caz said, turning back to her. "We're buying it. It's all white. You're the saint. I'm the feline sinner. We're perfection in our representation of room 412."

"Are we sure about this?" Taryn asked.

"Yes," the two of them said in unison.

Deciding to trust just her friends' instincts about these things, she exhaled and closed her eyes, ignoring the fear, longing to be Taryn the Brave for once. "How can I argue with that?" She also decided to trust *her own* instincts and scooped up the old Nikon she couldn't stop admiring. Of course, she'd have to score some film but didn't mind the extra step. "I'm gonna grab this, too."

Caz eyed the camera. "Are you a hipster in disguise?"

Taryn paused genuinely. "I'm not sure. But, um, I told you I was interested in photography, remember. I love the courses I'm taking, and I'm going to declare it officially."

"Dude, I'm starting to really like you." Caz batted her colorfully made up eyes. "Let's all get iced coffees and be introspective."

Taryn laughed. "Lead the way."

Four hours later, long after the sun had dipped behind the horizon and early evening melted into night, Taryn followed Sasha and Caz and several of their friends across the lawn to a large two-story house with the letters *TKE* above the door. She could already feel the loud music pulse beneath her feet as they approached the scene that could only be described as brash and chaotic. One guy hung out of the second-story window yelling what sounded like rhyming poetry. Two girls were huddled on the sidewalk in front having some sort of dramatic conversation with hands on hips. A couple made out up against the brick pillar of the house, and another guy swung shirtless from a tree branch as a group below cheered him on. Most everyone was holding a red Solo cup, which Taryn had always kind of assumed was a college party cliché, but evidently wasn't.

"Hot," a dude said in her ear as he passed her in the doorway.

She looked down at her vest, which showed off way more skin than she was used to. Thank God her boobs weren't huge or she never could have pulled off the look. "Thank you." Was that what one should say? Maybe she should have just nodded instead. She'd workshop it.

Before she knew it, Caz appeared at her elbow with a red cup containing something purple and mysterious. Taryn raised a skeptical eyebrow. "What is this, and was it in your possession at all times?"

"Trash can punch. Harmless. And yes." Caz sipped from her own cup and nodded happily at the results. "Okay, that's good. Really easy. You'll love it."

Taryn took a hesitant sip but was surprised by the sweet, near Kool-Aid-like taste. She hadn't been a huge drinker up until this point, so sipping would be the name of the game. She'd turned twenty-one in March, so the idea of drinking without looking over her shoulder was still a satisfying and new experience. Once they got settled in, she took a more generous swallow and caught the beat of the music. Now that combo was nice. She tossed in a very subtle head bop and caught the eye of a girl across the room who joined her, sending a sexy smile her way. This place was a vibe, and she felt herself starting to relax and enjoy the party.

"Like, where are you from?" a random guy in the kitchen asked her twenty minutes later when she went to refresh her drink. He was shirtless and wore a beauty pageant sash that said *Mr. Sinner* along with a backward black baseball cap.

"Oh, um. Dyer. Ever been?"

His eyes went wide and he slapped the counter probably harder than he meant to. That had to smart. "Isn't that where they found a bunch of those crop circles?"

She frowned. "No. No, I don't think it is."

"Cool outfit." His gaze dipped without apology to her chest. Dudes were so predictable. She could almost guess his next question. "Wanna see my room?" Yep, that had been it.

"Hmm. Can't say I do." She flicked her pointer finger at him. "Work on your game. It's missing the whole middle section. Said with care, not judgment. Excuse me." What was it about alcohol and talking to guys that zapped any and all trepidation? She decided to ride with it, which was helpful because the rest of the night was sadly the same. Drunk frat guys trying to make conversation, but clearly working with another set of motives that involved separating Taryn from her clothes.

"You're hotter than my mama," one guy called to her as she crossed the room to Sasha.

"What?" she asked, turning to him. "Play that sentence back. It's disturbing."

Even Caz, who apparently had a thing for people with glasses and gaming knowledge, was over the tired repetition. "The guy in front of the window? I thought he was gonna be a contender. He's a beast at Fortnite but can't tell me what color my eyes are after half an hour of conversation, ya know?"

"Too well. At least he didn't compare your heat index to his mom's."

"What?"

She slowly lifted her cup to her lips. "Exactly."

Taryn was on her third cup of that fruity punch and feeling so much looser because of it. Honestly, it was actually pretty marvelous stuff that had her enjoying the music and the freedom to dance and hang out. She should drink more frequently and let the good times happen because life was too short for third-act anxiety just when it was supposed to get good. She found a corner of the room and let herself groove to the music, which, to the frat brothers' credit, wasn't entirely awful. It was from that corner she first spotted the gorgeous blonde in jeans, brown boots, and a casual white blouse with flowy sleeves walking across the room. *Hello.* She didn't fit in. At all. She was dressed for dinner out, not Friday night at the TKE house, and that snagged Taryn's attention along with something vaguely familiar about her. Her confident carriage. The dimple on her right cheek that appeared when she smiled and waved at some girl she recognized as she glided through the room like she owned it. She was clearly on a mission, and no one was paying attention. Fueled by courage made of trash can punch, Taryn followed the blonde into the kitchen because she wasn't quite ready to pull her gaze away.

She didn't know why or what she hoped to accomplish, but something dragged her like metal to a beautiful magnet.

"Excuse me," Taryn said. The blonde turned. "Are you looking for someone?" Not that Taryn would be able to help even if she was. She'd figure that part out later.

The girl offered a smile. Luckily, it was a few decibels quieter in the kitchen that was now littered with empty beer cans and red cups. At least they didn't have to shout. "Yeah, my boyfriend. He's around here somewhere. I'm supposed to meet him." The blonde quirked her head and Taryn was circling the familiar factor once again but couldn't quite land on how.

"Do we know each other?" Taryn asked, squinting.

"Hmm. No. I don't think so." Her blue eyes were large and beautiful, but it was the voice that did it, linking the treasure trove of summertime memories to the face in front of her right now all these years later. Was it actually possible?

"Charlotte. Are you Charlotte?"

That seemed to catch the girl off guard. "Yeah. Charlie. Wait. How do we know each other?" It had been nearly eleven years, and Taryn hadn't even gone through puberty the last time they'd seen each other. It made sense that Charlie wouldn't recognize her.

"Sorry. I should have led with that. I'm Taryn Ross. Don't laugh, but I think you were my babysitter."

"No." Charlie's jaw dropped, and she covered her mouth. "Stop. You're Taryn? Little Taryn from Dyer? Uh-uh." She reached out and gave Taryn's hand an affectionate squeeze, a smile blossoming.

"Not exactly little, but yes." She laughed because she now had two inches on Charlie. This was surreal. She attended a frat party and ran into Charlotte-the-babysitter, who she used to worship? The world was strange and wonderful. She wanted to ask a million questions, to stand in that kitchen and catch up with Charlie, stare into those blue eyes a little while longer, because what were the odds of this run-in actually happening? Something about the whole thing felt…ordained. The night had definitely taken a turn for the better.

❖

Charlie was floored. She'd noticed the brunette to her left when she'd walked across the gathering room of the frat house. Mainly because the girl was incredibly striking and wearing an outfit that most people couldn't pull off. Except she had. And looked amazing, like a model right off Instagram. Now, as Charlie stood in that kitchen, she was supposed to believe that this truly attractive, sophisticated-looking young woman was actually Taryn, that energetic, silly kid from all those years back? It seemed almost laughable. The two simply couldn't merge in her head.

"Do you go to school here?" Charlie asked.

"Are you at Hillspoint, too?"

They'd spoken at the exact same time and laughed. Taryn motioned for Charlie to go first. But Charlie was knee deep in catch-up mode, all the while trying to keep her eyes on Taryn's and not on the very noticeable neckline on that vest. Her cheeks went warm at the acknowledgment, her stomach tight. What was that about? Certainly an unfamiliar response, but she was human, mature, and could certainly appreciate a beautiful woman. Nothing to write home about, right? Who wouldn't notice Taryn when she looked so amazing?

"I am," she said, trying to regain her line of thought. "I'm in my last year of graduate school. Danny, my, um, boyfriend, is one of the TKE advisors, and I told him I'd swing by and pick up a book we share." And now it felt strange talking about her boyfriend in the very next breath. Best to just press forward. "There's a reading due for class tomorrow, so no time to waste. I just had no idea it would be such a scene here."

"Not a frequenter of frat parties?" Taryn asked with a sideways grin that took Charlie back in time. There she was.

Charlie shook her head, grinning at the chaos around them. "It's been a few years." A round of loud cheering erupted from nearby, so Charlie leaned in close and raised her voice. "You're, what, a second year?"

"Third. But a new transfer. My first semester here." Taryn smelled like vanilla and honey. The ends of her long, dark hair tickled Charlie's shoulders, due to their proximity.

"Which would explain why I've never run into you. You're a *junior*? No. How is that possible?"

"I don't know what to say. I am. Time is a constant." Taryn's brown eyes seemed even bigger and more expressive than she'd remembered. Suddenly, she looked thoughtful.

"You said you're a grad student. What are you studying?"

"Creative writing. If all goes well, I want to write books until I'm an old woman who can't see the words on the page anymore. There are a few other steps between then and now, of course." She looked around. "I feel like I should knock on something."

"Somehow I don't think you'll need it."

"Thank you." Charlie nodded her head in the direction of Taryn's cup. "Careful with that stuff, okay? It sneaks up on you."

She tilted her head. "Aww, still looking out for me."

"Old habits and all." She looked around, realizing her original mission, yet Danny was nowhere to be found. "Enjoy yourself, okay? But not too much." Charlie passed Taryn a smile and squeezed her hand. "I'm gonna go find that book."

"Good to see you, Charlie." Charlie could tell she meant it. Taryn was glowing, and Charlie likely was, as well. This was too fantastic a discovery.

"Campus isn't that big. I'm sure it won't be the last time." Charlie paused for a moment, not really wanting to walk away just yet, feeling the loss of a moment that seemed important. She shook herself out of it, offered a wave, and headed into the backyard.

It didn't take her long to locate Danny. He stood in the back corner with three undergrad girls gathered around him in awe. Typical. She smiled and covered the short distance, waiting a few feet away, arms folded.

"What's it like having Monica McHenry for a mother? It's so cool that you're a writer, too," the first girl said. Bleached blond hair with a full spray tan in late September.

Danny shrugged. "I think I probably picked up some of her talent, but our styles are quite different." He ate this kind of attention up, always had. Harmless enough. She knew she had nothing to worry about. Danny very much valued their relationship and Charlie as his partner. Yes, he got a lot of attention because of his last name, but Charlie honestly wasn't the jealous type. If anything, they fed his ego so she didn't have to.

He caught her eye and held up a finger to his adoring crew. "If you'll excuse me."

"Having fun?" she asked with a knowing look.

He had the decency to look sheepish. "Shooting the breeze with the kiddos. New first-years."

"I could tell." She unfolded her arms. "I'm here for the reading."

He pulled the tattered textbook from the backpack he'd stashed a few feet away. "It's pretty dry stuff, and you can skip the last five pages because it's all a retread."

"Good tip. How much longer do you have, you think?"

"I'll hang out another hour and then leave the party in the hands of the distinguished and slightly inebriated brothers."

Charlie winced because the party was picking up steam by the second. "It's a madhouse in there. But I ran into a girl I used to babysit in high school."

"Is she a fan of Monica McHenry?" he asked with a playfully sly look.

"Stop that right now."

He laughed and kissed her lips. "I'm glad you stopped by." He gave her a twirl. "Looking good, too, Adler."

"Thank you," she said, not loving that move. "Gonna dive into what sounds like a thrilling read and turn in. I'm teaching in the morning. See you tomorrow?"

He nodded and placed a hand over his heart. "Always." It was possible he'd had a cup of that trash can punch.

She headed back through the house, understanding Danny would likely return to his fawning public for a few more strokes to his ego. More power to him. She had a reading to tackle and a career to prep for. It took more for Charlie to be noticed in the literary world, which meant she had to work harder, write better, and elbow her way to a seat at the table. The exciting part was that she was up for the challenge.

"Yes, people. Tare's ready to turn it loose," Sasha yelled as Taryn tossed both hands in the air, swaying her hips to the beat. "Back that ass up, T." Taryn laughed and danced alongside the girls from Alexander in the center of the room, losing herself in the music, the hypnotic rhythm beneath her feet, and the sense of finally being in the midst of it all, surrounded by people her own age. She was on her fourth or fifth cup of punch, which let her say good-bye to her inhibitions. Friends were meant to celebrate together, right? The room felt newly vibrant and fun, and even the frat bros seemed to chill the hell out for a minute and have a legit good time. Laughter topped the music until someone turned it up another three notches. The room took on a dreamlike quality, overrun and vibrating with people. Another two and a half Solo cups later, and maybe the space around her didn't seem as stable. Taryn sensed her error and tossed her current drink into one of the overflowing trash cans in the corner, but even that little bit of movement made the room lurch.

She gripped a nearby table, absorbing the feel of the cool surface like a lifeline.

"This party is dope," Scarlet called to her. She lived two doors down and binged historical romance and reruns of *The Kardashians*.

No. Couldn't agree. Wasn't feeling dope. More like dizzy and reminiscent of an extra-loud funhouse on steroids. "I think I better slow down."

Scarlet gave her a hard knock on the shoulder that nearly sent her over the edge from okay to not at all. "Been there. You'll rally."

Taryn wasn't so sure. She didn't drink often, leaving her tolerance low. Her stomach churned, and the spinning room made the nausea worse. In the midst of the loud music and crowded room, her orientation fled like a felon. "Gonna grab air," she called to Caz.

"Oh fuck. You drink too much? I got you. Want me to come with you?" Caz's dark lipstick had faded entirely, revealing the innocent, youthful face beneath. Her cat ears were now crooked and tired. Taryn wanted to straighten them but couldn't seem to come up with the proper execution. Bad sign. Bad, bad sign.

"No, you have fun. Be a happy cat. I'm real good. See?" She tried so hard for casual and unaffected but only manifested as weird and wobbly. The reality was she was getting drunker by the second. That was probably fine, right? People got drunk. She just didn't usually, but new experiences were super good for growth, and who didn't need to learn and gather a variety of experiences? Oh, look, a plant. Did it have a name? She could call it Melvin. So incredibly green and leafy.

While she couldn't remember getting there, a few minutes later, Taryn realized she was sitting on the lawn as partygoers streamed in and out of the frat house. She remembered the scene she'd walked up on when they'd arrived and realized she was now a part of it. She blinked and took a deep breath, realizing she should probably walk home, but wasn't sure her Jell-O legs would make it.

"Hey, look at me." A soft hand touched her chin. "You okay?"

She turned and her eyes collided with big, blue ones. "Yeah. Hi." An angel was looking down at her. A pause as her circling brain caught up. "Charlotte. I mean, Charlie." Charlie was kneeling in front of her, perfectly sober and mature. Why couldn't Taryn be those things?

"That's me. Where do you live?" Her voice was soft and caring. Taryn wanted lean in to it because Charlie would make sure she was okay. Didn't they used to do that for each other?

"Alexander, but I'm so very fine. Promise. Just taking a little breather, ya know?" She added a semi-athletic stretch, which, on second thought, probably didn't help her case.

"Oh, I know those breathers. Too well." Charlie paused, seeming to make a decision. "Idea. I'm headed that way. Let's walk together."

"Cool, cool," Taryn said as relief descended.

Charlie looked behind her at the house. "Before we leave, is the girl with the cat ears your friend?"

Taryn nodded. "And my roommate. Caz."

"Caz. Even better. I'll let her know." Charlie disappeared for a moment and then reemerged a minute or two later. It also could have been twenty. Time was weird. "Here we go. You steady?"

Taryn stood but wobbled considerably. The world tilted like a tricky carnival ride. "What a minx."

"Me?" Charlie asked.

"No! Ha. The ground. It moves. I think. One can't be sure what's real."

Charlie laughed. "Okay. Executive decision. Give me your hand."

Taryn stared at Charlie's offered hand, caught off guard, and placed her own inside it. The contact was instantly exhilarating, like a zap of electricity had just moved through her arm. She was holding hands with her former hot babysitter while wearing possibly the most revealing outfit she'd worn in her entire life. What a surreal experience.

"So. Did you get your book?" Taryn asked, pretending all was normal and she was simply making conversation. Why? Because embarrassment overtook her like a tidal wave as she tried unsuccessfully to get her jumpy vision to behave. All the while, Charlie held on to Taryn, keeping her steady. She adeptly guided her away from the frat house and onto the winding sidewalk that worked its way around the perimeter of campus.

"I did. And I got to see Danny in action in his advisor role. It was…something."

"Right. Your boyfriend. Serious?" Taryn closed one eye thinking maybe that would help. She noticed herself leaning in to Charlie for added support, swallowing back the nausea that bubbled.

"It is serious. We've been together a few years and are planning on many more. Anyway. How are you feeling? Do you need to stop? Do you feel sick?"

"Definitely feel sick, but stopping seems ill-advised." Instead,

Taryn focused skyward. "The clouds are so much more noticeable at night here in academia. Pillows hovering above our heads like haloed professors. Man, I'm poetic when I drink."

"Is that right?" Charlie laughed. "Hovering professor pillows. Intriguing descriptor."

"You would know, being a writer and all. And those people over there, do you see them? Whoa. Look how small. Tiny little folks." They were so cute. She waved and called to them. "Hi. You're adorbs!"

Charlie squinted. "Well, that's just because they're far away."

"Like little figurines poised for war." Taryn laughed at her own assessment, imagining the battle play out on the manicured lawn. But then she tripped on the sidewalk, saved by Charlie, and that brought her back to the present. "Whoops! Shouldn't do that. This is embarrassing."

"It's okay. I've got you." Why was Charlie's voice so smooth? Like warm butter. Taryn remembered her boobs from all those years ago. The white blouse she wore tonight said they were every bit as awesome now.

Taryn sighed. "This is going to be mortifying tomorrow, isn't it? I'm going to wake up in horror and have memories like a patchwork quilt. God, I really like those things. Do you like quilts?" Taryn asked on the steps of Alexander, gripping the railing tighter than customary. Time was still fluid and rebellious. How were they already here? They'd just started walking.

"Quilts? Well, this has taken a turn." Charlie shrugged. "Sure. I can appreciate a good *quilt*."

"I knew you would. I did. It was a lock."

Charlie laughed. "Also, I think you'll be fine tomorrow, other than a well-earned headache."

"Will you, though? You won't hate me. That would be the worst." She was bold to ask, but this was Charlie, whose opinion had always mattered to her. She shielded her eyes in horror. "God, that's intense." The fluorescent light outside the dorm was exceptionally bright, making her shift so the light didn't make her want to squint like Dracula in the sun.

"Why don't we turn you this way?" Charlie angled her so her back was to the light.

"You didn't say if you were going to be okay tomorrow."

"Me?" Charlie turned to look at her, and even in the drunken haze, Taryn spotted the reservation behind her eyes. "Is anyone ever really fine?" Hmm. Maybe things hadn't gone so well with the boyfriend tonight. Obviously, she'd side with Charlie without a shred of information.

"Oh. I'm not really sure. Aren't they?" Taryn wanted to ask more. Actually, she wanted to know everything about Charlie. Her intrigue overflowed, but her communication skills weren't at their best, so she abstained.

"You're probably right. Hey, let's go up to your room."

That perked Taryn up until she decoded the true meaning of the sentence. "No, I can make it on my own. You don't have to escort me."

"It's not really an option I'm comfortable with." Charlie continued walking. Or gliding. She had such an easy, graceful way of moving. Taryn remembered that from years ago, the way Charlie floated through rooms. Thereby, she had no choice but to follow her, well, anywhere.

When they stepped off the elevator, Charlie craned her neck and called out, "Got an overserved client for ya, Gray."

Her RA, who Taryn had only spoken to a couple of times, peered around his open door at the end of the fourth floor. He had messy light brown hair and a tendency to wear a lot of plaid. "You know Gray?" Taryn asked in awe.

"He was a TA for a class I taught last semester. We became friends."

"Because everyone likes you. Even Gray the RA." That cracked her up. "Totally rhymes. He's a lumberjack with all that plaid."

"Yep, totally drunk," Gray said, coming into the hallway.

"Ya think?" Taryn called back, feeling more laughter bubble and take off. She honestly couldn't stop. "I'm sorry. It's probably not as funny as it seems, Gray the RA." She would have to call him that for the rest of time. "I'm aware enough to know that I'm a drunk skunk. Don't hate me." She placed a hand on her forehead as they watched her. "You know what I'm going to hate? The incoming hangover which is so clearly en route. Whoa. I do not hate the artwork on that girl's dry-erase board, though." She squinted. "Wait. It's porn." A pause. She turned her head sideways. "Still not bad."

"Which room is hers?" Charlie asked, pulling her along.

"412," Gray said, proving he knew his charges.

Taryn widened her eyes. "Color me impressed, RA Gray."

"I can take it from here," Gray said. He was so tall. Unnecessarily so. Who authorized that?

"Nope. All mine," Charlie said, and something about that statement made Taryn warm and happy and okay with Charlie manhandling her.

In fact, she'd welcome more of those hands on her body, anywhere Charlie wanted them. She let them inside after three failed attempts to unlock the door and walked straight through the sitting area to her room and found her bed.

"Oh, this is good. Hello, bed. If the ceiling wouldn't spin, it would be even better." She heard a noise in the living room. "Charlie, are you rifling through my fridge right now?"

"Yes, I am." A moment later, Charlie appeared with a bottle of water in each hand. "I want you to drink one now and leave the other one next to your bed. You're going to wake up with a dry mouth. It's the worst. Grab one of these and take at least four swallows."

While the fact that she had to be chaperoned home was embarrassing, Taryn had a soft spot for Charlie's bedside manner. "You got prettier."

"What do you mean?" Charlie asked, removing the cap from one of the waters so it was ready to go.

"You were the prettiest girl in town back home. But you're prettier now. My thoughts are just talking. Are they allowed to do that out loud?"

"Great question." Charlie paused, bottle still in her hand. "But that's sweet of you, Taryn."

Taryn shrugged. "Just drunk honesty. Cue the regrets."

"Why would you regret honesty, especially if it's kind?"

"And it's because you're too smart and gorgeous and sophisticated to hang out with me, and I'm over here gushing."

"You told me I'm pretty. Thank you."

"You're welcome." They exchanged a smile and held it. Taryn felt that moment all the way down to her toes, which she now curled. "I'm so out of my league."

"Your league?" Charlie frowned. "I don't have a clue what you're talking about. We've always hung out just fine. You think you're going to be okay?" She slid a strand of Taryn's hair behind her ear softly and stood up. Taryn wanted her to do that again.

"Ima be just fine," she told Charlie. Though she had a feeling she was only getting drunker. "Did you know this whole time you were friends with Gray?"

"Shocking, but yes."

"I mean that he's the RA guy here and loves chips."

"I knew that, too." A quiet laugh. Taryn smiled at the sound.

"Good night, Taryn. Drink that water. I put my number in your phone in case you need anything. Gray is just down the hall, too."

"You're so nice. A good walk tonight. And quilts. We both like those. So, thank you."

Another quiet laugh. "No problem. Sleep well."

The door clicked shut, and Taryn exhaled. She closed her eyes, but the spinning room let her know that was not in her best interest. Nope. Instead, she lay there and replayed as much of her conversation with Charlie as she possibly could. *Charlie. Right here. So exciting and surreal.* There really was no one like her, and she was everything Taryn remembered about her at a minimum. But with both of them now grown, would their dynamic be different? She wondered if they'd be friends, then laughed that right the hell off. Charlie was a grad student who'd just done Taryn a favor. End of story. Close the book. Pay the check. It's not like they were gonna hang out.

As her stomach roiled, she played music from her phone and tossed a hand over her head, escaping into the angsty sounds of her Chill the Fuck Out playlist until the world finally slowed down. It had to have been a couple hours later when Caz woke her up. She and Sasha flipped on the light in the living room, laughing and shushing each other as they attempted to eat what had to be an entire bag of excessively crunchy chips. Feeling better after the passage of time and two bottles of water, Taryn grinned at their giggles, curious about all they'd seen and done. She'd find out tomorrow. That was the great thing about this place, her new home.

CHAPTER THREE

"But it's the metaphor of the little boy that I'm struggling with," Danny said across the conference table from Charlie. Their handful of classmates looked on, nodding as if he'd made the most notable point. Lawson scribbled a note onto his pad. Their critique session was entering tense territory, and Charlie had to remind herself to remain calm in the face of her classmates' criticism of her short story, especially since she was incredibly proud of it. But that's what grad school did, tore you down so you could learn and be better for it. As much as it hurt, she wanted to be the best writer she could possibly be, and that meant listening to the advice of other writers who perhaps could see what she could not.

"What has you struggling, exactly?" she asked, attempting to remain detached. Her blood pressure was up, however, and she could feel a hint of sweat bead at the back of her neck. Every little sound in the room seemed amplified right down to Lawson tapping his pencil on the table two seats down. She wanted to break it but exhaled instead.

"The wildfire that takes over the city one building at a time is representative of the little boy's passion and creativity that we see spark until it takes off."

"Right. I'm with you." She nodded.

Danny pressed on. "Then, we pull back and see that he was the storyteller all along. I just think that kind of parallel and reveal has been done so many times. It's tired."

Charlie nodded, rolled her lips in, and made a note. "I hear you. I'm processing. I do think it's an element of the story that's vital, however, and I wish that—"

"No need for you to offer a response, Charlie," Dr. Stewart said.

"You can ask a clarifying question or thank your classmate for the note. The session is about taking in information."

"Got it. Thank you, Danny, for the note."

He smiled and sat back. Maybe he was right. Everyone always seemed to think he was. But did he have to appear so smug about it?

"The prose is gorgeous," Emerson said, clearly attempting to inject a little bit of positivity into the discussion. You could always count on Emerson to find the rays of sunshine and hurl them at you. "I got goose bumps several times during the read because of your imagery. The rhythm is also to be admired. I mean, wow. It kept me guessing and thinking, which is what you want in a good short story."

Charlie wrote down the note, grateful for the compliment, but taking it with an Emerson branded grain of salt. "Awesome. Thank you for the note."

"True. Except it did get to be a lot," Danny said. Charlie swiveled, tensing. "And when I can see the author's footprints, it pulls me from the journey. You were trying too hard. That's how it read to me. Purposely shoving beautiful language in my face until I wanted to roll my eyes."

"Yeah, I gotta agree with Danny's assessment," Lawson said. "I felt hit over the head with the fire licking and spreading and spitting and twisting."

"Thank you for the note." She focused on her notebook and the construction of words even though their meaning didn't make a ton of sense to her right now. This was a hard one.

"Self-indulgent," Danny chimed in as if finding the characterization he was searching for. She blinked, regarded him, and contained her frustration. The critique from Danny came off incredibly harsh, and she couldn't help but wonder if he was extra-aggressive because it was her. Or maybe this wasn't about her story as much as it was about Danny retaining the title of strongest writer in the room. She'd never admit that to him, but the suspicion clawed at her daily.

Their classmate Richie joined in. He'd always been levelheaded but also trailed after the other males in the program, not quite a part of their club and aware of it. "I think the metaphor is viable. The little boy's creativity influences all those around him in the same way the fire's destruction touches everyone in the community." He turned to Charlie specifically. "But they're right in saying you're not giving the reader any credit. You don't have to drive the comparison home quite so hard." He held his thumb and forefinger close together. "Mildly insulting."

"I never intended to insult."

"No responses, Charlie."

"Yep. Understood. Thank you for the note, Richie."

The critique continued for another forty grueling minutes, and Charlie left class feeling like a beat-to-hell punching bag. Her nerves were frayed, her confidence zapped, and she wanted more than anything to stare at a wall until it all fell off her. Yet it was only the morning, and she still had a full day ahead. She'd walked into class with such hope and excitement, but the story she'd worked on tirelessly for four straight days and nights without much sleep had been shredded by her classmates in record time. *That's okay. Breathe it out.* High-level writing courses tended to encourage shredding, she had to remind herself. While it didn't mean the story was awful, she had to give credence to some of her colleagues' points, especially the ones they'd had in common.

"Don't take it personally for one second," Emerson said, catching up with her in front of the Modern Languages building. "If anything, the session just offered a few signposts, so the story can find its legs and run. It's good, Charlie. Really good."

"Working on getting there," Charlie said, shielding her eyes from the sun. She took her work seriously, and wading through criticism was part of the process. She had to be good enough to make it in the cutthroat writing world she was set to enter in less than a year. She also had to be strong enough to handle rejection. However, the detail that she couldn't quite reconcile was that Danny, who was supposed to be her person, had led the charge that day with gusto. He'd never been that harsh on any other classmate, ever. In fact, he'd delivered his notes with a pompous gleam in his eye that made her feel like satisfaction lurked. That had been his ego talking, probably inflated by his time at the writers' colony, and it wasn't attractive. "Can I ask a question?" She whirled around and faced Emerson, the dam breaking. "Was it just me, or was Danny not just out for blood, but *my* blood specifically."

"Well." Emerson took a breath and waffled. "I think Danny seemed extra-talkative today. And he had a lot of criticism to impart about a story that was honestly impressive." She shifted her weight from her right foot to her left. "You might be right."

"Thank you." She held her arm out and let it drop with a smack to her side. "So I'm not imagining things, because the look on his face, Em? The smug gratification that radiated off him with each piece of criticism he flung was so foreign and infuriating. I wanted to throw my laptop against the wall."

Emerson frowned and stepped forward. "Pause. Babe, no throwing. This is not like you."

"No. I don't think I've ever thrown anything at a wall before, but the inclination might be worth embracing today, don't you think?" The emotion flowed freely now, a strange feeling. "Why would he not have my back or at least put on the gloves first?"

"I'm not sure. But you can't let Danny get to you," Emerson added with a nod. "He's the type of guy who comes from writing royalty and knows it. He sometimes takes that as a license to throw his status around. But I really thought the story was a gem worth holding on to."

Charlie perked up. "You do? I know you like to stay on the positive, but I'm searching for your honest opinion."

"Yes. In fact, I chased you down to say I think you should submit it somewhere. Do some tweaking and send it off." She shrugged. "I have to get to work. Are you on this afternoon?"

Both she and Emerson worked part-time on campus at the library. Surrounding herself with the works of the greats had served as fantastic inspiration. "Yeah. I'm scheduled four to nine."

Emerson sent her a soft smile. "See you there. First rounds of exams are hitting, so it should be crowded."

She could imagine the reference section now. "My favorite."

Just as Emerson waved good-bye and headed across the grass mall that stretched in the shape of a rectangle across the center of campus, Danny and Lawson appeared. Conferring for a moment, Lawson offered a fist bump and jogged in the opposite direction, which left her and Danny staring at each other. He covered the short distance, making his hair bounce across his forehead, and a smile touched his eyes. "Hi, you."

"Hi." She placed a hand on her hip. "So, that was brutal."

He glanced behind him as if just then remembering the events in class. "Right. The session. I know. Hey, I was an asshole. I just got going and—"

"Couldn't stop. What's that about?" She masked her frustration, shooting for curiosity.

He let his head drop back and searched the tree branches for some sort of whispered answer. "I think I just want you to be the best writer, and sometimes I should examine my tactics a little more carefully."

"You would never have critiqued Lawson that way. Or Richie."

"That's not true."

She exhaled, not wanting to fight but believing her point was valid. "Isn't it?"

Silence reigned.

His jaw tightened. "Thank you for pointing this out to me. I will certainly work harder at how I impart my thoughts." She stared at him for a moment and watched his eyes finally soften. "But I still think you're the raddest human I know, and the most beautiful woman on the planet."

Better.

She sent him a smile back. He was a good guy but sometimes needed to be nudged back to an even playing field. He didn't always have to assert himself as the smartest person in the room, no matter how gifted the world had already decided he was. "Can we remain on the same team? Especially in critique when you know how hard those can be?"

"Yes. And we will." He ran a hand through his hair, and she watched it fall back to his forehead haphazardly. She used to think he was so cute when he did that. He still was, but the summer on her own had altered her perception somehow, equipping her with strength and independence to maybe not need him so much. The time away had given her a newfound confidence to see the world as so much bigger than just Danny McHenry. "But the metaphor is heavily hit. Lawson was right about the fire imagery, too."

She sighed. "Yeah, I know. I'm gonna rework and minimize."

"I'll take a second look if you want."

She nodded, appreciative of his willingness to help. He deviated from her in style, but his prose came right off the page. He specifically dazzled in his creative arrangement of words that took her breath away. His writing was one of the things she most admired about him. No disputing that part. "Yeah, I'd welcome that."

"I miss you," he said and exhaled slowly. "We feel distant lately, and we should work on fixing that. My body misses you, too." He stepped in to her, making it apparent. She couldn't go there with him. Not now.

"I miss you, too." But she tried to keep her voice lighthearted. Her feelings for Danny hadn't suddenly leapt back to life as soon as they'd returned from the break. They'd had sex a couple of times since, but it had been lackluster, making her search for other tethers. Their families were the main link, their shared history. With her mom gone, Danny's family was about all she had left. The water was warm by his side, and the two of them made such sense together. Their mothers had such rich history, and that knowledge nestled warmly in her heart, sanctioning her relationship with Danny. In so many ways, it made her feel like she was doing right by her mom, honoring what could almost be called a dying wish: that she ride off into the sunset with Danny.

"I want you to remember what we were like together," he said. "We can be that again."

"We can. I've been off lately." It was more than that, but her thoughts and spoken words weren't matching.

"It's okay." He was standing so close. Why did she have the urge to take a step back and put space between them? She tried not to panic. Maybe these were growing pains, and she just needed to shake it off and grow the hell up.

"But I have to go."

"I'll come over tonight. We can have some quiet us time." He meant sex, and the thought sent her down a path she didn't want to be on.

"Yeah, maybe."

"It's been a bit." He dipped his head and found her eyes.

"No. I know. It has." She glanced over her shoulder, disentangling herself. "But for now, I better get going. Busy day. I'm not sure about tonight. Let me see how much of that reading I get done for tomorrow."

"Okay." He kissed her once. "See you soon."

She slipped her hands into the pockets of her green quilted jacket, intent on taking a walk before starting the day's assignment and then heading to work. Her heart shifted uncomfortably. There had been a time when she couldn't imagine a world without her and Danny forever and always, and now she was hesitant to so much as encourage a night alone. It's not that she wasn't interested in him or not attracted to him. But there had to be more than just…this. Something new to spark excitement in her life and fill the gaps that were more and more apparent each day.

She could take up dancing. Video games. Or maybe even make a new friend.

Whatever came Charlie's way, her new plan was to embrace it, try it on, and see if it fit. She would run with the signs the universe placed in front of her, and keep her mind open to any and all open doors because the path she was on didn't seem like it was hers.

The very next opened door just so happened to be on her way into the library for her shift. Quite literally. An undergrad had run ahead of Charlie and opened the door with a flourish and a bright smile. "For you."

"Oh, awesome. Thank you," she said and met his gaze purposefully. A little young, but definitely cute with beautiful eyes.

"Anytime," he said smoothly. She enjoyed their semiflirtatious exchange and started off her shift in the circulation section with an extra dose of energy. She wasn't on the market, but the brief connection resonated, reinforcing her need for more.

An hour into her shift up front, she was called to the chaotic reference section as backup. Just like she and Emerson had theorized, it was beyond busy because anyone and everyone was gearing up for the first round of exams. Her line at the circular desk in the middle of the room was long and slow. Even though her feet ached and her brain was getting foggy, she pressed on with a smile, answering questions, directing students to particular reference books, and checking out articles and readings that professors had reserved specifically for their classes.

"Hi, there. What can I do for you?" she asked her next in line.

"Hi. I'm supposed to request the reading material for 1357: Intro to Photography."

Charlie reached behind her for the folder containing the printed article she'd already checked out to a half a dozen students that night. She raised her eyes and paused because the big brown ones looking back at her were familiar. "Taryn Ross."

"Yeah. Hey. I wasn't sure if you'd remember me." A grin bloomed on her face and made Charlie automatically happy. Well, that was something to note. She looked amazing, too. Charlie couldn't keep herself from taking in every detail. Her dark hair was down and swept to one side, resting on her right shoulder. She wore lip gloss and mascara that made her features pop without looking like she was wearing makeup. Her clothes were unremarkable on their own, jeans and a lightweight black V-neck sweater, but on Taryn they were anything but.

"You weren't sure if I'd remember you? I was literally tucking you into bed a couple weeks ago." There was something about Taryn that still grabbed her heart. She'd thought of her several times since that night and wondered when they'd run into each other again. She was so happy they had. In fact, it perked her right up from her mind-numbing shift.

Taryn laughed. “Some things never change.”

“Ha. Good point.” They stared at each other for a moment, and Charlie realized she was still holding the reading. “Right. So, you’ll need this.” She slid the sign-out sheet to Taryn. “Are you a photography major? They have a great department here.”

“I’m officially a part of it. I declared last week.” She shrugged. “I love finding the interesting perspectives that most people gloss over.”

“When the everyday is made special.” Kinda like the outfit Taryn wore. “You’ll have to show me some of your photos someday.”

Taryn’s cheeks warmed to pink. “Let me get a little better first.”

“No way. Then I can’t be there for the artist’s journey from the very beginning. How am I supposed to compare you to your future self without knowing where you started?”

Taryn looked thoughtful, biting her bottom lip with her brows drawn. “Do you really want to see my shots? I’m totally giving you an out if you’re just being kind.”

“I’m not at all kind.” That pulled a laugh, and she relaxed into a smile. “I really do. Let’s grab a coffee together since I’ve seen how you handle alcohol.”

“That’s fair. And really?” Taryn’s smile was tentative and cute. Everything inside Charlie stood at attention, committed to this conversation one hundred percent and enjoying herself.

“*Really*. But it’s fun how you ask me to affirm everything twice.”

“I’ll stop doing that. And yeah, I’d be in.” Taryn looked behind her. “But I think I’m holding up your line,” she whispered.

Charlie flicked a glance. “You are, and they’re about to start throwing things at you.”

“Terrifying.” Taryn winced. “But you’re on for that coffee. I’ll even buy.”

“It’s my lucky night.” She offered her best smile, aware of their unique energy.

“I hope the rest of it isn’t too rough. I’ll be up till at least three.”

“Ouch.”

“S’okay. My own damn fault. Scrawl *procrastinator* across my forehead and make me walk in shame.”

“I’ll get my lipstick. Bye, Taryn.”

“Bye.”

As Charlie assisted the next student with how to go about their Nexis search, she spotted Taryn at a nearby table, poring over her article. With one hand pressed to the side of her forehead, she was lost in concentration, her lips pursed. Charlie could still see glimpses of the young girl she once knew, but the present-day version was so very, very different. She walked with a certain level of confidence she didn't used to have, her movements measured as if she had all the time in the world. Was it swagger? Did Taryn now have that intangible assuredness?

"How's it going?" she asked Taryn, two hours later as she passed by with a stack of reserved books to shelve.

Taryn looked up at her, bleary eyed. "I don't think I'm cut out for this place. Pat my head and send me home."

Charlie placed a hand on Taryn's shoulder and gave it a squeeze. "Yes, you are. Just don't wait so long to cram next time." She gestured with her head to the stairs. "You know, there's a café in the basement open until midnight. Maybe you need some calories or an energy boost."

"Caffeine might save me. When do you get off?" Taryn asked, following Charlie's progress to the nearby shelf.

She checked her watch. "In about twenty minutes."

"Abandoning me."

They were becoming less formal. She enjoyed the playful back-and-forth, almost like a tennis match. "Well, some of us parcel out our schoolwork, which does this amazing thing—allows for sleep."

"Overrated. What about tomorrow?"

"For sleep? I plan to get it then, too." She sent a victorious smile. One point for her.

"No. For our coffee get-together extravaganza. If you're too busy, I get it."

"Hmm. It's Thursday, which means a full day of classes for me. I teach as well."

"You teach, too? What classes?"

"Creative Writing. First year composition." While her schedule was packed, and she'd be exhausted, she couldn't seem to pass up the opportunity for more of…whatever this was. "But I can go to the extravaganza after. Five o'clock?"

Taryn brightened, an adorable puppy all of a sudden. "Five is great. Put your number in my phone, I'll text you, and you can tell me where to meet."

She accepted the phone and typed her number. "I like the plan. Take care of yourself, little Taryn."

"The second time you've called me that." A pause. "Not as little anymore. Or didn't you notice?"

They held eye contact for an extended moment. For whatever reason, the interaction sent warmth down Charlie's spine that she didn't hate. "I actually had," she said quietly.

"Good. I'm gonna go grab that caffeine downstairs. See you tomorrow?"

"You will."

Charlie stood there watching after Taryn, struck by her remarkable and unwavering eye contact that made Charlie feel as if she could see straight into her. She wasn't sure she'd ever experienced anything like it.

She drove home with the music at an overly healthy volume, very aware that she had rebounded nicely from her uncomfortable conversation with Danny and the critique session from hell. Maybe it had been that undergrad opening the door for her with such chivalrous intention, or the steady stream of students that kept her busy shortly after. But she knew beneath it all that the reason for her improved mood were the interactions with Taryn that kept her smiling and grounded. Taryn was a little link to simpler times, and not only that, she emanated a soulful light, which Charlie found contagious. She was interested to hear more about Taryn's life since they'd last connected, what her goals were, what kind of music she listened to now, and what brand of comedy made her laugh without fail. Maybe they'd even become *actual* friends. Wasn't she just imagining making a new one of those? So, she'd chalk this night up to a win and work toward more just like it. The ground felt too unsteady lately, and Charlie could use all the anchors she could gather. Maybe Taryn Ross, her smokin' hot new friend, had crossed her path for a very important reason. Time would certainly tell.

CHAPTER FOUR

Taryn didn't have a lot of very specific talents, but one of them was hiding her nerves when she needed to. Whether it was speaking in front of an audience, taking an important exam, or waiting to hear her father's medical results, she was able to harness her fear and project a calm demeanor. It didn't mean she was calm, however. Inside was a very different story, which meant her reputation as a confident person was flattering, but wholly false. For some reason, Charlie Adler brought out an entirely different side of her. By all accounts, Charlie, who she found beautiful and amazing, should have made her more nervous than anyone, yet the opposite seemed to be true. She could only assume it was Charlie's warm and nonthreatening personality that somehow calmed Taryn's seas, but the effect was a welcome one.

"Well, you look incredibly relaxed and at home."

She knew that voice well. Taryn looked up as Charlie approached her table for their coffee meetup. *Here we go.* She grinned and sat up straight. "Me? Just enjoying the tunes they have going here."

"I kind of thought you'd like the place. Not sure why."

"Well, you nailed it. I'm never leaving."

They shared a smile before Charlie took a seat across from Taryn.

The coffee spot Charlie had suggested, the Bump and Grind, was off campus by about two blocks and maybe one of the most chill places Taryn had encountered since arriving at Hillspoint. Lots of space between tables. Tall ceilings. Calm lighting. She'd definitely be back to sample their creative list of coffee and espresso. Half their menu featured standard coffee classics, but the other side was full of riffs and fancy-free offerings they'd clearly created for the shop. A maple bacon latte? Not her normal fare, but she could congratulate them on the outside-the-box thinking. They also had their own roaster looming large and proud at the back of the dining area, signaling the shop's absolute legitimacy. Even the song on the sound system was a bop she'd be searching out later.

Charlie laughed. "You don't even have coffee yet, and look at you, already in your happy mode."

"I'm in my zone."

"It suits you," Charlie said, using her hands to create the four sides of a frame around Taryn. "Isn't this what you photog types do? Framing? I'd capture this shot right here and call it *Carefree Coffee Connoisseur*."

"The alliteration is a fantastic touch." Taryn grinned and sat up. "And, yes, framing is key to composition. It offers your subject power or takes it away. I'm learning a lot."

"And it shows. What's the best part?"

"I love the way the technical and artistic work together."

Charlie nodded, studying her unabashedly, taking her time. Taryn felt her stare all over and wondered what she was about to say. "You're different these days," were the words Charlie finally chose. "You used to come with this vibration of energy just below the surface, like a sweet puppy dog. Now you seem grounded and unaffected."

"I'm deciding whether you just threw a rock at me. Ow."

Charlie laughed and leaned forward lightning fast, arm out in apology. "No. Not like that. In a really impressive sense. I'm saying you know who you are now."

"Well, I was a kid all those years ago. Lots more energy. Plus, it's a total act. Don't buy any of this. I'm a bundle of nerves half the time. For some reason, less so with you."

"Really?" Charlie seemed intrigued by the confession.

"Oh yes."

Charlie shook her head in mystification. "If you say so." She wore a blue knit top that nearly made her glow and brought out the vibrancy of her eyes. Her blond hair had lazy beach waves, which meant the curls had likely loosened as the day wore on. Taryn liked the look a lot. Too much, apparently, because a tingling sensation engulfed the lower half of her body. Here was the thing. She had a mad crush on this girl. Correction, *woman*. Then again, she likely always had without realizing it back in the day. Charlie was hot and smart and charming, and Taryn's entire being took notice in her presence. Her only hope was that she wasn't broadcasting her feelings.

Charlie pointed at the bar behind Taryn. "I'm going to grab a coffee. What can I get for you?"

"No. I'll get it." Taryn leapt up and then forced herself to slow her movements. "What would you like?"

"Oh." Charlie pulled her face back. "You're gonna buy *me* a coffee?"

"I am. The extravaganza calls for it."

She sat back. "Incredibly sweet of you. I'll take their cookie crumb latte."

"Okay, but that's not a coffee." Taryn winced at the beverage choice and her own blunt response. Her filters didn't work when it came to coffee.

"It's not?" An amused grin. "Well, I'm learning so much. Tell me, Taryn, what is it then?"

"It's a hot milkshake with, I don't know, a sprinkling of caffeine for decoration."

"Oh." She leaned forward. "In that case, I guess I'll take"—Charlie pursed her lips and made a show of contemplation. It was a stunning sight to behold—"a milkshake in hot form with a sprinkling of caffeine. Sounds amazing." She sat back, pleased.

Taryn grinned, put in her place and loving it. Charlie knew what she liked and owned it. Badass. "Coming right up."

She tapped on the bar as she waited on their order, more bonus energy. All the while, she stole glances back at their table, just so damn happy to be in Charlie Adler's presence again. She was hanging out with the cool girl from back home who used to make Taryn feel exponentially more sophisticated by proximity. Throw in the way Charlie's boobs filled out her top, and Taryn might be in over her ridiculously lust-spun head.

"Show her you," she said to herself under her breath. "And no objectification."

The barista slid the drinks her way and followed her gaze to Charlie. "You got this," the girl whispered.

"Oh." She straightened. "No. It's, uh, not like that."

"Mm-hmm," she said with a knowing look on her face. "Whatever you gotta tell yourself. But she's a snack. I say go for it. Leave no crumbs."

"Ha. Yeah. I hear you, but it's never going to happen. Not like that, anyway."

"No? Have you not looked in a mirror?" she asked, turning with the milk jug and placing it back in the fridge. "If it doesn't work out with her, come back sometime. I have a friend I could fix you up with. She'd be all about you."

"Oh. Really? Thanks." Taryn did her best to absorb the compliment and harness its effects. She carried the drinks back to Charlie, feeling an inch or two taller and a lot less on edge. The problem with the barista's advice was that Charlie was the straight girl poster child. She had a serious boyfriend, gave off zero queer energy, and used to flirt with the guys around her lifeguard chair in high school. Sadly, Taryn wasn't exactly her type and knew it. Even if she had been, why would Charlie be interested in an undergrad she used to babysit, for fuck's sake? There was a babysitter barrier she didn't have the ability to hurdle. Something about the no-shot-in-hell realization took the pressure right off. The stakes were nonexistent, so she should relax and enjoy Charlie's company. That helped.

"Hot dessert for you," Taryn said, with a sly grin.

"Look at you. You've grown into a coffee snob."

"Guilty." She slid into the chair across from Charlie's.

"Does your sweet mother know?"

"I think you mean my loud mother." Taryn laughed. "And there's nothing she doesn't know. Martie Ross is intrusive and makes no apologies." She slid a strand of hair behind her ear and leaned in. "My only real time away from my house the past couple of years was studying at coffee shops, the origin of my coffee opinions. I really looked forward to that decompression time, and I ordered everything on their menus. Learned a lot about beans and their roasting processes from conversations with the baristas. Nothing compares to freshly roasted, which is why this place is already getting high marks."

Charlie peered into Taryn's cup and her eyes went wide. "Is that black?" she practically shrieked. "You're drinking black coffee?"

"It's not a horror movie."

"I'm sorry." Her voice was exponentially quieter, making the comedy that much better. "I'll try to compose myself. Are you a mob boss?"

"Not yet," Taryn whispered. Charlie nodded with a knowing gaze as she sipped her liquid dessert. She definitely knew how to enjoy herself, and it was refreshing. Taryn didn't remember her having the unexpected funny side. "Listen, it's the absolute best way to experience the true flavors of the beans. You should try it sometime."

"I don't think I will be. And who are you right now?" Charlie asked around her cup. "This is a glow up."

Taryn made the keep-it-coming gesture. "Say more."

"No way. I will not give you a big head." Charlie squinted in study mode. "You're just a lot more…worldly than I would have imagined at what, twenty?"

"Twenty-one and half, thank you very much."

"Oh, and a half? My mistake. Can't forget the half." She patted Taryn's hand, which just made Taryn feel all the younger.

"Stop that." She vowed to prove her maturity to Charlie one day soon and started brainstorming all the ways to do it. "And you're twenty-six. I remember the age difference."

"You were paying attention, huh?"

"Big-time. I thought you were the coolest." She shrugged. "And I don't mind you getting a big head. Go ahead. I'll wait and sip."

Charlie went still. "And what do you think now?"

Taryn felt a ripple in her stomach, and she resisted the inclination to shimmy against it. There was a very powerful energy bouncing between them that was better than the caffeine high. "So far, you're living up. Dessert style coffee excluded."

"That's fair. What else?" Charlie rested her chin in her hand as if ready for all the details. When the light caught her eyes, they shone such a vibrant shade of sky blue it forced a lump in Taryn's throat. "Catch me up on all that's happened over the years."

"Well, my dad experienced a pretty significant stroke. That's been the headline. My senior year of high school. So you could say everything went sideways. Our plans came to a halt. My mom, who is as strong as a California redwood, was destroyed."

"God." Charlie sat up straighter. "I'm so sorry, Taryn. I had no idea."

"Totally okay. How could you? We didn't plaster it on social media in order to keep his privacy intact, and it's not like you lived in Dyer anymore."

"That must have been absolutely horrific."

Taryn felt the uncomfortable memories swarm. She shoved them away. "It was the worst thing that's ever happened to me." She had to purposefully distract her brain from jumping back in time to the night he'd not been able to speak to her just before crashing into the glass coffee table in their living room. They didn't know if he'd live or die after the ambulance rushed him to the closest hospital. As a family, they'd had to figure out how to maneuver through the life-altering adjustments that had to be made to care for him in that first year. "But he's climbing his way back. He's the most determined person ever."

"Is that why you didn't start at Hillspoint as a first year?"

Taryn hesitated and swallowed the reality. Confessing to Charlie that she'd actually made the decision to bail on school before her father's stroke seemed too embarrassing an admission. She was a coward still in so many ways. The world just didn't know it. "My mom needed my help. For a while, he wasn't able to stay on his own. Mobility and short-term memory issues." The answer, while also true, made her feel like a fraud.

"So you put your world on hold for them. You're a good person, you know that?"

Taryn shrugged. "I think it's what anyone would do for someone they love." She was selfish and hated herself for it, hiding behind her family's misfortune.

"And how is he now? Self-sufficient?"

She softened, because the answer made those scary memories so much more manageable. "Mostly." She touched her chest. "He's working part-time at a new dealership, so it made sense for me to get back to life as scheduled, too."

"I think you're meant to be here at this exact point in time. I'm not sure why I feel that way." Charlie squinted, grappling to explain. "But I do."

Taryn grinned when she thought back to running into Charlie for the first time. "I have to say, spotting your babysitter when you're overserved at your first college party is a little surreal."

Charlie raised a brow. "So is finding my charge drunk on the sidewalk."

"Not my best look."

Charlie opened her mouth and closed it. "You didn't look bad. Trust me on that."

Taryn lifted a brow. "Oh?"

Charlie focused wide-eyed on her cup. "Quite the outfit."

It was probably an innocent comment, but it still made Taryn go warm. Correction, hot. Her blood ran hot and bothered, and she swallowed before searching for proper communication. "I appreciate you trying to make me feel better, but I don't plan on any repeats of the episode."

"Rite of passage. You checked yours off the list."

"So what do you do here exactly? I've heard both student and teacher," Taryn said. She'd been wanting to ask and had even attempted to Google-stalk Charlie but hadn't been able to turn up too many details. "I mean, you're friends with my RA, you've got a boyfriend, you write, and you're a librarian. Do I have all that right?"

"Funny, but I am not the university librarian. The part-time job does help pay for my school loans, however."

"Helpful."

"My main focus is my MFA, everything else is just supportive." Pride flickered, replaced quickly by vulnerability, which made Charlie human and relatable to Taryn. "I don't want to be just a novelist, but a very good one."

The thought of Charlie concentrating in front of a laptop with a candle lit next to her was the sexy image that arrived. *Don't go there.* "I'm impressed by your drive. I have a feeling you're a great writer."

"Well, I hope to be."

"I want to read your work. Do you have anything with you?"

"No. You don't have to read my stuff." A pause. "Really?" Charlie seemed surprised. She pulled her face back as if judging whether the question had been sincere.

"I'm dead serious. Give me something. This second."

The skepticism hung on as she lifted her cup to her mouth slowly. "Not a lot of people are eager to read me. It's like homework when you're close to a writer."

Taryn stared, unwavering. Silence lingered.

"You're sure?"

"I promise. If I'm volunteering for more reading beyond the ridiculous number of pages I've been assigned this semester, then I'm really into the idea." In fact, Taryn couldn't wait to curve into a chair with Charlie's words. She might even indulge in a glass of wine because that seemed scholarly somehow.

"Okay, then." Charlie reached for her bag with slight hesitation. "I have a short story with me. It's about this boy, and…Well, I'll just let you read for yourself. Ten thousand imperfect words." She handed over a hard copy held together with a thick black clip at the top.

Taryn made a show of holding the story, bouncing her palms. "Feels heavy. Feels like serious work."

"I don't know about that." Charlie's eyes met Taryn's, cloudy and regretful. "My class tore it apart in oral critique, but I'd be interested in an outsider's take."

"Why would they do that? Give me the numbers of everyone in their extended families."

"Comes with the grad school territory. We learn, work on developing a thick skin, and try harder next time. I think they do it on purpose, trying to drive us to greatness."

"I don't think I could do that to someone else's creative effort. I wouldn't want to."

"You're a kind person with a big heart. I've never known you to have a mean or judgmental bone in your body."

The words moved through Taryn like heated silver. It was a glimpse into how Charlie viewed her, and she liked it. "I just happen to think the world's better when we're nice to each other. I might be weird."

"You're refreshing."

She sighed. "But if I move forward with photography or photojournalism or whatever, I'm bound to encounter harsh opinions. I guess I might need to toughen the hell up, too."

"Maybe." Charlie studied her, her big blue eyes searching. Taryn liked being studied by Charlie. A lot. "But I kind of prefer the soft edge."

"And soft coffee." The lighthearted comment was her way of remaining a normal, functioning human, deflecting from the things a simple gaze from Charlie did to her. Too late. Her hands itched and her cheeks flamed.

Charlie glanced down at the cup in her hands and rolled her eyes. "You're not going to let this die, are you?"

"Probably not. No." Taryn shook her head and then tossed in a grin. "Just playing, though."

"You're going to keep me on my toes, Taryn."

The sentence indicated they'd be hanging out more. She refrained from her happy dance. There was always later. "Can I say something?"

"Always."

"I don't know. It's just nice to have someone who knew me before Hillspoint." Taryn attempted to find the right way to explain what she meant. "You have to teach everyone about yourself when you come into a new environment. But you *know* me."

"Let's make a deal," Charlie replied immediately.

"A bargain?"

"Exactly that. Let's check in on each other. You can keep me young and cool and on my toes, and I'll be that tether to home. Your safe place to fall if you have a rough day. Or the person you call in the case of unfortunate inebriation." She offered a playful wink.

"I like where you're going. And how do we do that?" Taryn had plenty of ideas that would live in her fantasies but none she'd ever have the courage to voice.

"A regular check-in like this one?"

That didn't sound bad at all. In fact, it delivered Taryn a burst of happiness and warmth in her chest, imagining getting to see Charlie on a regular basis. "I'd love that, actually. I could really use it."

"Then let's do it." An idea seemed to pop into Charlie's head. "Come to my place next week, and I'll make you dinner. I know you don't get anything home-cooked when you're living on campus."

"You have no idea how awesome that would be."

"Then we're definitely doing it. Thursday again?"

"Yeah. I'm free Thursday night."

"How do you feel about savory chicken and pasta? Maybe a linguini."

Taryn's response was delayed because she was picturing Charlie in a sexy apron tasting the sauce like a pro. "I feel like Thursday is so far away."

That pulled a laugh. The sound was brief but Taryn let herself enjoy its melody, feminine and authentic. She wanted to hear more of it and be the root cause. She vowed then and there to make it happen. A new goal, rising easily to the top of her others.

Today had been a good day. She'd scored an A-minus on her digital media exam, sat on the curb with Caz and watched in fascination as the sorority pledges avoided the grass they weren't permitted to walk on, scored some amazing shots of the window washers scaling her residence hall, but the best of all? This coffee date with Charlie.

Taryn couldn't stop smiling as she strolled across campus, hands shoved into the pockets of her black leather jacket. Theirs was easily the best conversation she'd had since arriving on campus. Charlie was still Charlie, and when she directed her attention to Taryn, it felt like the sun was shining on Taryn's face. She was loud and cheerful when she arrived back to the dorm, rifling through the mini fridge and commenting on every potential snack item.

"I do love a good string-cheese stick. But I could also go for a little chocolate milk and a cookie. Pickles offer a nice crunch."

Taryn caught Caz watching her from the doorway to her bedroom. She wore pink socks up to her knees. "Why are you smiling at the food?

Did you take something? I told you I wanted to be there when you get high for the first time."

"I'm entirely sober. I just happen to be in a good mood. And hungry."

Caz pointed at her, arm outstretched. "Yeah, but you never glow. You're the chill one who's affected by very little. There are tiny beams of light literally shooting off you."

Taryn popped a La Croix and took a couple of sips. "You just *think* things don't affect me. I'm secretly freaking out about fifty-four percent of the time."

"But not today. You're broadcasting jubilation." Caz straightened. "Do you like my eyeliner? I'm trying something."

Taryn squinted. "It's got a purple hue."

"That's on purpose. Pink and purple." She gestured to her socks. "Do you like it?" She blinked several times to show off the eyeliner. There were people in the world who wanted to fly under the radar, like herself, and exhibitionists like Caz.

"On you? Yes, please. On others, questionable."

"I take that as a compliment."

Caz was hard to offend, which was one of the things Taryn had grown to really like about her. They were compatible roommates and already pretty good friends. She was lucky to find herself a Caz, clearly a leg up from the gods.

"As well you should," Taryn said. "You're adorable. You going out tonight?" Caz opened her hand for a Le Croix and Taryn tossed her one.

"I wanted that guy Noah to call, but he's been live on TikTok for two hours, going on about his PS5. So I texted Sareen from my statistics class, and we're going to steal a moment at the dive bar on Fourth with the peanuts. Toby the Tiger's."

"Sareen. You've mentioned her before. Is this a romantic outing?"

"Oh yes. That's why I chose the purple."

"Noted. You gonna hook up with her?" Caz's dating life was endlessly interesting. She was a romantic butterfly, flitting from one potential partner to the next, and operated with very little stress about it. She didn't have a preference when it came to sexuality or gender identification, which meant she had no true pattern or type. Caz didn't care about labels or explaining herself to anyone. Admirable and refreshing. In fact, Taryn wanted to be more like Caz and care less about other people's opinions or perceptions.

"I'm not ruling it out. Love her style, a super feminine type but keeps wearing ties to class, and I can't get enough of these ties. I forget to pay attention and miss half the lecture. If she wears a tie tonight, Taryn, I'm a goner. She's like this little hot banker, and I love bankers."

"Wildly specific."

"You're not into bankers? What's wrong with you? With the little pads? I just can't with them."

"I've never pondered *bankers*."

"Do." Caz turned to the mirror on the back of their door. "My horoscope said I should prepare myself for the unexpected, so I'm going to do that."

"I root you on. What does mine say?"

Caz dashed back to her laptop on the coffee table. "The highly heart-driven Aries." She skimmed her findings. "You should be on the lookout for a blast from the past because they just might hold the key to your future."

"My babysitter," Taryn blurted. "Totally."

"Excuse me?"

"I just had coffee with my old babysitter. She was the one who walked me home from the party that first month of school. Remember that?"

"It's familiar but hazy. I was so fucking hungover when you were telling me, which was likely a deterrent to detail retention. Many apologies retroactively."

"It's okay. Charlotte, also known as Charlie, used to babysit me back home. I was eleven. She was sixteen. I was in awe of everything she said and did. Don't get me started on how she looked in a swimsuit. I'll just say it was formative."

"And she's here and she rescued you from the drunken clutches of Tau Kappa Epsilon?"

"Yes! And tucked me into my literal bed, something I wish I had been a little more lucid for. So much regret."

"I love this. You've got the hots for the babysitter?"

"You're ahead of the story."

"Sorry." Caz zipped her lips and sat on her hands.

"Then I ran into her in the reference section of the library. She apparently works there part-time as work study for her grad school program. She's a writer."

Caz unzipped her lips. "Already hot." She promptly rezipped them and sat on her hands again, offering a nod for Taryn to continue.

"Anyway, she invited me for coffee and we had the best conversation." She closed her eyes, ready to go there. "Here's another big admission. I didn't fully realize it at the time, but Charlie was likely my first crush."

"Ah yes, the babysitter crush of many a youth."

"Yep. And wait, there's more. I'm still crushing."

Caz leaned in. "I love this saucy library-slash-coffee tale. Did you two kiss? Open-mouthed or closed? Say open and offer the specifics slowly so I can record them in my mind."

"No, no. Nothing even close to that. We're very platonic, and she's super straight. A boyfriend, even. No hope there."

Caz moved to their mini fridge and found a stick of string cheese she began to peel. "First of all, that's a defeatist attitude. Second, it's impossible to blatantly label someone because of past partners. Unless she's handed you her sexuality, you can't claim it for her. Thereby, Your Honor, hope lives on. I rest my case."

"When did the attorney motif enter the chat?"

"Just now. I improvise, baby."

"Well, Counselor, I hear you, and you're right. But I'm going to rely on the evidence I have until proven otherwise. All signs point to straight. If they didn't, my head would explode and I wouldn't be here anyway, so…" Taryn blinked unable to imagine that scenario under any terms. "Conclusion—I won't make that leap for Charlie, but I also just can't go there. Too many goose bumps. Too much stomach tightening."

"This is going to be a soap opera of a year, isn't it?" Caz took a long drink from her can. "I'm going to relish it."

"I promise I'm more boring than that. Don't get your hopes up."

"The quiet ones always say that." Caz shook her finger at Taryn. "I have a feeling your world is about to open the hell up. Stick with Charlie. If nothing else, you have a cool new older friend who might set aside books for you at the library. Think of the literary scandal."

"I love your appreciation for reading, Caz."

"I love a good story both on and off the page," she deadpanned and winked. "Don't let me down. Now"—Caz set her drink on the small table—"I have a date that might pull in a few sexy details of its own. But more likely a decent beer with a side of peanuts." She stuck her arms out to slow her roll. "Not gonna get ahead of myself. This is so chill. Look how chill I am. Even around ties. Give me the awards." It was Caz's own brand of pep talk, and Taryn smiled at the rare display of vulnerability from her roommate.

"You're gonna have the best time. Don't get in your head."

"A sage, you are. Okay, bye now."

Taryn sat back and watched her friend bound out of the room into the worldwide festival of dating that she wasn't yet a part of. Yes, her time would come, but her little gay heart wished it would hurry the hell up. In the meantime, she had a boring date with her nemesis, the Spanish language.

Chapter Five

Charlie's world was plummeting into chaos. She loathed having too many balls in the air because at any moment, one was going to fall like lead, straight onto her face. Today, she had the gnawing sensation that she'd forgotten something pressing, but as she drove quickly from her afternoon teaching gig back to her apartment, her brain was too scattered to land on just what. All she knew was that she had a very important departmental cocktail hour the next evening and absolutely nothing suitable to wear. She'd need a dress, and not one of the same two she'd already worn to these things countless times in the past. She killed her engine when her phone vibrated.

Are we still doing today? After five and no you.

Oh fuck. Taryn. No, no, no. That was the thing she'd missed. They'd decided to put off dinner until next time but were supposed to check out the walking trails at Jameson Park, and her overcrowded brain had blanked.

Sooooo sorry. Any chance you'd want to shop instead?

It was the best Charlie could offer without canceling on her entirely, which she didn't want to do. She'd actually been really looking forward to seeing Taryn again, a bright spot on her week's agenda. They'd had such a fun time at the coffee shop the week prior.

Grocery?

Dress. The cocktail variety.

The dots danced while Charlie waited. *Um. Really bad at that. Never really been a dress wearing kind of girl.*

Dress would be for me.

She touched her forehead and exhaled, attempting to slow down. Tame the chaos. Moving through her day so quickly was what caused her to blank on Taryn in the first place. *Get it together*. The good news was that the hard part of her day was done, the lecture that had her on edge was now over, and she could just coast with Taryn, her new/old friend. Decided, she thought with an exhale. She would chill the hell out and coast.

When Taryn didn't immediately answer, Charlie hit the call button and decided to give her an out. "You don't have to come," she said immediately. "But I have an event tomorrow and nothing to wear. A true emergency."

"I think I get it now," Taryn said. She had such a smooth voice with the tiniest rasp. It sent a tingle to Charlie's ear, leaving her a little drunk. "This is an elbow-rubbing English department dress." A pause. "I mean, I could try to help."

"Really? You'd be down? I could definitely use a second opinion."

"Well. Don't get too excited. Let's take me to a store and see what happens."

"A mall. We're headed to an actual mall." Charlie smiled into her phone. "And that's what I was hoping you would say."

A quiet laugh. "I don't like to disappoint."

Why did Charlie break out in goose bumps after that statement? Why did she want Taryn to say it again? She eased herself out of it. "Get over here. Now. I'll drop a pin and my address."

Taryn laughed. "Yeah, yeah. On my way."

Ten minutes later, and they were driving together in Charlie's Nissan Rogue to the nearest department store with the meager remnants of her checking account and Taryn on music duty. Apparently, she wasn't having much success. As the station flipped for the sixth time, Charlie turned to her. "I feel like you're hard to please over there, or you're just determined to torture me because I'm making you shop."

Caught, Taryn's brown eyes went wide. They seemed extra vibrant today, highlighted by the gold knit top she wore beneath her black leather bomber jacket. Her dark hair was down but had a few waves today, which made Charlie imagine that's what her hair did when she chose not to blow dry, which she should definitely do more often. The untamed look worked on her. "I'm so choosy about music."

"I'm gonna make the leap that you're choosy about everything," Charlie said. "I haven't forgotten your coffee opinions."

Taryn's cheeks went rosy in a cute display. "I think you're roasting me."

"Is that a coffee riff?"

"Like I would miss this opportunity," Taryn said, pleased with herself. They were at a red light, which meant Charlie didn't have to tear her eyes away.

"I'm affectionately doing just that. Yeah." She relaxed. "What kind of music do you like?"

Taryn sat taller and abandoned the station flipping, invested in the conversation now. "That's the thing. I'm all over the map. My grandparents had me hooked on James Taylor as a kid. My parents blasted Motown in an unlikely matchup, but I was into it. I was just as die-hard for local emo bands as a teenager. Some of the Top 40 work for me. Rap, if it's good."

"Eclectic." The light turned and Charlie pressed the gas.

"I'm currently living in the highlights from practically any era, hanging out with what was popular at different points in time." Taryn shook her head. "I'm easily influenced, but when all is said and done, I love the one girl and a guitar vibe. It's my current go-to."

"Really? You're an old soul, Taryn Ross."

"I'm taking that as a compliment even if it wasn't meant to be."

"Except it was," Charlie said sincerely and pulled the car into a spot near the front door of Carrington's. "Hopefully, we can be in and out quick."

"What do you need from me?" Taryn asked with honestly the most sincere eyes. She clearly wanted to make sure she did the best job possible, which was sweet.

"How about your honest opinion? Tell me which dress makes me looks like someone impressive, yet also personable enough over a glass of white wine."

Taryn slowed her pace, processing the task. "That's incredibly specific, but yeah, I think I'm up for it."

Charlie laughed and looped her arm through Taryn's. "I know you are."

They moved through the racks, Taryn offered up her choices, and Charlie collected a few dresses of her own. It turned out, Taryn had quite the eye. Once Charlie was inside the dressing room on her own, it was Taryn's contributions to the pile that truly stood out. Charlie turned to the side wearing a turquoise fit and flare and realized it was a definite contender. It was the fourth dress she'd tried on, and it made her feel pretty and smart, a combination that had always worked well for her. She opened the door and walked to the sitting area that offered a full-length mirror.

"I think I really like this one," she said to Taryn, who was seated quietly on one of the couches. Charlie smoothed the fabric and regarded herself in the mirror. "What do you think?"

Taryn stared for a moment before opening her mouth and closing it again. "It's a beautiful dress." She swallowed. "Buy it. Whatever it costs."

Charlie laughed. "That's quite an endorsement." She turned to the side. "Do you think it's giving too much boob access?"

"No," Taryn said without delay. "I don't."

Another laugh. She turned to Taryn, whose eyes had gone wide. "Again, you know what you like."

"Yeah," Taryn said. "I guess I do."

Charlie felt warm with Taryn's gaze on her like that. She was suddenly a little self-conscious and aware of her own skin. Weird, and honestly a little embarrassing. "Wow. It's like they're running the heat pretty high in here," she said, looking up at the vents as a means of deflecting attention from what felt like a strange moment. She had no definition for what she'd just experienced, either. A passing few seconds in which Charlie felt like she'd floated right out of herself.

"Right? Not just me then," Taryn said, standing and rolling her shoulders.

"No, not just you." Charlie added a laugh to fill the unexplainable space. Her eyes connected with Taryn's, and just like that, she felt like herself again. "I think I'm going to take this one."

"There really is no other choice." Taryn ran a hand through her hair. The action rearranged where her part fell, giving her a very sexy edge. What a difference a mindless flip could make. Taryn executed it expertly.

"What are you staring at?" Taryn asked. She looked behind her.

"The way you flipped your hair just now made you look like a rock star. One little gesture and you changed your whole look." As she passed Taryn on her way back to the dressing room, she gave her hair a playful tug. "There has to be an analogy for life in there somewhere."

"What's the thing my mom used to say about my dad's stroke? Things can change on a dime."

Charlie paused in the doorway of the small dressing room, the concept loosening a memory. "Isn't that the damn truth? When I was nine, my family was having spaghetti and meatballs for dinner. My absolute favorite. I had been excited all day waiting for my mom to call us to dinner." Taryn smiled at that. "My mom served me my helping, which I remember being very generous, several meatballs. She knew how much I adored spaghetti. Just on cloud nine, I reached for the Parmesan cheese and knocked my glass of milk over in the process. It spilled all over my plate and some onto my father's. He backhanded me so fast I didn't even see it coming. Didn't realize it had happened until I found myself on the floor stunned. A total one-eighty moment. Like you described." The room was silent. Charlie realized her mistake. "Changed on a dime," she said with a lot less volume.

Taryn blinked at her, sadness and shock crisscrossing her face. "Charlie," she said quietly after a moment.

Oh fuck. Why'd she have to go and do that? They were having a nice time, and bam, she'd just served up a memory she'd long since tucked away. Embarrassing. She scrambled for a smile to save the mood. "I know. Pretty awful story." She shook her head, amazed that the whole thing had just tumbled out of her mouth. "I have no idea why I decided to share that, but here we are. Tell you what. Let's move on. Dresses! Yay!" She tossed in a laugh. Taryn didn't join her.

"Were you okay?"

"That time?" She scanned her history. "Um, actually, no. My jaw was fractured, and eating was an ordeal for a few weeks. All good now. Leagues better. Not as big a meatball fan anymore, though."

Two women entered the dressing room in a flurry of energetic conversation, which put an end to theirs. They stared at each other, solemn and stuck in the aftermath of the exchange for a couple of long moments. "Anyway," Charlie said with a shrug. "Things *can* certainly change on a dime. Even this conversation."

She paid for the dress she wouldn't have even tried on if it wasn't for Taryn, and they began to walk the length of the mall in silence. A cloud hung over them that Charlie wasn't sure how to remedy. Finally, Taryn looked over at her, her eyes big and melancholy. "I remember your father. He always seemed like such a nice guy, almost jolly. Everyone loved him. He'd come over for beers with my dad after work."

"I remember that, too." Charlie reflected back on the days when her dad was still living with them. "He was incredibly charming. And manipulative. It's why he sold so many cars. I'm not surprised your dad liked him so much. He was good at fooling the world. Hell, even my mom fell for his act at first."

"Forgive me for being in awful amazement right now. I'm looking back on everything differently."

Charlie turned to her. "Well, don't look at me differently."

"I wouldn't."

"Good. Because I'm far past those days and not looking back." It was an optimistic statement because Charlie was aware of the effects her childhood still had on her outlook and behavior. She didn't let herself reach for too much because she was confident it would be taken away. And when she finally did grab hold of something wonderful, it wasn't out of her character to self-sabotage or decide she didn't deserve it. Charlie was a work in progress. Years of therapy had helped until she finally decided she needed a break.

"Here's the thing. I don't want you to get caught up in my less-than-ideal childhood. I'm okay. See?" She brightened into a grin that she hoped conveyed her current mental health, which definitely resided in the *just fine* column.

Taryn's expression didn't follow her lead. "I'm a little pissed off on your behalf. Are they still together?"

"My parents? No. I lost my mom to stage four cancer a few years ago."

"Charlie. I'm going on about my dad's stroke and you didn't say a word."

"It's not my favorite topic." She nodded as they walked. Somehow the movement made diving back into these details easier. She smiled at the memory of her mom, the biggest cheerleader she ever had. "She was my favorite person. The only one I knew I could depend on. Danny's mom was her best friend and has been great to me since Mom died. She's pretty well known, an author. Monica McHenry. Heard of her?"

"I have. The novelist who writes the mysteries." Taryn turned, surprised. "They just did a movie from one of her books."

"That's her. My famous stand-in mom. I'm lucky in that sense."

"And what about your dad?"

"Once we moved to California, everything got worse. My dad's dealership never came to fruition. He was angry about that and choked some guy in a bar, which got him three months in jail. Luckily, the space gave my mom the courage to hire an attorney and get the hell out. My last year of high school was the best ever. My mom and I had so much fun and felt what it was like to just breathe and laugh and relax in our own home, which was this cute little two-bedroom cottage that was perfect for us. I don't have a clue where my dad is now and don't want to know. He could be living it up in Beverly Hills or in a jail in South Carolina. Who the hell knows?"

"God, I hate him now." Taryn was still rigid, her fists balled and tight.

"Come here a sec." Charlie took a moment and pulled them onto a nearby bench to see if she could get their night back on track. She hooked a strand of hair behind her ear. "One thing I've learned about trauma is that sometimes it sneaks back up on you, like it did me in the dressing room back there. The healing isn't exactly linear. I'm sorry for bringing our night down. I hope it won't happen again, but I should warn you that it might."

"No, no, no." Taryn put her hand over Charlie's, which was more comforting than she would have predicted, a surprise anchor in the storm. "Please don't apologize. You don't have a single thing to be sorry for." Her voice was quiet and steady, which made it really easy to believe her.

Charlie nodded, her heart somersaulting. "Thank you. You're right. I know that deep down." No one deserved to be hit or insulted. Yet she still lived with the feeling of embarrassment that came with victim status. She remembered wondering as a child what she had done for her dad to hate her so much. She tried to be more like her friends in elementary school, imagining their dads loved and took care of them because they'd done something right. She thought she could have that, too, if she just tried a little harder. It was ludicrous, looking back now, but at the same time, old habits died hard. To this day Charlie often *felt* unworthy of love even when she *knew* she wasn't. It was a mind fuck that kept her moving in circles and hesitant to let others in.

"In fact," Taryn continued, "I'm feeling like a special person right now because you *did* share that memory with me when you didn't have to. You trusted me, and I want to say thank you for that."

Charlie blinked. That was certainly new. She was used to making other people uncomfortable whenever she mentioned anything too real from life with her dad. Certainly, no one had thanked her before. "You're welcome seems like a strange thing to say back."

"Honestly, you can say whatever you want, and I'll listen." Taryn took her hand and squeezed it. "I've been told I do that kind of thing well."

Charlie looked down at their hands and pulled her gaze back to Taryn's captivating brown eyes. "I've always thought you had the prettiest eyes. They seem lighter these days. Little flecks of gold within the brown."

"Oh yeah?"

"Yeah." Charlie forgot herself in their connection, and wow, Taryn excelled at eye contact. The world felt hazy, slow, and off balance in its wake. The edges of her vision faded. In a strange turn, it seemed like they were the only two people in that mall in spite of the crowds moving busily around them. An oasis if she'd ever found one. Finally, she blinked, looked down, and offered a slight smile, honesty bleeding straight through. "I feel like I know you better than I do. Isn't that weird?"

"Well, you do. We have true history, ya know. You were instrumental in my youth. Probably a lot more than you realize." Taryn seemed to be leaving the details out, but this felt like a confession of her own. Maybe it was just that kind of evening for them.

"You mentioned that at the coffee house. Why is that? Because I gave you lemonade slushies and middle school advice?" It was hard to equate this put-together human with the eleven-year-old from back then. In actuality, both versions were mature for their age, now that she thought about it. Taryn had always been both wise and kind. That hadn't changed.

"No, because you gave me someone to look up to, who also made me feel special and seen. I thought you were just about the best thing since I discovered Sour Patch Kids at six years old."

"First comparison I've ever had to those things. What a day."

"That's odd. I compare them to everything." She regrouped. "But the truth is, I was thrilled every single time I heard you were coming over. Charlotte Adler was cooler than cool, which is why it was such a blow when you moved away so unexpectedly."

Charlie sat with that information for a moment because she'd honestly had no idea. Realizing that she'd had a larger impact than she'd understood relaxed something in her chest. She was both moved and slanted with regret. "I'm so sorry. I would have stayed in touch if I'd known. You must have thought I didn't care, and I promise you, I did."

"Stop. Your life was much bigger than mine back then. Popular, pretty, and good at everything. All my friends wanted to be you. Guys were obsessed with you." Taryn turned to her more fully, energized, and with a smile. "They used to stalk your lifeguard chair. Were you aware of this?"

"Maybe some did." Charlie had relished her social world in high school. It was true. She'd had friends, a job, and all of it had served as a nice escape from the homelife that kept her on the edge of most any chair. "Everything probably looked perfect. I get that." She tilted her head thoughtfully as a toddler raced ahead of his mother, pointing at the mall's Halloween display. "But I think that just goes to show that *all that glisters is not gold.*"

"Quoting Shakespeare. A true writer."

Charlie turned in surprise. "I'm impressed. You knew the quote that quickly?"

Taryn beamed and shrugged. "I like his stuff. We read *R and J* in high school, but I picked up a few more after."

"Oh, just a little light reading for a high schooler." She shook her head. Taryn continued to offer up surprises. She was this really interesting onion with layer upon layer waiting to be discovered.

"You're maybe one of the only people I know who thinks I'm awesome for reading plays."

She nudged Taryn's shoulder with her own. "Good thing I'm the one sitting next to you, then."

"Speaking of writing, I loved your story. I devoured it that night and then read it a few more times."

Charlie went still. "You did? I hope it wasn't out of some sense of obligation to make me feel better after I confessed what happened in my class."

"I wish I was someone who responded to overhanging obligation. Maybe then I wouldn't procrastinate so much. My grades would be much higher if I subscribed to *have to*. Which means, in your case, I *wanted to*."

"I feel better, then." Charlie would have loved to have been cavalier about Taryn's thoughts on her story, but her heart overruled her. "You don't have to be polite about your impressions. I have a pretty thick skin these days."

"But here's the thing. I was truly enraptured, hooked, and annoyed with you because I was supposed to be writing an analysis on a pivotal photographer," Taryn said, a softness coating her voice. Charlie was learning to like the gentle side of her. She was a quieter person, which made her harder to get a read on. But when Taryn *melted* in the way she just had, Charlie did, too. She had a definite soft spot for this girl, unique in the way it made her feel. "The contrast between the two stories was hugely impactful. The boy. The fire. You wove it with a true seamlessness."

"My peers felt the metaphor between the boy and the fire was heavy-handed."

Taryn blinked. "I couldn't disagree more. I'm not an MFA writing candidate, but is that who you write for at the end of the day? People who set out to find perceived weaknesses, or someone like me who just lets the story wash over them?"

"Well, when you put it that way, you. Most definitely you." She internalized the concept. "This is a valuable reminder that the larger world won't be reading my work with the same fine-tooth comb my classmates do." She exhaled. "I really look forward to an audience shift." She covered her eyes, remembering the stress of those critiques. "That will be such a relief."

Taryn smiled. "Just here to offer a preview. I especially liked the scene where the boy sat with a paintbrush for the first time and learned he could create." She shrugged. "It's a weak comparison, but I've felt exactly the things you described recently."

"Tell me when."

Taryn got a faraway look in her eye, transported. "I picked up a camera at a resale shop earlier in the semester and have taken quite a few shots around campus." She gave her head a shake. "The realization that I'd captured something that hadn't been there moments before really struck me. It was almost like I was meant to read your words. I mean, you illustrated the feeling I had perfectly."

With her gaze locked with Taryn's, the world went still again. She'd never get used to it. She wanted to touch Taryn's cheek, her hair, take her hand. She didn't dare. First of all, this was *Taryn*, the kid from back home. Emphasis on *kid.* Second, Taryn was a girl. Third, Charlie had a boyfriend. None of the urges that seemed to be swirling could be given any kind of credence. "I'm so glad." She focused on the conversation, keeping herself in the midst of the topic at hand. No more *thoughts* of Taryn. "There's a true beauty in the creation of art, isn't there? I'm honored I was able to exemplify the feeling for you."

"Me, too. And I'd love to read more if you're willing to share."

"I just might be if you show me some of your shots in return."

"Okay, but I'm aspiring at best." Taryn blinked, and Charlie caught sight of her long, dark lashes that had no right to be so beautiful. Actually, Taryn herself was. Charlie noticed more and more with each moment they spent together. It made her nervous and vulnerable in a strange sense, and dammit, she was doing it again. But it seemed like Taryn saw every part of her, straight to her soul. Jarring and hard to ignore.

Charlie shifted, off center with butterflies crisscrossing her stomach. Her skin felt sensitive to the touch, and her mind wouldn't obey even the simplest rules. None of this was like her. "I like to support aspiring artists."

"You'd have to go easy on me. I don't know if I'm good or not. But at least my professor seems to think I have an eye. I'm holding on to that compliment, if you couldn't tell."

"I have a feeling your professor is right. When can I see them?"

"Um, are we doing next week?" Taryn asked, keeping to their schedule.

"I don't want to wait until next week." In this moment, she couldn't imagine doing so. The time they were spending together felt like water in a desert.

The sentiment seemed to catch Taryn off guard. She sank into a smile. "Okay. Sooner than that, then."

"I have work at the library tomorrow, but what about the day after? I'm free after four."

"Damn. I have my hours in the photo lab. The darkroom is hard to reserve."

"Then don't lose your slot. I get off at ten tomorrow. You could come over to my place. I usually make a late dinner. Something quick and easy like pasta and chicken marsala."

Taryn nodded, stone-faced. "Yeah, I know when I think quick and dirty dinner, a chicken marsala is always at the top of my list. So basic."

She winced. "I heard it once I said it."

Taryn laughed. "Do you pop in a soufflé for dessert? Beef bourguignon must be saved for the weekend."

Now Charlie was laughing as well, which, after their earlier conversation, helped lighten her mood immensely. "I promise I'm not a culinary elitist, but I have a very savory palate, and anything with wine in the sauce is a warm embrace, okay?"

"I'm that way with cheese, which is why the famous chefs from Kraft always make my macaroni with the utmost care and packaging," Taryn said quite seriously. "I prepare it on medium in the most delightful cooking mechanism called a microwave. I pronounce it *mee-cro-wav*. I'm not sure if you're familiar."

Charlie tapped her chin with one finger. "Vaguely rings a bell. So, are you coming over or not, weirdo?" Why was Charlie practically holding her breath?

Taryn relaxed back into herself. "For chicken marsala in the middle of the night? Not sure how I could pass up such an opportunity."

Charlie exhaled. "You really can't."

"And I wouldn't want to."

"Done." Charlie lifted her bag. "So let's get out of here and get you back to your homework."

"You still think I'm a child."

Charlie grabbed Taryn by the back of the neck and gave her gentle shake. "Trust me when I say that I don't."

Chapter Six

Her parents were thankfully doing okay.

That was the headline Taryn took away from every FaceTime call she had with the two of them, multiple times a week. It gave her peace of mind to see them bustling around the house, bickering about dinner plans, and acting like every decision of hers belonged to the group for discussion.

"Are you getting enough nutrients, though?" her mother asked for the hundredth time since Taryn had arrived at Hillspoint. "You never pay much attention to what you're consuming, and you need to take care of your body, or you'll simply shrivel up like a college-aged raisin. Is that what you want?"

"I had an omelet for lunch at the dining hall and so far no shriveling. I keep checking, too. Just waiting for bam, raisin status. But nothing. It's weird."

"Still have your same sense of humor, I see. One omelet on its own is not enough."

"I'll have three next time. Maybe four." She offered a cheeky smile.

"Thank you. A side of fruit will do." Her mother's face filled the screen as she leaned in, reminding Taryn of one of those fun house mirrors. "You never know who you might have to fight late at night in a parking lot. Do you have plans tonight? Take your pepper spray. I'm dead serious."

"Later on tonight, I'm getting together with Charlie. I'm not going to pepper-spray her, though. It's rude."

"Your old sitter?" her dad asked.

"Remember I told you? She's a grad student here."

Her mom reclaimed the screen. "How is Charlotte?"

"She's a badass writer now. I just read a short story of hers and feel like I have offered very little to the world in comparison. She's so talented, Mom."

She saw the corner of her dad's face edge in. "Ronnie's daughter, right?"

Taryn tensed at the mention of the man's name. She'd still not gotten past what she'd learned about him from Charlie. In fact, it kept her up half the night prior. "That's the one."

"I wonder how he's doing. I heard they divorced."

"I heard he went to jail for assault at one point. Charlie doesn't really talk to him these days."

Her father's smile faded. "He always did run a bit hot when things didn't go his way."

"Sounds like more than that, Dad."

"Is that what she said?" her mother asked, clearly not liking the implication. Her parents were pushy, but in a good way.

"With a few more unfortunate details. I hope I handled the situation correctly."

She watched her mom's features soften. "You're a good person, Tare. I know you did. Be her friend. It's the best thing you can do for another human."

"Working on it. Trying to find the right mix of available but not annoying."

"You'll get there," her mom said.

There was a lull at that point. The awful topic seemed to have left all three of them grappling for conversation.

"So…how's being gay?" her dad asked.

She laughed. "Wow. Thank you for asking." She exhaled into sincerity. "It feels good to just be myself. Not that I'm a *practicing* lesbian."

"Yet," he said with a great deal of enthusiasm.

Her mother was a little more timid on the subject, which was interesting because there was rarely anything timid about her. Taryn remembered her mom's reaction to first learning Taryn was attracted to women.

She'd been sitting on their green couch, clutching a throw pillow to her chest tightly. "I love you so much. I just don't want anyone to ever hurt you or say anything unkind. I will tackle them like a linebacker and beat them with my Lillian Vernon bag. I swear to God, Taryn, I will do it. I might go to jail."

"But that's your favorite bag," Taryn had said and patted her mom's knee. "Pick a different one for the beating, okay?"

"I just want the world for you, Tare-Bear, and if there's a woman holding your hand through it rather than a man, that's every bit as wonderful. But I just pray she likes our Frito Pie Sundays because who doesn't?" Her mom seemed genuinely concerned about Frito Pie popularity.

"I'm sure she will, Mom, whoever she is." Taryn had sighed. "First, I have to work up the courage to announce myself to the lesbian and bisexual population of the world." It had taken her years to even get to this point.

"You take your time," her father had said from his spot in the entryway. He was more of a lingerer than a full conversation joiner, preferring to shout things and retreat. "You have a clean slate coming up when you head to Hillspoint. That's the best thing about college. You get to start all over."

"Yeah. I'm really looking forward to that part of things. Being me. No hiding."

That had been months ago, and Taryn now lived as a happy young gay, very much looking forward to gay life, gay kissing, and allowing herself to feel all the gay things without guilt or shame. So far, so good. She was more than ready for the next step, which was someone potentially to share it with. She'd kissed exactly four people in high school and only one of them had been female. Bianca Mack. They'd first kissed just outside the gym door fifteen minutes after school got out for the day. Bianca had flirted with her countless times, and Taryn finally shut off her brain and took the leap. It had been fun sneaking around for a bit, but in the end, Taryn grew tired of Bianca smoking weed all weekend, and Bianca thought Taryn had weird taste in everything down to licorice flavors. So they'd let things between them fade without anyone ever knowing they were fooling around. Yet Taryn couldn't help but wonder what an actual relationship would be like with someone she *was* compatible with. Would she count the minutes until she could see her again? Get nervous, excited, and extra-talkative in her presence? Would Taryn be an affectionate partner? A romantic? She had a feeling all of those things would prove to be true and looked forward to finding out.

"I've not really found anyone I'm interested in at this point, but there's still time in the semester to maybe dip my toe in."

Her dad popped back onscreen. "Try one of those apps on all the commercials. Guppies in the Lake. Something like that."

"Minnows Abound," her mother chimed in with a laugh.

"Sharks in a Pond," her dad countered.

"Thanks, you two. I'll see how I do on marine-inspired dating apps."

Her mother blew a kiss to the screen. "Love you, Tare-Bear. You're our gift and don't you forget it. I'm gonna send you a striped sweater I saw on Amazon that is very *you*."

"And I'm not the least bit terrified. I love you guys. Dad, take care of yourself, please."

He offered a salute. "Doc says I'm close to fighting shape. You'll be surprised when you see me again."

"I don't doubt it."

They said their good-byes, and Taryn slid off the call, leaning back against her headboard, phone pressed to her chest. It always took her a minute to disconnect from her world back home and float into the present again.

While it was hard being away after having experienced so much with her family in the last two and a half years, the near-daily conversations with her parents kept Taryn going and reassured her that they were both doing okay without her.

She exhaled slowly and allowed herself to look forward to the next part of her night. She checked the clock again. Charlie would be getting off from the library about now, which meant she should head over to her apartment in about twenty minutes. Nervous energy zigged and zagged. An extra hit of exhilaration threaded itself on a needle and wove through her system.

"You're smiling," Caz said when she poked her head into Taryn's bedroom. "Want to hit up Toby's for a pool tournament with the fourth floor? I suck but they don't need to know that."

Any other night and she would have been down. But canceling on Charlie was not exactly in her DNA. "I have important plans," she said with a wince. "Sorry."

"Is it a date? Is that why you're grinning?" Caz asked, coming fully into her room and plopping down on Taryn's bed like it was hers. Taryn loved that.

"Nope. Late night dinner with Charlie. She just got off."

"I see now. It's all becoming clear," Caz said with a shoulder shimmy. "Maybe you could get her off, too. If ya know what I mean. What?" She looked around the room. "Who would say something like that? Oh, right. Me. I would."

Taryn stared her friend down and shook her head. But in spite of the jokes, Caz was proving to be a decent sounding board. Her advice was always measured and mature. "Here's the thing. I need to talk this out a minute before I head over there. Can you help?"

Caz's eyes went wide and she popped to her feet. "I'm so ready. Born for this. Go." She placed her hands on her hips and proceeded to pace the room in listening mode.

"I love spending time with Charlie, but she treats me like one of her best girlfriends. She asked me how her boobs looked in a dress at the mall and circles her arm through mine when we walk, like we're two really chummy gals about town."

Caz paused her walk, whirled on Taryn, and pointed. "And that's not where you are at all. You don't want to be her chum!"

"No! It's so not a mirror of the urges I'm feeling, which—I might add—are beyond the scope of real possibility. I'm not delusional."

"Because you're still convinced she's straight."

"All signals lead there. But there's this tiny little *what-if* that's sneaking up the back of my spine based on a couple of our interactions."

"Like?"

"Prolonged, meaningful eye contact."

"Fuck. That's a buying sign."

"Don't get ahead of yourself," Taryn said, pointing at her. "But there's also been moments where I wondered if she'd been checking me out."

"Double fuck."

"I know. And if it's not a figment of my imagination, I want to make sure she has me in the correct box."

Caz shrugged like she'd just been asked a ridiculously easy math problem. "Then you gotta paint the box in red for her so there's no mistaking it."

"I don't know how to highlight the box."

"Kissing her face off might offer clarity," Caz said, dropping her hands.

Taryn closed her eyes. The suggestion was so far from plausible but, at the same time, offered up a visual that turned her the hell on. Not exactly helpful. "I appreciate the advice. I will work on ways to paint the damn box red."

"Have it your way, but will you keep me updated?" Caz asked in a much more sincere tone. "I know I'm a sarcastic ass sometimes, but I really do think you're rad and want to help in any way I can." She offered her fist up for a bump, which Taryn took her up on.

"I think you're awesome, too. Thanks, Caz. Beat everyone at pool."

"From your adorably full lips."

Half an hour later, when she arrived at the navy and white Sailor's Sound apartment complex, Taryn had made the decision that she simply had to loosen up around Charlie and show more of who she actually was. Honesty was best.

When Charlie answered the door in a pair of gray joggers and a gray and black snuggly hoodie, Taryn melted. She looked both soft and hot, and the combination sang the song of sexy to Taryn's heart. The way strands of blond hair fell out of Charlie's ponytail and framed her face made Taryn want to stand there and admire her forever. Luckily, her social skills overrode her cartoonlike longing.

Taryn gestured to Charlie's outfit. "You're already changed and much more comfortable than I am. I missed the memo. Boring jeans. So many regrets."

"Not at all boring." Charlie sent her a smile that could calm any storm and tilted her head. "Also, one can't cook unless one is relaxed. The food simply wouldn't taste good." That's when the aromas wafted onto the porch. Something savory and amazing was sizzling on the stove a few yards behind Charlie. "On that note, get in here. I gotta get back to my pans." Charlie grabbed Taryn by the front of her shirt and tugged her inside.

"You know how to welcome a person."

"Would you like a drink?" Charlie winced. "But go easy. I can't tuck you in tonight." She tossed in a playful wink.

"A soda would be fine. I'm only an occasional drinker, as probably evidenced by how hard it hit me that night."

"Wise." Charlie opened her fridge and presented her soft drink options, to which Taryn grabbed a can of Sprite and poured it into the iced glass Charlie provided on the spot. "Sauce on top of the chicken and pasta or on the side?"

Taryn stared at her. "On top. I'm not a monster."

That scored a laugh. "My kind of girl. Not that I would have judged otherwise." Charlie ladled the sauce and held their plates in her hands. "How do you feel about a coffee table picnic?"

"I'm intrigued."

"Just a more relaxed approach to midnight dinners. Follow me. I'll teach you my ways."

Taryn did, taking a seat on the carpet, catty-corner from Charlie. Their plates were placed on the coffee table, which turned out to be the perfect dining height. Who knew? Taryn didn't mind the cozy, comfortable setup in the slightest. Nor did she mind the food. After one bite, she turned to Charlie, fork in midair.

"You're not a culinary student, so explain yourself."

"Wow. A big compliment if I've ever heard one," Charlie said, covering her mouth as she chewed. "At least, I think. I'm learning to speak Taryn."

"You speak it just fine. You cook even better. Are you married? Because…" The words were out before Taryn had fully had a chance to okay them, and now there they were, floating around the room like a bubble about to pop.

"Shockingly, no. No one has proposed just yet. Writers are notoriously high-maintenance." Maybe it was the stressed look on Taryn's face that she couldn't quite smother. Maybe it was just Charlie's intuition. Either way, her smile faded to sincere. "So, do you date girls? I realize it's not something we've talked about."

"Yes," Taryn said, probably too quickly, her opportunity to spray-paint red all around that box. "I'm not exactly straight. At all."

"Cool. I didn't know." Charlie focused on cutting another bite of chicken. "Is this something you've newly discovered, or…" She paused, fork suspended in the air as she waited for Taryn's answer. Such a casual conversation about something Taryn had been overthinking unnecessarily for days.

"No. I've known I was a lesbian for years. Just hadn't looped other people in until more recently. So I guess you can consider yourself looped." Why was her heart pounding so loudly, and had Charlie noticed?

"I'm glad you're telling me. I hope I haven't made assumptions when we've talked." She frowned. "Straight shouldn't be the default. I'm sorry if I made it that way."

"No. But remember when you asked me how your boobs looked in the cocktail dress?"

"The perfect dress that you picked out? I do. I still owe you for that assist."

"That could have led to an awkward moment."

"Why? You don't like my boobs." Charlie flashed a dazzling smile that became a kind one. She covered Taryn's hand with hers. "I see your point, and I will refrain from putting you in any potentially uncomfortable scenarios about boobs."

"No, no. I didn't feel uncomfortable. I just want to make sure *you're* not uncomfortable, and that means all the cards on the table, and one of those cards is my sexuality. If you're going to ask a question about your boobs, I just want you to know who's answering. That's all."

Charlie nodded definitively. "I hear you, and I think it's really impressive that you're now your full self. I admire you. You're ahead of a lot of people at Hillspoint."

"I'm not," Taryn said flatly. "I'm wildly behind. Couldn't even go away to school, when it was all I wanted." Apparently, confessions were pouring out of her tonight.

"What do you mean?" Charlie asked softly.

Taryn closed her eyes. "Everyone thinks I stayed in Dyer because my dad was recovering. The truth is that I backed out of school way before his hospitalization. I choked. I got cold feet, had trouble leaving my house for a period of time. It was all so overwhelming, and the idea of failure was…too much."

"Taryn." Charlie stopped eating entirely, her features soft and sympathetic. "What did it feel like?"

"Paralyzing. Like the world was crashing in on me." This wasn't something that she talked about much.

"It sounds to me like you were experiencing anxiety. You're not alone. Lots of people struggle."

"I use the words *crippling fear*, but yeah." She exhaled slowly. "I get in my own head and set it off, working on ways to overcome trepidation. That's why it's so ironic when people comment on my confidence. If they only knew."

"I think you can be both. Confident people can get scared."

Taryn turned the idea over in her mind. "I like that take."

"I believe it, just like I believe you're going to be okay, Taryn, and are to be admired for how far you've come."

"I still can't seem to find my way to the dining hall. That's why I'm eating dinner at midnight." She blinked, refusing to crack a smile.

Charlie laughed. "Your delivery kills me. You never break."

Taryn tossed Charlie a grin and raised a shoulder. "Yeah, well, your chicken marsala left me dead ten minutes ago. This whole conversation is from the beyond."

"Then cue my grief. I happen to like you."

God, this woman had eyes that sparkled when she enjoyed herself. Taryn had heard the descriptor before in books but had never actually witnessed sparkling eyes in real life until Charlotte Adler flipped her world on its head at the beginning of the semester.

"I like you, too. You cook me amazing floor food." She stole another bite and sank into the wonder response it pulled. Could she ask for a pint of this sauce to go? Would that be rude? She wanted to be invited back.

"I'd be happy to teach you a few cooking basics. You seem impressed, but I don't think you realize how simple this dish actually is. But I do like the fangirling." She made the keep-it-coming gesture.

"Is this offer you still taking care of me?"

"No. I have a feeling you're more than capable on your own these days."

Taryn rested her chin on her knee. "Now I'm blushing." The room was thick with tension. Taryn wasn't imagining it this time.

Charlie looked up from her plate as if she just had to see for herself. "You are. Look at you."

Were they flirting? God, she hoped so because this was so much fun. The ping-pong match helped Taryn relax. She was proud of herself for coming out to Charlie, and the reality had been so much more chill than what her imagination had conjured. Not a single stumble or awkward exchange. If anything, she wished she'd been open about her sexuality sooner.

"Tell me more. Are you seeing anyone?" Charlie asked. "What about the girl with the cat ears from the party? She was worried about you that night."

"Caz. She's my roommate and a good friend, but there's nothing romantic between us. I haven't dated anyone since coming to Hillspoint."

"No? I would think this would be your time to go kid-in-a-candy-store. Shall I fix you up?" Charlie asked with an arched brow.

"Yes. I'm taking any and all recommendations." So maybe they weren't flirting. Taryn didn't confess that the dynamic of her crush setting her up with someone else might feel like a letdown, but she was also determined to keep her mind open. Especially since Charlie was off the table.

"Tell me your type."

You. "Oh, um, can't. I don't have a type."

"Try."

"I like people who don't take themselves too seriously." She eased a strand of hair behind her ear. "I'm into kindness when it's not mandated. They should probably understand the importance of a good binge-watching session on long weekends, and maybe visit the zoo on occasion for peace and because they love animals."

"Specific." Charlie nodded sagely. "What else?"

Taryn went up on her knees, energized, enjoying the game. "They don't like surprise parties and never loiter."

"Everyone hates pesky loiterers." Charlie nodded as if taking mental notes.

"They likely once played an instrument but don't have to anymore. Sleeping in the nude is always a plus."

"Now we're getting scandalous."

"Did I go too far?" Taryn asked.

"Not at all. Let me find you a binge-watching flute player who sleeps naked and visits the zoo without loitering there. Shouldn't be hard. I'll go through my phone and construct an extensive list."

Taryn laughed and placed a hand over her heart. "Please tell me you know that I'm joking."

"If you say so. I'm gonna binge-watch something mindless until I get sleepy. Hey, that's one of your qualifications. You in?"

"You've come to the right person," Taryn said, liking the extension of their time together. "My first class isn't until ten a.m. tomorrow."

Charlie's mouth fell open in outrage. "I miss undergrad life. I want you to revel in rolling out of bed in joggers and racing to class midmorning."

"It's a pretty nice life."

Charlie flipped on a medical drama Taryn was mildly familiar with. Within twenty minutes, she was hooked and snuggled up on the couch one cushion away from Charlie.

"Why is everyone acting like that doctor isn't ridiculously hot?" Taryn asked.

"Because in the medical field on television, everyone is either hot or on their way to being hot. See that woman? She'll be hot next season. They take turns."

"So intriguing."

The next thing Taryn knew, she was blinking sleepily into a dimly lit room. A strange room. Where in the world was she? Light slanted in through a window to her right, and it appeared she was on a couch covered in a wonderfully soft purple blanket. Who'd covered her with a blanket and was making coffee nearby? The aroma was from heaven. She stretched her limbs, feeling rested and satisfied.

"Sorry. I hope I didn't wake you. I'm teaching this morning and have to get out of here." Charlie. She was behind Taryn in the kitchen, packing up a black leather laptop bag. A turquoise thermos of coffee sat on the table.

"Did I fall asleep on your couch?" If Taryn wasn't so ridiculously comfortable, she would have had the decency to be mortified. "I really like it here. This is a good couch, Charlie."

"Thank you." Charlie walked over. "We both fell asleep, so I covered you up and snuck off to bed. You smiled and nodded when I told you what I was doing, so I figured you were okay with the crashing."

"Crashing? What are you talking about. I live here now." She offered a sleepy smile.

"I see you're playful even in the morning. Good to know. Would you like a black coffee?"

"Yes, please. But I'll get it." She pushed herself fully into a sitting position.

Charlie waved her off and poured the hot liquid into an oversized orange mug and presented it to her on the couch. "Cereal's in that cabinet, and milk is in the fridge. Help yourself and just press the lock when you leave. I gotta run." She placed a kiss on Taryn's head. "I like the bedhead. Adorable."

Taryn nodded numbly, a warm feeling infusing her chest. Everything felt homey here, and she liked it very much. She made sure to memorize Charlie leaving the apartment in black pants and a white blazer, which reminded Taryn that Charlie was teaching that morning. Now *that* was fun to think about. Taryn set her mug on the coffee table, fell back onto the couch, and tossed an arm over her head. Next, she let her imagination wander to Charlie walking across the front of a classroom in a position of authority. Lecturing. Gesturing with her hands while making one intelligent point after another. The fantasy was PG, but what it did to her body was anything but.

"Fucking hell," Taryn murmured and laughed. Because she and Charlie weren't going to ride off into any sunset together. It was fun to think about, though. In fact, she had a few extra minutes…

Chapter Seven

Just a reminder that your persuasive papers are due on Tuesday." The students, eager to be dismissed, began gathering their belongings, which meant Charlie had to speak a little louder. "Here's a tip. Read your work out loud. If you're getting bored, guess who else might? Look for endless and confusing sentences. Hearing the words will also help you spot grammatical mistakes. I promise." She saw several nods from the more committed students and some jotting down of notes. "If you have questions, hang around after." She checked the clock. "I have ten minutes, and I'm happy to assist. Good class today. Have a great rest of your morning."

Charlie watched as the thirty-two students in her freshman comp section packed up their belongings and moved to the door. Only four or five hung back.

"I'm struggling with a compelling thesis statement," Zane Mullins said. His hair was disheveled as always, but that seemed to be the look he was going for. He shoved his printed-out draft in her face. There were scribbles in the margins and crossed-out lines throughout. Just the kind of revisions she'd hope to see on a draft. He really did try, which scored points. She read the introductory paragraph and nodded.

"You lay out the reason for your argument nicely, but watch out for repetition. That's why your thesis isn't packing the punch you want it to. You've already gone there earlier in the paragraph. It's a rerun."

"A rerun. Which is unexciting." His eyes went wide. "That makes so much sense. Thank you." He accepted the paper and backed away slowly like she'd just handed him the keys to a new car.

"He has it so bad for you," Ellie Tremble said with a shake of her head. Charlie smiled politely but chose not to respond. Instead, she looked over Ellie's shoulder to her laptop screen to answer her question about formatting. She enjoyed the one-on-ones with her students and often wondered if teaching might be something she'd be interested in continuing beyond grad school, should her writing career not go the way she hoped it would. The life of a teacher didn't seem so bad at all. She was feeling unusually optimistic today and wasn't quite sure why. She had a tiny hunch, however, that it was the dinner around her coffee table she'd had with Taryn. Their unexpected friendship had swiped her completely off guard, injecting interesting conversations, playful banter, and a new, intriguing pull in Taryn's direction. Charlie wasn't sure she'd ever experienced such a judgment-free zone in her adult life. Everyone she knew came with some kind of agenda these days. But Taryn? She was all heart, and in many ways, it felt like she'd filled an empty space Charlie hadn't even known needed to be filled.

She finished up with her students and checked her watch. She had an hour break and should rush home to grab an early lunch so she wouldn't have to carve out time later. She was actually a little sad that Taryn wouldn't be on her couch right where she'd left her that morning, looking sleepy and like she belonged. As she walked across the spacious lawn full of lounging kids and a group of guys kicking a soccer ball back and forth, she fired off a text to Taryn.

You didn't fall back asleep, did you?

Moments later, the dots danced beneath her message, which made her stomach tighten and a bolt of electricity hit. What was that? Why did contact with Taryn have such a powerful effect? She was simply at its mercy.

I'm shocked I didn't. My review is already up on Yelp. Five stars. How was class?

Charlie smiled, warm and on a high now as she typed.

Persuasive papers are due so lots of guidance needed.

Damn those dots and the happy anticipation they inspired. She rolled her shoulders and allowed herself to melt as she waited. Totally okay. Not everything needed its own analysis. Couldn't she just enjoy a new friend? She was going to.

You need to help me with my homework.

Charlie didn't hesitate. *Anytime.*

She slid her phone into her bag as she arrived at her car.

"Who's got you so smiley, ma'am?"

Emerson. Caught. Damn.

"I didn't even see you there." Charlie rested her back up against the driver's side door and attempted to deemphasize her grin.

"I know because you were somewhere else entirely. Somewhere kind of sexy, I would say."

Charlie felt her eyes go wide. "No. Nothing like that. I was texting with a…new friend."

"Oh yeah? For a minute there I was wondering if you and Danny were scheduling a midday meetup, if you know what I mean." She bounced her eyebrows.

"Unfortunately, no. I've got a busy day." And she and Danny had never done anything of the sort. Not that he wouldn't welcome it. There was a time when she would have, too. Everything felt different now.

Emerson nodded. "I feel you on that. I wish we could find a way to just slow things down a little. Enjoy each other. I'm jealous, if I'm being honest, of what you two have, but I have no time to date. Aren't we a pair?"

Charlie paused, attempting to translate. "Oh. You mean what I have with Danny?" It was a concept that caught her off guard. "You want to date someone like *Danny*?"

Emerson shrugged. "I wouldn't mind having something so set in stone. You and Danny are a lock, and that's something you can depend on beyond grad school."

Charlie blinked. "Right. That's true." She circled around how she felt and couldn't quite land. Part of her wanted to argue that things in her world weren't perfect. There was something missing, a click that never quite manifested. The fire, the passion, the hurricane of emotion that she'd always expected to catch up to them never quite had. But she could never admit that to Emerson.

"Well, I'm glad you're smiling. That's the headline," Emerson said, nodding toward Charlie's phone.

"Right. Totally." Charlie hooked a thumb over her shoulder, feeling strangely uncomfortable, as if she'd been spotted enjoying a rated R movie when she wasn't yet old enough. "I gotta run. Hope your day is a good one."

"That's the goal, but this semester has me questioning my entire slate of life choices." Emerson beamed through the proclamation, but Charlie didn't. Her stomach turned because she felt the same way. There was something just beyond the edges of her understanding that called to her, tapping her on the shoulder and asking to be noticed. A faint voice in the wind she couldn't quite decipher.

"I think we're all in that spot about now. Maybe it's because we're about to be shoved into the great big world without a net."

"That's gotta be it," Emerson said. "Take care of you, and keep up the amazing writing. And the Danny thing? Play it by ear."

Charlie blinked because was Emerson that intuitive? She understood that she was supposed to say something like *What are you talking about? We're completely good.* But she was feeling disoriented about her trajectory, and Emerson's advice actually landed. "Thank you. I think I will."

Charlie slid into the driver's seat of her used Nissan Rogue and did the one thing that might bring a smile back to her face. She messaged Taryn.

When do I get to see some of your photos?

Like water to the parched, it only took a few moments before she had her reply.

When are you free?

❖

The hallway was empty as Taryn sat outside her professor's office studying the photographs that lined the hallway in 17x20 inch frames. The work all seemed to come from past students whose work had been deemed worthy of display. The choices were good ones and left her feeling inspired. She studied the captivating image of a ballet dancer midperformance. She was bending at the waist with her back leg extended, the stage light in the corner of the frame pointing directly down on her. The lines were beautiful and full of tension. She tilted her head, taking in the use of highlight to direct the eye impressively. Taryn wanted to be that good, to capture a moment, ice it with beauty, and create interest in a subject otherwise overlooked.

"Taryn, are you ready?" She stood from the uncomfortable black metal chair, ushering her thoughts back to the here and now. Her professor, who'd asked the class to call him Roger, stood in the doorway to his office. She was his two o'clock and more nervous than she probably should have been. Each member of the class had been asked to sign up for a time to meet with Roger to go over their progress before moving toward final projects. In many ways, she felt like she'd been playing catchup. Most of her classmates had experience before Roger's narrative photography class. Meanwhile, she'd been relying more on instinct than technique, scurrying to apply technical skills they already seemed to have. To compensate, she'd been reading beyond the given assignments, tearing through trade magazines, online message boards, tech articles, absorbing as much on her own time as she could.

"Have a seat. Have a seat." Roger often said things twice, she'd found. He was also a nice enough guy, if intense when it came to craft. His office certainly mirrored his personality. The walls were dark. A futuristic-looking lamp stood tall in the corner and served as the only light source in the room. A variety of photographs, likely his work, hung in metal frames on the wall. A black-and-white portrait of a child. Car headlights in close-up. A group of people leaping into the air at the same time in the middle of a forest. She tried not to stare but also attempted to gulp it all in. "How do you like the class?"

"I love it," Taryn said without even thinking. While she still had a couple of basics to get out of the way, the three courses in her field of study kept her energized, learning what her future just might have in store. She wanted to capture and create. After a few months of living in the photography world, she was gone on the art form. "I just sometimes feel like I'm winging it."

"I don't think so," Roger said, frowning. He thumbed through a series of shots she recognized as hers, along with their attached specs and notations. "The series from the on-campus protest is compelling. What made you choose to cover it?"

She nodded. She'd been on her way to class and came upon a group of students protesting a speaker on campus. "I saw their angry faces, jagged movements, and the way they stood united and knew there was a visual story there. It made me late to my Spanish class, but I think it was worth it."

"You weren't wrong about the story." He set one photo on the desk and slid it in her direction. "This one in particular resonates." It was a shot of a girl who'd sat down on the lawn, her sign face down in front of her. "Defeat."

"That's exactly what it was."

"You have an eye for the quiet moments. That's been your most powerful trend." His finger pressed just shy of the photograph. "But don't get too poetic. That's a trap. The grit is every bit as worthy. I'm going to encourage you to get messy. Get ugly. You said the word *jagged* earlier."

"Right. That's how it felt."

"I like the inclination. More of that. More of that." He met her eyes with a fire and vigor in his.

Taryn understood the note and also knew it was contrary to her nature. She wanted the world to be a beautiful place, so perhaps that's the reason she seized the quiet humanity within a tense situation, like the angry protest. "I hear you. I will work through the urge to soften."

"I also want you to continue to work on the technical. Use foreground images for orientation in your darker shots."

"Okay." She wrote a note. "I hear you."

"And get yourself more practice in the darkroom. Sign up for extra slots, and I'll okay them. You're overexposing your photos by a hair. Pull back."

"I can do that, too. What else?" She was hungry for this kind of feedback. It motivated her in a way she hadn't been prepared for.

"Make it a goal to learn from the others in the department." He sat back, both hands resting on the back of his head. "The truth is I see a kernel of something really cool going on with your work, but you're green as hell."

A compliment and deflater in one. "I know. I feel it."

"What would you say to me pairing you up with a student mentor? We've done it before to great success."

"I'd be all-in. I want to get better." She was sitting on the edge of her chair. Her heart pumped double time, excitement building. If Roger, who she very much respected, saw something in her, then maybe she wasn't off base in her pursuits. "Great. I think I'll have Ashley reach out. She's a semester from graduation and one of my top students. She's got a good eye and well-developed skills behind the lens. I think you two will hit it off."

"Thank you. Awesome. I'll wait to hear from her." She stood, sensing their chat had come to a close.

"Thanks for stopping by. And Taryn?" He leaned forward.

"Yes?"

"You're doing great, okay? Work on the things we talked about. Get uncomfortable, and I don't just mean in your work. Push yourself. Fucking push yourself." He stared at her, letting the point linger in the air. "That's how you achieve what you never thought possible. You hear me?"

She turned the words over in her mind. She was committed to taking his advice and would search out ways to push herself beyond her comfort zone behind the lens and in life. "Every word. I'm gonna do just that."

"Hit me up with whatever questions you have. I'm happy to be your cheerleader or worst nightmare of a critic."

She paused. "I think I need both."

He laughed, low and full. "Let's talk again in a couple weeks."

"Cool. Thank you." She left Roger's office more energized than ever. She vowed to keep her camera with her whenever possible and find the messy side of reality just as often as the picturesque. Energized by their meeting, she spent an hour walking through campus, grabbing shots, experimenting with shady spots and her f-stop. By early evening, she had an email from Ashley Wendell, asking her if she'd want to meet up in the lab in a couple of days. Roger had delivered on his promise to pair her up with a mentor. Taryn couldn't type her acceptance fast enough. Things were truly starting to come together, and doors were opening. Was it surprising that the first person she wanted to share her news with wasn't a member of her family, or Caz, or any of her new friends, but Charlie? No, because some things never changed.

An hour later, she paused in front of Charlie's apartment, her portfolio tucked away in her bag. She raised her hand to knock and froze at the sound of Charlie's voice. "It's open. Come on in."

Taryn opened the door and searched the empty living room for Charlie. "You're invisible. Where'd you go?" Taryn called.

Charlie jutted a head out from the hallway bathroom. Her hair was wet, and she wore a fluffy white robe that crisscrossed her chest, offering a generous glimpse of cleavage. *Whoa. Okay.* Taryn swallowed and glanced away as nonchalantly as possible, ordering herself not to steal another eyeful. Yet she did anyway. *Holy fuck.*

"I grabbed a shower. Give me five." Charlie frowned. "What's going on? Why are you looking at me like you almost just got hit by a car?"

"I'm not." Taryn focused all her energy on the dark television screen, gathering herself. Yet Charlie was likely naked beneath that robe, and she couldn't unknow it. *Pivot.* But when she turned back to Charlie in an attempt to change the subject and mask her overt reaction, she saw Charlie's features change. She looked down at her neckline, and back to Taryn. Her cheeks flamed and she held up a one-minute sign before disappearing behind the closed bathroom door.

Taryn tried to swallow back the regret but was unsuccessful. If she'd made Charlie feel uncomfortable or objectified, she wanted to right things between them at the soonest possible opportunity.

Embarrassment swarmed as she paced the small expanse of the living room, searching for words that would bury the last five minutes. Her face was still hot and her palms itched. Her crush on Charlie was beginning to cause problems and interfere with their friendship, and that meant Taryn had to do everything in her power to kill it. She would, too.

"Fuck," she said quietly.

❖

Alone in the bathroom, Charlie gripped the pedestal sink. Her heart thudded, her mind raced, and her body was turned the hell on without anyone issuing permission. What was happening and why? This wasn't like her in any way, shape, or form. The white robe that had felt fluffy and light just moments before now oppressed her overly sensitive skin. She loosened the tie and let the robe fall open. *Deep inhale*. Her breasts ached ever so slightly, and her thighs were trembling. She touched her cheek with her palm as if to erase the heat. The desire to be touched then and now rocked her.

She couldn't have this reaction right now. There was a guest in her home, and not one that should bring on such an overwhelming sexual response. Would Taryn be able to tell? None of this was ideal, but at the top of that list was the source of her attraction. A kid she used to take care of? Okay, well, maybe not so much a kid these days, but *still*. They were at different stations in life, which placed caution tape all around Taryn. *No. No. Nope.* Time to move the hell out of this whole line of thought. Just as she tried, the memory of Taryn's gaze moving across her exposed skin flashed, and her limbs went liquid all over again. The way Taryn had immediately looked away, respectful of the boundary, only added to the allure. A forbidden moment.

Charlie dressed quietly, leaving her hair to air-dry, and chalked up the reaction to an isolated anomaly. She was likely in the midst of some kind of hormone surge and should check her calendar.

Deep breath. She forced a smile on to her face and shook off the strange event. "Sorry about that," she said, as she emerged from the bathroom. "But I'm ready now."

Taryn, standing across the room in the kitchen, whirled around, and her dark hair swung and landed on her shoulder. Effortlessly gorgeous. Luminous brown eyes and thick dark hair. She naturally appeared more thoughtfully moody than thrilled with the world, and damn, it worked for her. That was Taryn. Unaware in her brooding perfection. Until today, Charlie thought she was jealous of how cool Taryn presented. Today, she felt more confident that another reason crept beneath the surface. "No problem. Just studying the, uh, backsplash." She touched the wall. "Love this green and gray tile. The craftsmanship is just… top."

"I'll tell the rental office." She gestured behind her. "I just needed to stand under a warm stream of water and decompress for about twenty hours. Have you ever done that?"

"More times than I care to count. They're also great for crying." Taryn's gaze hit the floor. She got the feeling that Taryn regretted the confession seconds after she'd made it. She remembered Taryn's anxiety and the struggle to tame it privately, which maybe explained why she held it in until the shower. Heartbreaking.

"You wait until you're alone?"

"Yeah," Taryn said quietly with a nod.

"You don't have to do that, you know? Come cry here. I have a shoulder." Charlie moved closer, took Taryn's hand, and squeezed it. When she did, something vital clicked in place and the vibrations of the world around them went quiet. Charlie knew unequivocally that their connection was meant to be. They were destined to be *something* together. She could feel it all over the second their hands came together.

"You don't understand how much that means to me." She attempted to continue but couldn't, emotion strangling her words. Her hand fluttered to dry the tears that had gathered in her eyes. Charlie gave her hand a squeeze and waited patiently, allowing the moment to move at its own pace. Finally, Taryn lifted her gaze and sent a grateful smile. "If it helps, there's less shower crying these days. Since you." That statement brought on an avalanche of feelings Charlie didn't know how to receive, sort out, or handle. She stared at their hands and made the choice to let go, unequipped in the moment. To distract them both, she walked to Taryn's attaché on her kitchen table.

"Show me your work. I've been excited to see it."

"Okay," Taryn said, as if waking from a dream, and joined Charlie next to the table. "I'm a little nervous."

The only thing that hinted at nerves was the quiet quality of Taryn's voice. Charlie was learning her signals. Her hands were steady and purposeful—beautiful, really, now that Charlie was focused on them. Her nails were neatly manicured, and her slender fingers were graceful in their movement from one side of the portfolio case to the other. She already knew how *soft* Taryn's hands were after just having held one.

Charlie flashed on an image of their fingers intertwined, Taryn's on top and Charlie's resting on the sheet beside her as she looked up into those determined brown eyes. Her stomach dipped and clenched. Yep. She'd just gone there.

"Should I ask again or just give you a minute?"

Charlie blinked a few times and found her anchor in the here and now. Taryn had just said something. "Sorry. My bad. I drifted."

"You're having a day, aren't you?" Taryn asked gently. Everything about her was.

"Yes," she said, seizing onto the lifeline. "It was a really grueling afternoon, but I'm happy to be here with you now."

"Are you sure? I can go if you'd rather some down time."

Charlie bumped Taryn's shoulder with her own. "You better not. I was promised photos."

They held eye contact a moment. It was rather wonderful, and Charlie didn't look away. She was learning to not be afraid, but it was a process. "I was just asking if you wanted to see examples from my narrative photography class or my portraits."

"Let's start with portraits."

Taryn flipped to the right side of the case and pulled out a stack of 8x10s. As Charlie took in the first one, the world went still. It was a photo of an older woman, maybe in her early eighties, standing in front of a window, her face turned to the camera. The light clung to one side of her face, bringing every detail of the life she'd lived into startling focus. Her gaze was trained on the camera with a hint of a smile directed at the lens. "They brought in a handful of men and women from the assisted living center over on Delmont to pose for us. That's Annie. She was amazing." Taryn tapped the photo reverently. "She made me work for it, but her face had so much to say."

"I can't even imagine the stories she could tell." Charlie couldn't stop staring. There was something haunting about the shot, and triumphant at the same time. "I feel like she's been through a lot and has emerged victorious." She nodded at the photo, absorbing every detail of the moment Taryn had so elegantly captured. "I suppose in a way I identify."

Taryn paused.

Guilt struck. "I hope I didn't make you uncomfortable."

"I just didn't imagine my shots having an effect on anyone." She met Charlie's eyes. "It's an honor, in a way."

"I like that better, because this is a very moving photo, Taryn." She went through the rest of the shots, laying out her favorites on the table and offering her insight and reaction to each because Taryn seemed to gobble it up, just like Charlie did when someone read a piece she'd written.

"You don't think the distance causes a disconnect?" Taryn asked about her photo of a rather happy-looking man sitting sideways on a chair.

"No. That's the best part. The shape of his body in contrast to the chair offers a certain amount of…I don't know. Tension."

Every inch of the room seemed to tighten with that word, as if the walls might pull apart at any moment, giving way to something Charlie couldn't quite voice.

"Yes. I agree. Tension," Taryn said softly, her voice smooth and quiet. "It's powerful stuff." They shuffled through the remaining twenty or so photographs that Taryn had selected to print. Charlie was astounded. She wasn't an expert, but this didn't feel like the work of a beginner. "Are you sure you haven't taken courses in the past? Not even an intro back home?"

"No, but I'm eager to learn, so I spend most of my free time reading photography journals, even when they don't fully make sense to me, and fucking around with my camera."

"You might be the only undergrad I've ever met who grabs a journal instead of heading out to Toby's with their friends."

She grinned. "I like Toby's, too. I've always been the type to consume myself with new and exciting things, and right now that's photography. I'm actually meeting with a student mentor my professor set me up with."

"I love that," Charlie said. "Let me know how it goes, because these"—she picked up the stack—"have really surprised me. You have true talent, Taryn." She watched the color hit Taryn's cheeks.

"That means a lot. Thank you." The vibration of a phone interrupted their exchange, and Taryn grabbed hers. "Speaking of Ashley-the-mentor, she wants to know if I want to go on a shoot with her."

"And do you?"

Taryn hesitated. Charlie sensed she didn't want to be rude and flee the scene.

"Oh, don't worry about me. In fact, I think you should go. I'm just going to chill and probably be really boring. You're not going to miss a thing."

Taryn tilted her head. "Are you sure? I just want to show her that I'm eager." But Taryn had been zapped with a shot of energy the moment that text message had come in, and Charlie didn't want to hold her back.

"I'm sure," she said, pulling Taryn into a hug. "Go be great, and catch me up later."

Taryn's arms went around her, and Charlie went still because she felt them all over. Her skin tingled in the spots Taryn held her, and she didn't want the moment to end, which was the exact reason it had to. And fast. She dropped her arms, stepped back, and wrapped them around herself. Luckily, Taryn hadn't seemed to notice and busied herself gathering her photos.

"Thank you for having confidence in me." Taryn's eyes were soft, which meant Charlie's words had resonated. "It makes me want to get out there and prove you right."

"You will. I believe in you."

Taryn, in the midst of lifting her portfolio case, turned, grinning. "Yeah?"

"Definitely."

The smile expanded exponentially. It reminded Charlie of the sun warming her face on a cold day. "The way you smile," Charlie said, shaking her head in awe. "It's amazing. You should know that."

"That's funny. I feel the same way about yours." They shared a moment of eye contact that felt important.

"I'll talk to you soon, okay?"

"You definitely will. Bye, Charlie."

Chapter Eight

Wait. No. This couldn't be right. When Taryn arrived at the address Ashley had texted her, she parked the car she'd borrowed from Caz in front of a small white church with three wooden steps in front and a single black cross on top of the building. Simple, old fashioned, and secluded. The church was off by itself down a lonely road. Not exactly what she'd expected for their evening. She wondered if she might be murdered. She watched through her windshield as a family made their way inside. Then another. "What the hell?" she murmured. She climbed out of her car and surveyed the parking lot until she spotted a brunette in all black, pulling a camera bag from the back of an old Jeep Cherokee, the car Ashley had mentioned she drove.

"Ashley?" she asked as she approached. "Taryn." She touched her chest.

"Yes. Stoked you're here. Can you carry my light stand?"

"On it." She grabbed the stand and hurried to catch up to Ashley, who hadn't exactly waited for her. "Can I ask what we're doing here?"

Ashley looked over at her and grinned. "Should have led with that. My bad. I heard about this little church and its very dedicated congregation and made arrangements to shoot through their hymn sing-along tonight. Waivers signed and all."

"Awesome. Um…why?" Taryn wasn't criticizing the choice. She simply didn't have all the pieces of the puzzle.

Ashley hooked a strand of her long dark hair behind her ear and tossed her long wispy bangs. She looked every bit the part of photographer. "Senior thesis. You'll have one, too. Art is capable of communicating the unending range of human emotions. My project is about presenting them in their most specific form to gain understanding of the array. We've all seen glorious photos of happy people, sad people, even mad as hell, right?"

"Right." Taryn was intrigued, and especially captivated by the gleam of passion in Ashley's brown eyes as she spoke.

"But what does *sublime* look like when captured in its most individual state? What about awe? My project is an exploration of all the in-between."

"Wow. Okay. I like that idea a lot."

"I needed an extra pair of hands today. If you could cover me on lighting and manage the reflector, that would be great. But I'm happy to walk through my steps." Ashley paused as if something snagged her attention from the topic at hand. "You're a lot to look at."

Taryn rolled her lips in, dissecting the comment. She wasn't sure if the implication was good or bad. "I don't know what that means."

Ashley laughed. "You're pretty. And maybe new to this? Just a guess."

"To photography?"

"To being a queer." She winced. "I get the vibe you are, but I'm so sorry if you're not. I hate overstepping. And of course, you don't have to say." Ashley's brown eyes were friendly when she said it, and no one had ever read Taryn so quickly before. It caught her off guard but simultaneously thrilled her, being seen.

"I am a lesbian, and yeah, it's kind of new." And now she was smiling, too. "I'm impressed that you just knew."

Ashley nodded. "It's one of my few gifts." She walked on, leaving Taryn to wonder if Ashley was a lesbian, too, and had she just flirted with Taryn? She really had to get better at this stuff.

They spent the next forty-five minutes moving around the small church, made up of eight rows with one center aisle. The members of the congregation sang loudly from their hearts as Ashley worked to capture them in various states of worship. Taryn did her best to keep up, using what lighting knowledge she'd picked up in class, and followed Ashley's quietly offered direction. But seeing the experience play out through the lens of Ashley's thesis was a truly inspiring experience. Each emotion-filled facial expression, whether it was a woman singing her favorite hymn from childhood, or a child mesmerized by the stained-glass window near the altar, had something important to contribute, a moment in time not to be overlooked.

"That was amazing," Taryn said on a high as they made their way back to the parking lot, gear in hand. "There was this visual energy just pinging everywhere, and when I think about the individual moments and their assembly, there are so many different stories that could be told. It all just depends on the angle of the approach. The narrative would be entirely different depending on who was shooting and what photos they selected to showcase and in what order."

"Exactly that. Yes!" Ashley said, matching her enthusiasm. "For that very reason, I always seek out places where people feel something important. I'm not even a religious person, but the combined energy of people coming together for something that has meaning to them is a powerful thing."

"You don't have to convince me. Did you get some good stuff?"

"So much. I can't wait to go through it all." She touched Taryn's wrist briefly. "You were awesome, by the way. Roger was right about your eye. You saw things I would have missed in there." She leaned against her Jeep and turned her head to Taryn. "So, what's your story, if you don't mind my asking." She offered a friendly smile. Ashley was easy to like, respectful and talented and kind.

Taryn searched for the high points. "My first semester at Hillspoint. I'm made a handful of friends and spend way too much time on my photography classes. But I've always worked hard in school."

"Common problem. And you're recently out?" She placed a hand on her own cheek.

Taryn nodded. The conversation had her in her happy place, affirmed by someone she respected and was beginning to like. "That part has been, I don't know, encouraging in many ways."

"I remember coming out my senior year of high school. The most liberating and terrifying thing I've ever gone through. If you ever need anyone to chat with or a sounding board…"

"Awesome of you to offer. I'll remember that."

"You're also incredibly pretty. Have you been kissed since you've been here?"

"No," she said automatically. A car pulled out near them. A breeze hit. Taryn blinked.

"You could tell me to go to hell, but you seem really cool, and I very much want to kiss you right now."

"What's stopping you?" Taryn asked after a beat. They were alone in the parking lot. The fluorescent street lamp buzzed overhead. She was aware of it all.

"Yeah?" Ashley asked, turning to Taryn and meeting her eyes unabashedly. This girl was unflappable and so incredibly smooth.

"Yeah," Taryn said, enjoying the moment. Ashley had a very nonthreatening vibe about her that quelled a tad of Taryn's anxiety.

A sweet smile appeared on Ashley's face, and she leaned in, paused, and captured Taryn's lips in a slow, lazy kiss. "You're a really good kisser."

"Yeah?" Taryn asked. Her body had gone warm, and she found herself in a dreamlike state. This had been entirely unexpected, but not at all unwelcome. She liked Ashley, and she liked their dynamic. The kiss didn't necessarily feel like anything other than what it was, a moment in time. Low-pressure.

"Mm-hmm." Ashley straightened. "Thank you for all your help today. I'm happy Roger thought we would work well together."

"Same," Taryn said, in slight amazement at what they'd just done and wishing she'd cobbled together a more eloquent response.

"Maybe we can work another project together sometime. If nothing else, I'd love to show you the final product of the shoot today."

"Yes. For sure. Thank you." Thank you? Why did she have to exist?

Ashley laughed. "You're cute and really awesome, Taryn. Have a good one, okay? Let's talk soon about your next class project."

"I'd love it. Good night!" Taryn stepped away from the Jeep and watched as Ashley started the engine and pulled away, her headlights shrinking into the night.

Alone in the parking lot of an old church, Taryn touched her now sensitive lips and smiled. She needed to learn to expect the unexpected, apparently. Either way, that kiss made her feel like she had joined the land of the living. Was Ashley Taryn's type? Not exactly. But she'd made Taryn feel special, and hot, and noticed, which counted for a whole hell of a lot. Maybe they'd kiss again. Maybe not. Either way, Taryn felt alive and happy, enjoying her little gay life, going on shoots, kissing girls in parking lots like it was no big deal. Big, happy sigh. She could really get used to this.

❖

"Are you nervous or something, babe?" Danny asked, his eyes on Charlie as she adjusted the place settings for the third time. His mother would be there in under twenty minutes, and as much as she adored the woman, she certainly had strong opinions for days. As her own mother's best friend, Monica was the closest thing she had left to a parent in her life, and Charlie wanted to impress her more than she had even fully admitted to herself. Monica's opinion mattered. It just *did.*

"I'm not nervous, but I do want tonight to be nice. I want her to be comfortable and see our life and think that we're doing just fine because we are." She wanted to believe her own words, but Charlie knew better. Something wasn't right between her and Danny. They were best friends who'd made the leap to a relationship, and now it was up to her to fix what wasn't working.

"And it will be." He opened the bottle of cab she'd set out and allowed the wine to breathe. He thought of those details that she sometimes missed. "Can I pour you a glass?"

"I think I'll wait."

She'd been looking forward to this dinner for weeks now, but the trepidation was starting to overtake the joy. Seeing Monica always drummed up memories of her mother, so many wonderful, happy, welcome reminders. But Monica also stirred up her grief, something she worked hard to contain. She missed her own mother more than she could quantify and knew unequivocally that she would feel it most potently today.

Two hours later and they'd already covered any and all small talk. Charlie's nerves were at ease, and she had to admit, it was really good to see Monica. Plus, the pot roast had been a hit, and the burgundy sauce was perhaps the best Charlie'd ever made. Even Monica had thought so.

"So…do we have anything important to discuss?" Monica asked and then looked expectantly between the two of them. "Any exciting plans? You know, for the future." She didn't come right out and ask if there was an engagement, but the insinuation was clear.

"Mom," Danny said.

"What? I'm a mother." She laughed, loud and warm. "And a future for you two kids was all Deirdre and I ever wanted, so I might be overly excited to see it all coming to fruition. I just wish she was here with us to enjoy it as much as I am."

"Totally allowed," Charlie said, placing a hand over Danny's. "And I like to think that she is." She exhaled slowly. "I think we're just hyperfocused on surviving the semester and not murdering each other in the midst of class critiques."

"If he's being too hard on you, you call me," Monica said with an exaggerated glare. She tapped her mauve-painted fingernails on the table as if preparing for Mom battle.

"This is a helpful offer." Charlie turned to Danny. "I'll do it, too."

With that, he held up his hands. "Heard. I have no death wish. Now let me get those plates." Danny cleared their plates, and once coffee was served, Monica turned to Charlie. "How about a little one-on-one chat?"

Charlie grinned. "I'd love it. You got this?" she asked Danny, who stood at the sink in rinse mode.

"I can probably figure it out," he called over his shoulder.

Charlie led Monica to the small outdoor sitting area at the back of her apartment. It had been a selling point in the early days when she'd first visited. The back of the complex faced a wooded area thick with trees and a walking path. It was Charlie's peaceful place, where she came to think and decompress.

"This is adorable," Monica said, surveying the natural surroundings. "Your own little carved-out slice of nature."

"I sit out here a lot, actually," Charlie said. "Sometimes I even talk to Mom."

Monica's eyes went soft. "I guarantee she hears you. Whenever I talk to her, I get a little tingle on the back of my neck, and I know that's her way of giving me a nudge." Monica sighed. "She'd be so excited about you and Danny, Charlotte. You have no idea. We used to joke about you two growing up and making us grandmas, and I don't want to get ahead of myself, but I can tell you that I speak for the both of us when I say that it would be wonderful." She squeezed Charlie's wrist. "No pressure." The laugh she tossed in helped ease the weight of the comment, but she was, in fact, serious.

"She was always trying to get us together." A romance with Danny had seemed a foreign concept to her back then. But after her mom passed, Danny almost felt like a way of being closer to her. In many ways, it seemed like she was fulfilling a wish of her mom's. That part felt really good. She just had to find a way to make their relationship spark the way it should. She needed to feel…off-center, excited, giddy, or downright flushed, the way she had the other day after her shower when Taryn—

The thought came to a screeching halt on command, but there was already heat creeping up her neck. She sipped her coffee, hoping the action would distract her brain, but she wound up choking on it and sputtering like a lunatic.

"You okay, sweetie?" Monica took the mug from Charlie's hand

and set it safely on the table. She raised an eyebrow and waited until Charlie regained control. "That snuck up on you, didn't it?"

"You can say that again," Charlie said. Because dammit, had it ever. "Sorry. Sometimes talking about Mom brings it all rushing back." She exhaled slowly, a confession bubbling. "I miss her so much my chest hurts at night when I think about all I didn't get to tell her that day."

"That makes you a human being. And the next time that happens, you call me. Tell me all about your day. Danny or not, you're my best friend's little girl, and I will always be here for you. Do you hear me?" Her voice was coated in conviction on that last part.

"I hear you. And it means more to me than you'll ever know." Monica made her feel not alone, a mother figure when she could really use one. Her voice had lost half its strength and an uncomfortable lump arrived in Charlie's throat because Monica's eyes were now wet and full. Grief was swift in its arrival. Always had been. That was one thing she'd learned over the past three years. A single moment could be turned on its head the second grief entered the chat. She'd never get used to it. Ever. Her mom should be here. Why didn't the Universe take her asshole father instead? "And if it makes you feel better, Danny and I talked about rings not too long ago." She was trying to throw Monica a bone, longing to make her happy. The truth was that he'd asked what kind of ring she might be interested in when a commercial had come on television one night. She'd completely evaded the topic, surprised by how wildly uncomfortable it had made her.

Monica drew in a loud, excited breath. "I knew it. I don't know how, but I knew you two were quietly making plans." She held up a hand as if to stop herself from going too far. "But I don't want to rush you. Just know that if Deirdre was here, we would have to run around the side of the building and squeal a little. We would have been the hippest grandmas together."

"I believe it." Charlie smiled, basking in the joy that now radiated off Monica because of the truth she'd stretched. Charlie had always been a people pleaser, probably going back to never wanting to ruffle any feathers when her father was in the vicinity. Like the perfect little soldier, she did what she could to keep peace in the house, not just for herself but for her mom, too. Old habits died hard.

"What did I miss?" Danny asked, joining them.

"Charlie and I were just discussing the very bright future," Monica said and bumped her eyebrows at Charlie. "And I don't think I've ever been happier."

Danny looked slyly from Charlie to Monica. "Anything you'd care to share?"

"Absolutely not," Monica said. "Just between us girls. Isn't that right, Charlotte?"

"Definitely," Charlie said, sinking into herself a little more with each moment that passed.

She had trouble sleeping that night, unsure why she felt like she couldn't move when she had all the space in the world to stretch and breathe. Danny slept at his place because he planned to work out early and knew it was her day to sleep in. She touched the pillow, realizing she should probably miss him. Instead, her mind wandered to Taryn and how things had gone with her mentor. She hadn't heard from her in a couple of days and decided she'd reach out in the morning.

When she woke, she blinked at a message from Taryn on her phone.

Good morning, Charlie.

That was it. That's all the message said, but those three words put a smile on her face that stayed with her all morning. Her classes flew by, she laughed a little easier, and when the afternoon rolled around, she was still riding high. The only thing that could make things any better was blowing off her afternoon writing session and catching up with Taryn in person. Yes, she was leaning in to the good feelings, a very unexpected happy spot in her life, and calling it an experiment in flying by the seat of her pants. Giving in to the urge to spend time with this new friend made her feel like there was finally an abundance of air in the room. Taryn didn't expect or demand anything from her. In Taryn's eyes, she was an amazing writer and an even better cook. Not only did she feel like a superstar of a human in Taryn's presence, but she craved time in Taryn's presence as well. "So, let's see what she's up to today."

Want to stare at some trees?

Charlie waited on the playful dots, her stomach tight and her heart ready to take a small risk.

Chapter Nine

It was cold outside, but you'd never have known it. With a week left until final exams, which would lead them into the holiday break, Taryn found herself flat on her back, head beside head with Charlie Adler, staring up at the red-leaved branches of two intermingling maples.

"But the thing about studying at the library, specifically, is that I always want to peer over and see what you're doing."

"I get that," Charlie said seriously. "The work I do is highly intriguing. Most people can't look away."

Taryn laughed. "You do whip those reference books around with a great deal of flair."

"That's my middle name. Charlie Flair Adler."

Taryn peered over because Charlie delivered the line with such believability. "No, it's not. The side of your mouth is twitching, which means you're lying."

Charlie turned and met her gaze. "You're already on to my tells?"

"I know. This friendship is getting serious."

Charlie laughed quietly and dropped her head. "Do you ever notice that when the afternoon edges toward evening, the campus turns copper? Look how everything is lightly touched with the most golden light."

Taryn took a moment to marinate in the perfectly articulated description. "You even talk like a writer. But yes, I have. I've even tried to capture it on film, but it's an elusive quality. So I try to just enjoy the thirty minutes or so we get of it each day." A pause. "I've never thought of it as copper before, but that's exactly what it is. This place is copper."

"So are you."

"What?" Taryn grinned and her heart squeezed. She had to hear more.

That's when she noticed Charlie watching her. No, *studying* her, causing her skin to tingle and her limbs to warm. "You have an adorable dimple on that left cheek. Has anyone ever told you that?"

Absently, she touched her cheek, needing to experience what Charlie was fixated on. "My mother is a big fan. She's the only one, unfortunately."

"Not anymore."

Okay. That sent a potent tingle up her spine. There was a surprising openness to the way Charlie was interacting with her today. It was markedly different and, in all respects, quite wonderful in Taryn's opinion. "I had no idea you were an admirer of dimples."

"There are a lot of things you've yet to discover about me." She didn't look away, and neither did Taryn. If this had been a date, Taryn would have kissed her after that remark without hesitation, hoping to learn one more thing and then another, starting with how Charlie kissed, what she tasted like, and what kinds of things made her murmur in appreciation.

"Did you hear what I said?"

Taryn blinked and rejoined the fold of the conversation. "I drifted away for a second, but I heard you."

"What were you thinking about?"

"Well, I can't tell you that."

Charlie offered a half pout. Adorable and sexy, too. Taryn understood that with the right facial expression, Charlie Adler could probably get Taryn to do anything. Not that she was prepared to share that information.

"Don't look at me like that."

"Like what?" Charlie turned onto her stomach and rested her chin in her hand while improving the pout. *Fucking dammit*. Charlie was doubling down, and it was doing things to her. As they watched each other, Taryn decided this was another situation where her intuition was completely off when it came to matters of the heart because she would have sworn this was a form of flirting. Why was she bad at identification? Because if Charlie was flirting with her, the world had just exploded into sunshine and lollipops. Her phone buzzed.

"I cannot be swayed," Taryn said as she checked the readout. Ashley checking to see how Taryn's lab session had gone. She'd taught her an awesome new way to batch photos to speed up the process and make the most of her lab time. She smiled and typed back.

"Who has you smiling over there?" Charlie asked.

Taryn sighed. She wasn't sure how to describe what was happening with Ashley. Since the kiss at the church, they texted on occasion, talked technique and style over text, but there was a big question mark around whether there was anything true bubbling between them. "Ashley."

"The mentor, that's right. How's it going?"

Taryn decided to just be honest. Charlie had a lot more relationship experience than she did and could maybe offer some helpful advice for navigating confusing waters. "Good, with a question mark sidecar."

"Interesting response. What's the question mark?"

"So, I went to the shoot last week, which was awesome and educational and all you would expect. Blah, blah, blah."

"The blahs are noted. You say them nicely."

"Thank you."

"Now to the mysterious sidecar."

Taryn sat up straighter, searching for the most effective way to describe what had happened. She had nothing creative or cute, so she just went for it. "Then we kissed."

"Oh."

"Well, clarification. She kissed me, but I definitely participated." As she spoke, Charlie's smile seemed to freeze in place, becoming a lifeless placeholder of what Taryn knew her true smile to be. Nervous now, Taryn described the scenario in more depth, probably providing too much detail. Charlie nodded. But again, the action seemed mechanical at best, as if Charlie was going through the motions of things a good listener would do. There was an indifferent glaze coating her features that left Taryn on edge. Should she not have shared any of this? Was this because Ashley was female? A feeling of dread trudged over her because she wasn't sure she could handle homophobia from her favorite person. "So I'm not really sure where we stand. Should I ask or just leave things as they are?"

Charlie took a moment. She nodded again, this time absorbing. "I think that depends on what you want out of it. Do you have feelings for her?"

"I mean, no. We don't know each other well."

Charlie's mouth made the shape of a small *oh*. "But you're attracted to her."

"She's definitely attractive. Not someone I would have instantly been drawn to, but there's something about her that's interesting. She's more confident than I am."

"I've always thought of you as very confident." The trees caught a breeze, and the branches swayed above them, jostling each other in their tangle. Taryn watched the way a strand of hair blew over Charlie's eyes, and Charlie casually brushed it away. Even her everyday gestures had a way of captivating.

"Then I'm doing my job well. But no, Ashley is all sharp edges and charisma. She comes to play. I'm more the reserved wallflower."

"You're reserved, but if anyone doesn't notice you, that's on them. You stand out, Taryn. Stop telling yourself that you don't."

She felt the corners of her mouth tug in happiness. Hearing that Charlie thought so was everything.

"I think flashy people sometimes seek out the less flashy. Maybe she saw that in me, or maybe she really just wanted to kiss someone and it'll never happen again. We're gonna grab dinner in a couple of days."

Charlie stared down, thumbing the blades of grass beyond the blanket.

"Are you okay?" Taryn asked. She seemed more and more pulled into herself with each moment that ticked by. The playful and bold Charlie from earlier was nowhere to be found. She missed her already.

"Do you mind if we head out? I'm starting to not feel so good."

Taryn widened her eyes, feeling guilty now. "I don't mind at all. Here. Let me grab the blanket and your bag. I'll walk them to your car."

"You don't have to do that," Charlie said softly, pushing herself to standing.

"Well, I'm going to." She picked up the blanket with the intention of folding it.

"Here. I can do it," Charlie said, reaching for the corner.

Taryn held tight. "What are you doing? Stop that. I got this."

But Charlie didn't. She actually ripped the blanket out of Taryn's hands and begin folding it herself without a word. Taryn watched in surprise, unsure what had prompted the move. But Charlie focused fully on her task without raising her gaze at all. In fact, it felt like she was purposefully avoiding Taryn and any and all eye contact.

"What just happened?" Taryn asked quietly.

Charlie's beautiful hands went still and Taryn was wildly aware of her heart beating double-time. "I don't know," Charlie said. "I'm working that out, and I don't think I can talk about it right now. I hope you understand."

Taryn nodded. "I do. I think. That's all right." She looked around, searching for the right words to say to move them out of this awkward moment and noticed that the copper quality of the afternoon had evaporated right along with their mood. Taryn felt guilty about anything she'd done to land them here, although she had no idea what that could be. In fact, nothing seemed to fit. She'd asked a friend for advice. Yet, the information that Taryn had kissed someone seemed to have upset Charlie. She went still. Because, no. There was no way in hell that Charlie was jealous. Impossible. Not eligible for the list of possibilities. Then again, she'd balked at the thought of Charlie flirting earlier. And now she was shoving away the idea that Charlie was jealous. What if she was wrong on both counts? Taryn placed a palm on her forehead as if searching for life's answer.

"Can I please walk you to your car?" Taryn asked.

Charlie's face was red, and it seemed as if she was embarrassed. "No. I'm good."

"Well, that question was only a formality because I'm doing it."

"Fine. I'm that way."

They walked in silence, an uncomfortable weight pressing on Taryn's shoulders. She usually enjoyed silence. Not this kind. "Will you let me know how you're feeling tonight?" she asked as they approached Charlie's Rogue.

"If you want me to. Yeah." Her voice was soft and friendly again, but she was noticeably more reserved than usual. Taryn had a million questions diving and circling her brain, but the perfect sequence of words never seemed to assemble itself. Instead, she offered a nod. "Yeah. Thank you."

She stood on the curb and watched as Charlie, the most beautiful and puzzling girl ever, drove away from her, taking a piece of Taryn's heart along with her. "What the fuck was that?" she murmured, at a total and complete loss.

Too keyed up to work, study, or eat, Taryn found the walking trail that circled the perimeter of campus, and with her hands shoved into the pockets of her leather jacket, she replayed the afternoon over and over again. She realized that night had fallen around her as she walked, and her stomach rumbled, uncomfortable from lack of food. Didn't matter. The more Taryn examined their interactions, the more she was convinced that maybe Charlie felt a sliver of what she did. And if that was the case, wasn't there a conversation to be had? She blinked as terror descended. *Oh, fuck no.* There was no way she could bring this up to Charlie. Everything about Charlie had signaled she was straight until this point, including a very serious boyfriend. Plus, God, what if she was wrong? The embarrassment would be never-ending. Nope. She paused under a streetlight and regarded it for help, finally coming to her conclusion: so much better to just wait and wonder. And that's simply what she would have to do. If Charlie felt anything for her whatsoever outside the boundaries of friendship, there would be more signals along the way. Her new trajectory would have Taryn paying close attention.

❖

The dog barking incessantly in the apartment above Charlie's had woken her up three different times the night before, and now she'd woken up grumpy and exhausted. Not only that, but her slow-moving status left her less than fifteen minutes to get out the door to teach her intro creative writing class, and no will at all to make that happen. Glaring at the walls and furniture, she moved slowly from her room to the kitchen, wearing one of her nicer suits in the hope that it would make her rise to the occasion and deliver a killer version of the lesson she had planned for her students, one she'd actually been truly looking forward to until today. The short lecture, followed by a group brainstorming session, and finally individual writing and sharing time was generally a hit with her students. It would be in her best interest to get it the hell together.

But the overactive portion of her brain—the other reason she'd been left awake half the night—wasn't exactly relenting. She took quick swallows of coffee and closed her eyes as it burned a trail down her throat. She needed it, though. Anything to jar her back to herself. She'd been on edge ever since she'd listened to Taryn describe her kiss with that Ashley woman, which she had no business caring about.

Yet she could no longer deny the fact that she had. Taryn made her feel things she hadn't expected and shouldn't feel, given where she was in her life. Danny was on the brink of proposing, she was nearing graduation, and until recently she'd believed herself to be an ally but certainly not a card-carrying member of the queer community. None of that seemed to matter to her mind and body. Her feelings had also joined the club because she didn't just lust after Taryn, she felt strongly for her, too. She loved listening to her talk and found solace in those big brown eyes. There was a string between them, a tether that tugged Charlie in Taryn's direction over and over again that she simply couldn't ignore.

Now what? She swallowed and checked her watch. There was no time to solve all of her life's problems on a Thursday morning in her kitchen, but it was time she stopped hiding from what continued to smack her in the face. She was deeply attracted to the grown-up Taryn Ross.

When she arrived on the second floor of the Saunders Building, her students were mostly assembled in their seats. She scanned the classroom and its raked seating that offered her a clear view of each student. With a smile, she deposited her belongings behind the small desk off to the side and moved to the podium to set up the slides she would run from her laptop. Something tugged at her, though, beckoning her to raise her gaze. She did. Seated in the back row on the far left side was a familiar brunette. She tilted her head in question. Taryn offered a four-finger wave and shooed her back to her job. She was crashing Charlie's class? Interesting turn of events that gave her a slam of energy. If she'd been looking for a motivator this morning, she'd certainly come upon one.

"Good morning, everyone," she said and made eye contact with several different students purposefully. A routine practice. Charlie had always believed that personal connection mattered in education. "How's the final paper coming?" The question was greeted by a chorus of uncomfortable sighs. She nodded hyperbolically. "Oh, really. That good, huh?"

"No clue how real writers do it," Trey Cobb said from the second row. Most of the students were hanging on by their fingernails, attempting to make it through the end of the semester. Final projects and exams loomed, demanding more from them than ever before. Care packages were arriving on campus, overflowing with snacks and notes from home. Travel plans had long been made for the end of finals week. Identifying, Charlie hoped to ease the mental load as much as she could.

"Well, I have news for you, Trey. You're a real writer."

"If you say so," he said half-heartedly. The kid was better than he thought, though, and before the semester was over, she planned to make sure he knew it.

"Well, hopefully a few of the tips I have for you today will loosen your brain, get your words unstuck, and have you writing the best work of fiction you've ever turned out. Who's with me?"

She saw the class sit a little taller and greet her with a few grins in response. "I'll take that. Let's get started." As she turned to her slide deck, she was aware of Taryn's eyes on her. As she began her short lecture, the glimpses she grabbed let her know that Taryn was sitting back in her chair, wearing a black shirt and plaid scarf. Too good.

She'd rested her chin in her hand and never took her eyes off Charlie. She'd make a good student, Charlie realized, feeling proud. The class was a successful one and rowdy by the end with the group coming together and offering suggestions to their classmates and encouraging one another, just the environment Charlie had been going for, and she smiled at the success. When class concluded, Charlie remained at the podium for private questions from her students and then packed her materials in her attaché, the one she never could have afforded on her own. Monica had purchased it as a gift once Charlie had been assigned her first class as an instructor. All the while, she knew exactly where Taryn was in the room without even fully watching. Apparently, it was her gift.

Taryn had repositioned herself near the door, arms folded across her chest, all assured and looking amazing. She's waiting for me, Charlie thought, suppressing a smile. Honestly, it was her first genuine smile since she'd heard Ashley had kissed Taryn. She gave herself a moment to savor the happy effect before making her way over to the door and Taryn.

"Well, this was a surprise. Hoping to pick up a few writing tips on the fly?"

Taryn's eyes were bright and she shook her head as if in amazement. "You had them eating out of the palm of your hand and then each other's. That was amazing."

Charlie felt her herself fill up with that compliment. She shrugged. "I think because I've been in their shoes and carry such passion for the subject matter, I'm able to work my way in. At least, that's my hope." She closed the classroom door behind her and led them down the hall.

"Have you considered teaching as a career at all?"

"Um…" The truth was she had but had never given the thought voice. "I have, actually. I think I want to get out there and give myself a chance to struggle and get my writing career going. Maybe down the road I can bring back what I've learned to the classroom."

"You have my vote if you ever get the chance."

Charlie had a feeling that Taryn would support her in most anything she attempted in life, from choosing an ice cream flavor to a risky career. "I'm glad you came. Brightened my morning." Instinctively as they descended the steep outdoor staircase to the sidewalk, Charlie looped her arm through Taryn's, feeling too light to stop herself.

"Well, watching you in your element completely brightened mine.

I don't think you understand how in awe of you I am right now, and I was already fairly impressed with you in general."

"Stick around. There might be more."

Taryn paused and an unreadable expression enveloped her perfect features. It made Charlie want to confess everything, that she was drawn to Taryn whether she should be or not. That she thought about her more than a friend thinks about another friend. That she was attracted to her physically to the point she'd experienced foreign reactions from her traitorous body. But what would that say about her relationship with Danny? What would it mean for everything she thought she knew about herself and what she wanted in life? But the unanswered questions were becoming tiresome, and Charlie wasn't prepared to battle them anymore. Because what did one do when they didn't have answers? *Seek them out.* She stopped walking and turned to Taryn, more determined than she'd ever been. They weren't alone on a busy sidewalk. Not even close. Students and faculty flooded the walkway between buildings, dodging each other, talking animatedly with their friends and classmates as they moved from one class to the next. Didn't matter. All Charlie saw was Taryn.

"I really like you, Taryn." She exhaled. It was a step.

Taryn stood taller, making the two inches she had on Charlie all the more noticeable. "Is that what we're talking about? Like?"

"I'm not sure."

Taryn hesitated, this time searching for words. "What does that mean? *You like me*. Because it could go a lot of ways, and I'd be lying if I said I hadn't wondered where your head was when it came to us."

She nodded. "Us." God, she liked the sound of that as much as it terrified her. "I imagine I've made things confusing. I can see that. But it's because I *have been* confused. In fact, to be specific—"

"Hey, Charlie." Trey Cobb stood at her elbow with a concerned look on his face. "Hate to bother you, but I left my notebook under my seat in class, and the door must have locked because I can't get in. Do you by chance have the key?"

"I do. Um…" She turned fully to Trey and blinked herself into the here and now of his plight. "I can walk you back up there. I don't think there's a class after ours."

"Thank you. I have a project due next class, and I need that folder badly."

She turned to Taryn, apologetic. "Can we maybe press pause?"

"Definitely. I get it." But her eyes held so many questions. While Charlie wasn't sure she had the answers, she was certainly willing to try to find them.

"Let's talk soon," she said, holding eye contact as she reluctantly walked away from the girl who owned all her thoughts these days.

Chapter Ten

Taryn walked into her apartment, closed the door, and stared at Caz and Sasha, who were seated on the floor, textbooks open. "Can everyone drop what they're doing and give me the best advice you've ever given anyone? I have girl problems."

"Don't we all," Sasha said, Red Bull frozen on the way to her lips.

Taryn also went still. "You have girl problems?"

"Newly. Didn't even know that was possible, but there was one at the vend-a-snack on the second floor who I'm pretty sure is my soulmate, but I don't know which room she lives in. The mystery is intense."

"Start knocking on doors in the name of love," Caz deadpanned with a shrug.

Taryn pointed. "That's what I need. Flat-out practical wisdom. Door knocking will produce the snack girl. But how do I get my babysitter to tell me her true feelings for me when I'm starting to suspect they're beyond just friendly?"

"I think you just one-upped me," Sasha said. "A babysitter trumps an unknown hungry girl."

"I can agree with that." Caz nodded. "Wait. What happened to the photography mentor? I thought she was who you were mixing and mingling with these days. The babysitter is straight."

"I need to take notes," Sasha said. "There are a lot of angles here."

Taryn blinked. The reference to Ashley threw her because she'd honestly not thought about her at all since Charlie had gone home from their tree-watching session. That had to say something.

"Nothing happened to Ashley. She's all well and good, but it's Charlie who is making my head spin, and I need a de-spinner."

Caz tilted her head. "Say more words."

"We need context," Sasha said, touching the floor with one finger. "My babysitter was sixty-two years old and not datable, so I find this confusing."

"Well, let me help. She's twenty-six, beautiful, kind, smart, and good at everything. I want to spend as many minutes as possible with her, and the more I do that, the more minutes I crave."

Caz nodded sagely as if to say *right on*. Sasha pointed. "How can I sign up for a babysitter like that?"

"You can't. She's rare and amazing and also really confusing. That's the problem. We were this close to having a real conversation about whatever it is that's bubbling between us—"

"I applaud the use of *bubbling*." Caz jotted a note in her phone.

"—when one of her students interrupted."

"She teaches, too?" Caz asked and fanned herself. "This just gets hotter and hotter. Maybe I need to start swiping right on grad students so I can have hot and sophisticated problems, too."

"Hot and sophisticated is not off base." She shifted her lips to the side. "Can't vouch for other grad students, but with us? Everything feels very close to igniting. Yet it doesn't, and there are good reasons for that. Did I mention she's practically engaged to a guy who thinks he's a better writer than she is?"

"We hate him," Sasha said automatically.

"Well, we're definitely not rooting for him," Caz said, a little more tempered. "I think you set up another time to speak with her."

"I do, too," Taryn said. "I need words, though. An angle that's considerate of her feelings, but honest about my own. I also need courage, because Charlie is someone I like most in this world, but also someone who intimidates the hell out of me."

"Because you're vulnerable to her," Sasha added, as if it was the most obvious thing in the world. "She's capable of stomping on your heart in a way no one else is."

They swiveled to her.

"Yes," Taryn said, amazed at the wisdom from an unexpected source. She hadn't been giving Sasha enough credit. She plopped down, mulling over her feelings. "I've been ignoring-slash-burying my feelings for months. Now I have this little kernel of hope, and it's causing all sorts of problems."

"Damn the kernel," Caz said. "But also, what if it leads to an awesome bowl of romantic popcorn? Who doesn't want their boring kernel to explode into wonderful?"

Taryn dropped her head back. "I just have a hard time believing that it could. At the same time, I don't want to give up my kernel now that I have it."

Sasha scrunched one eye closed. "I think you have to. Don't you?"

A big pause. They were giving her the space to answer for herself. "Yeah. I have to risk the lost kernel."

"You have to risk the kernel!" Caz yelled back in celebration. "*Let's gooo!*"

With a deep exhale for courage, Taryn nodded and carried her phone into the hallway. She could text Charlie, but a phone call seemed more personal. She waited as the call went through, aware of her own heartbeat and its vigor.

"You're calling me?" Charlie asked, her voice friendly. She was definitely smiling. "That's new."

Everything in Taryn relaxed. There was nothing to be afraid of. This was Charlie. "I wanted to hear your voice."

A pause. "Oh. That…makes me happy."

That had to be a good sign, right? "I was hoping you had time for a conversation. I could meet you for dinner or swing by your place."

Another pause.

Maybe she'd caught Charlie at a bad time. Maybe Charlie didn't want to continue their conversation. Her suspicion said otherwise as she flashed on Charlie in front of her classroom, imparting knowledge with a gentle confidence. She pressed her nails into the palm of her hand as she awaited a response, the pain holding her attention and keeping her from panicking. "Or we can skip it."

"No, no," Charlie rushed to say. "Um, we should. Right? Why don't you come over?"

"I can be there in fifteen minutes. Should I bring, I don't know, a bottle of wine? What's fitting?"

"I have wine. Get over here."

Taryn remembered to breathe. All was well. They would talk. Things would clear up, and at the very least, she'd know more than she did now. "On my way. Not at all afraid."

"Hey. Just me."

Warmth settled in the center of her chest. "You're right. And that's the best part."

"See you soon, Taryn," Charlie said, her voice a tad quieter.

When she opened the door to her room, she smacked straight into Caz and Sasha, who had been pressed against the door.

"Owww. How about a little warning?" Sasha asked, hand to her forehead.

"I feel like it's a fair trade-off for access to my call."

"There was no resisting the listen in," Caz said desperately. "We are on Team Taryn over here, and that means we can't be left out of this very important moment in your young, gay life. This might be a story we tell your grandchildren someday."

"We should probably slow down."

"Where's your sense of romance?" Caz asked.

"It's cautious in its approach. But thank you for the cheerleading. Now"—she grinned—"I gotta go."

"Yeah, you do," Sasha said, pulling her into a tight squeeze. "You're giving me so much motivation to find snack girl. Now, go turn your kernel into popcorn."

"I'm never going to regard popcorn the same again." Taryn grabbed her keys and backed out of the room. "You know that, right?"

"Nor should you," Caz said, handing her her bag. "Get out of here."

Taryn, with an extra shot of energy, did just as they said and covered the short distance to Charlie's place. The moon was full and lit her journey like a beacon encouraging her mission. She'd left her coat at home, making the walk to Charlie's door a chilly one, the cold blast actually helping her harness her nerves and focus. More determined than ever, Taryn knocked and waited a few moments before Charlie appeared and the world slowed the hell down. *Well, look at her.* Taryn's heart clenched, and she went all soft and gaga like a lovesick puppy. Charlie's hair was in a ponytail with several strands escaping. They framed her face with a gentleness that was the epitome of Charlie. She wore a pair of gray sweats with a pink stripe down the side that made her look adorable and cuddly and ridiculously cute. If this didn't go well, Charlie's whole look was going to make this exceptionally more difficult.

"Hey, you." Charlie looked behind her. "Come in. Come in." She scrunched her shoulders. "So cold out there."

"Hi," Taryn said, meeting her gaze. If she'd been nervous on her way here, it tripled as she crossed the threshold into the apartment.

"Red or white?"

"Always gravitated to red."

Charlie poured and presented her with a long-stemmed glass of cabernet. "I hope you like the cheap stuff."

"It's my favorite." She followed Charlie into the living room and took a seat across from her on the couch. "How was the rest of your day? Had to be downhill after being such a badass during that lesson this morning."

"That's the thing about grad school life. Just as soon as you find a little bit of confidence, it's dashed as you're humbled in the most public way possible. Danny's most recent short story apparently only got better with revisions while my classmates felt I hadn't gone far enough with mine."

"They're all just trying to make their way, and acting like they know more about that story than you do is just part of that routine."

"I'm not sure that's true, but you get so many bonus points for saying so."

"I'll take them." A pause. "After class, I felt like we were in the midst of something, I don't know, *key*."

"Key. That's one word for it." Charlie's eyes searched the wall as if the answers she was looking for were inscribed there. She downed half her glass of wine as if it was a lifeline to sanity.

Taryn set hers aside. "The last words you said to me on that sidewalk were *to be specific*, and I've played them over and over in my head more times than I can tell you, because this is important."

Charlie's eyes held anguish. She was battling herself, and Taryn could feel it the short distance across the couch. As if hearing Taryn's thoughts, Charlie stood and walked across the room and absently picked up a small statue of a lighthouse and studied it. "I was feeling so brave in that moment. Adrenaline left over from the successful session in class."

"Well, maybe I'm on adrenaline now," Taryn said, following Charlie and pausing behind her. "But I'm feeling brave." She swept a section of Charlie's hair off her shoulder to reveal her neck, smooth and perfect. She resisted the urge to run her finger across it.

"Taryn," Charlie whispered achingly. Her hands, still holding the statue, went still. "This could change everything." There was a vulnerability behind her voice that Taryn had not heard before. Yet that softness, Charlie's willingness to show herself, infused every inch of Taryn's being.

She was trembling on the edge and dying for that first touch, that first taste. She wanted to kiss Charlie into oblivion, stare into her eyes for hours without having to hide her feelings. When it was just them, the world faded to the edges, and she wanted to live in that space for as long as humanly possible. She took a step closer, her breasts now lightly touching Charlie's back. "I don't want to blow your life up, Charlie, but I know what I'm feeling, and it's all-consuming. You are. I know what I want and it's you and me."

Silence took over. Taryn was well aware of her own heartbeat in her ears.

Finally, Charlie turned and faced Taryn, and their connection locked into place. "Blow it up," Charlie whispered, her blue eyes dark and determined. She'd never looked more beautiful in her life. Gently, Taryn eased a strand of that blond hair behind Charlie's ear. She slowly lowered her lips to Charlie's, aware of the soft sound of her breathing, reveling in the warm tickle of her breath on Taryn's mouth. When their lips pressed, Taryn's knees almost buckled, her breasts most certainly tingled, and her body went hot with desire now unleashed—held back for longer than Taryn had even realized. She'd wanted this woman with a passion she hadn't even fully admitted to herself, and here she was, beneath Taryn's touch. As Charlie's lips began to move with hers in a perfect rhythm all their own, her body hummed and ached, finally where it wanted to be for so damn long. The heat, the sizzle, the unmistakable chemistry leapt every expectation Taryn carried with her. They kissed slow and deep, and it was Charlie who first angled for better access and slipped her tongue into Taryn's mouth, an act that exponentially challenged her legs' ability to hold her up. She was certainly unprepared for how Charlie's kiss would affect her. She would plan better next time. She hoped there'd be more.

"God, I love kissing you," Taryn said quietly, refusing to move from this very spot and her close proximity to Charlie.

Charlie nodded, a small smile playing on her lips. "Me, too." A pause and she dropped her head back. "I can't believe we just did that. Did the last few moments really just happen?"

"I think so," Taryn said. "Are you…okay with all of this?"

"I'm trying to be. I have these feelings for you that are new and awesome and alarming and not at all in any semblance of order."

Taryn could sense a *but* on its way. She braced herself.

"But we're a little out of order here."

The world came crashing in. "You have a boyfriend."

"Right. And we probably shouldn't have kissed."

Taryn absorbed the words she knew were true but didn't want to face. She wasn't someone who went around knowingly breaking up relationships, or kissing people who were already attached to others, but something felt…meant-to-be in this scenario, and she'd leapt with her eyes closed. "Do you mean ever or…?"

Charlie looked thoughtful. It was clear all of this was weighing on her, and Taryn hated to be any kind of stress in Charlie's world. "I need to talk to Danny. I need to think some things through. I'm a fish out of water right now and want to make sure I don't act impulsively."

She hadn't said she was ending things with him. If anything, she seemed confused, which was perfectly okay, but also somewhat devastating if you were in Taryn's shoes. "I can give whatever time you need, but know that I'm steady. I'm here and not going anywhere."

"But do we make sense, Taryn? I'm about to graduate."

"And in a year and half, I will, too, and then we'll both be out of school for the rest of our lives. This is just a blip of time. Not that I'm proposing, or getting ahead of myself." She held up her hands. "I don't want to do that."

"I'm five years older than you."

"You told me I'm wise beyond my years."

Charlie smiled and her cheeks dusted with pink. "Do you have an answer for everything?"

"Yes," Taryn said automatically, fully believing that she did. If nothing else, she was excellent at debate points.

Charlie laughed. "Why are you so cute?"

"I'd love to hear your theory on that."

"What about Ashley?"

"Who?" Taryn tilted her head.

"Good answer." Charlie reached for Taryn's hand and threaded their fingers.

She looked down at them, liking the look, feel, and reality of the physical contact. She would never get used to this. The perfect fit. "Is this a violation?"

"Hard to say, but I just wanted a moment of connection to you before—"

"You kick me out? You're about to do that, aren't you?"

Charlie met her gaze. "I don't trust myself not to kiss you again."

"You probably shouldn't trust me either. I'll go." She hesitated. "When will I see you again? I don't want to walk out of here, and we pretend like none of this happened. I don't think I could take that, Charlie."

"That won't happen."

"Then when?"

"Maybe we can have dinner soon. But I want time to think. To talk to Danny. To work things through." Her gaze brushed the ceiling. "Taryn, this is all so unexpected, and it's happening in the midst of my last year when there is already so much on my plate."

"That sounds ominous."

"Don't. I'm just being as honest I can be."

"I know you are." She offered a small smile. "And I don't want to make your life harder than it has to be."

"You make my life better," Charlie said without delay. "I'm more than clear on that portion." The comment hit Taryn in the chest and spread out, leaving her warm and happy.

"You, too. I mean that." She gave Charlie's hand a squeeze before letting go. Not the good-bye she'd have chosen if she'd had her way, but it would have to do. "Don't think too hard, okay?"

"Tall order. And aren't you the resident overthinker?"

Taryn turned back. "And I speak from experience when I say it sucks. I much prefer to feel these days."

"I won't if you won't."

"Deal. Good night, Charlotte Adler."

"Good night, Taryn Ross."

Charlie closed the door, and Taryn walked to the parking lot of the apartment complex in shock and awe. Had that really just happened? Had she made out with Charlie in her living room, and had it been the most intoxicating, wonderful experience of her entire life? Why, yes. To all of that. A resounding yes! And though nothing was figured out, squared away, or decided upon, she allowed herself this tiny moment in time to live in the wonder of it all. She wasn't alone in her feelings, and that felt like a validation she'd very much needed.

Standing alone on the sidewalk, she pulled her camera from her bag, turned it around, and smiled as she clicked blindly on the shutter. It wouldn't be the cleanest selfie ever shot, but she wanted to remember this moment and the way she felt in it for all time. Because she was Taryn, but she wasn't. In her place was this new version who now understood what it felt like to be fully alive. She turned in a small clichéd circle, smiled at the twinkling stars above, and made a promise to herself that whatever happened, tonight was more than worth it.

❖

There was no way around it, this was going to be hard. Charlie sat on the steps that led up to her door and checked her watch. How did you properly disappoint someone you deeply cared about? Charlie didn't know how she was going to do it. Her nerves were frayed, she was on very little sleep, and her stomach churned, but she had to be honest with Danny about what was happening within her. Was it a sexual awakening? A self-realization or discovery? Or was this just about the intense connection she had with Taryn in particular? She didn't have the answers, but she had to find them. Was she about to press pause on her assumed future on a whim?

No. That's not what this was. Her feelings were real. Time had proven them so. It didn't mean she was any clearer about how to handle all the intricacies of the situation. There were so many plans. Was she supposed to undo them all now? God, what would that even look like?

She placed her face in her hands and closed her eyes, waiting for the universe to shower her with the wisdom she needed to choose the proper path and answer all of these questions. But all she saw in her mind's eye was the moment she first kissed Taryn playing on a loop that made her so ridiculously happy. If that wasn't a sign, what was?

"Hey. You okay?"

She popped her head up and blinked. Danny stood in front of her wearing black basketball shorts and a baby-blue Nike Swoosh shirt, which meant he'd likely just come from a pickup game. He wasn't the most athletic of humans, but he had fun on the court and definitely looked the part.

"Sorry. Yes. I was lost in thought."

"Since when do you think with your head in your hands? You look like the picture of utter despair." Leave it to a writer to characterize her struggle. He slid onto the step next to her and didn't wait for an answer, which was honestly kind of standard. Danny often had a trajectory from which he didn't deviate. "Hey, Lawson has been getting close with that girl I told you about. Lindsey someone, and we were thinking that we could all get away for a weekend soon. Maybe one of those cabins along Lake Michigan. I've narrowed down a few options for you to peruse."

"I don't know."

He frowned. "Are you worried about your schedule at the library? I'm sure if you gave them notice, they'd accommodate."

"Maybe if it was you. Everyone accommodates you." He stared at her, and she regretted the statement, which had come with a bite in her tone. Why was she going there? There was no reason to lash out. Yes, Danny had things a little bit easier. He was talented and rich and well-connected. None of that was part of the reason she needed to step back. *Focus. Breathe. And explain.* She held up a hand. "I'm sorry. I've been on edge lately."

"I've noticed." He shrugged. "So let's break it down. We can get you back on track. Is it the workload, the writing, the stress of what's next?"

"All of those things. But Danny, there's more than that, and I need to be up front with you, hard as that may be."

"Okay. Then do that. I wouldn't want you to be anything else." He scratched a spot above his lip, a sign of his brain at work, which she used to find so endearing. She still did, but now it didn't feel like hers to appreciate. "I'm listening."

He took her hand and she let him. "You know my friend, Taryn." She'd once introduced them in passing at the library. He'd been uninterested at the time, mainly because Taryn had been quiet and seemingly not as impressed as most other people who'd met Danny McHenry.

"The undergrad? Yeah. Cool enough girl." He squinted as if trying to assemble the pieces ahead of time.

A pause. She didn't have the perfect words and decided to lead with facts. "We kissed two nights ago."

"She *kissed* you?"

"And I kissed her."

He was still for a moment. "Forgive me if I'm caught off guard."

"No, I get it."

He stood and walked a few paces away, hands on his hips. He was processing. She knew him well enough to recognize his cues.

"I'm sorry." It was all she had.

"You're sorry and you want me to forgive you, or you're sorry and you want to kiss this Taryn girl some more?" His eyes held hurt, not anger.

"Please don't say it that way."

He whirled around. "Fuck me. You're serious?" He shook his head because she hadn't reassured him. "You want to pursue something with her?" He had clearly not been expecting it to go that way. No one turned Danny down for anything, a stranger to rejection in all its forms.

"Maybe. I have real feelings that I've tried to ignore, and that seems to have made them stronger."

Danny took a breath, softened, and came to sit next to her again. "I get it. I've had the same feelings here and there, but you know what? It's just the pressure of all that's ahead. We're about to start life with all of its huge, suffocating demands, and it's easier to just fixate on something else."

He was explaining things to her as if she wasn't someone who could navigate this situation on her own, and it was exactly the behavior that had made it hard for her to breathe the past few years.

"Please don't minimize the way I'm feeling."

He nodded. "I apologize. I just think if you take a step back, you'll see that this is a wild hair that you will likely regret in six months. We're good, Char. You and I make sense. We're writers who see the world through a similar lens." He exhaled. "And it's what your mother wanted for you."

Low blow. She closed her eyes, shocked that he'd gone there. The pain slashed through her, nevertheless. Her mother's memory was a soft spot for her, and living in a way that would make her mom proud was her most important goal. And he knew that.

"I'm just doing the best I can," she said, emotion grabbing her throat, making words difficult. "But I owe it to myself to find *me*. Find my happiness. She would want that, too."

He stood, nodding. "What if I'm not here when you come to your senses?"

"It's a risk I have to take."

His hands went into his pockets and his gaze locked on hers. "Perfect. I guess I'll see you in class."

"Danny."

Her turned around slow, hands still in pockets, chin tilted back. There were so many things she could say in this moment to smooth things over, to give him hope, or to explain herself further. "What about your mom?"

"Don't tell her. She had a busy month, and this would break her heart."

Charlie nodded. It was a request she could grant if it would make this any easier on him. "Understood. I'll follow your lead."

He hesitated. "You sure you want to do this?" His eyes were soft, and it broke her heart. They'd had some good times together, and this felt like the end of an important era. She wasn't good with endings. In fact, she hated them.

"I have to, Danny."

"Gotcha." He offered one affirmative nod and rounded the corner to the parking lot, not looking back.

Now alone, and reeling, Charlie didn't move. She let the sadness, the fear, and the guilt wash over her. In a few minutes, she'd wipe her tears and think about what was next. But first, she needed to let herself come to terms with good-bye, not just for her relationship with Danny but for the person she no longer was. As she sat on those steps hugging her knees to her chest, she watched the sun sink in the sky, bursting into vibrant pinks, purples, and oranges in one of the more gorgeous displays she could remember experiencing. It was a stunning transition that resonated with her on such a personal level that it sent an uncomfortable lump to her throat and brought happy tears to her eyes.

Because no. She shouldn't just be grieving. She should also be celebrating the excitement of what might lie ahead. This very easily could be the first step in the rest of her ridiculously happy life, and she should mark it appropriately.

If this was a new chapter for Charlie, she wanted to give it all the effort and attention it deserved. She was both terrified and excited, and that was okay. But one thing she wasn't going to be was closed off or untrue to herself. That stopped now.

She stood, wiped her tears, and gave herself a small squeeze as the sun continued to show off its sky-painting ability. "And here we go," she said quietly.

Chapter Eleven

Taryn hadn't heard from Charlie in the three days since they'd turned her world upside down with that kiss. She'd given Charlie the space to sort things out on her own, but the suspense of what decision she would come to had been nearly unbearable, sabotaging her ability to focus, and making getting any sort of reading assignment done laughable.

She'd gone to a party and taken it much easier on the alcohol this time. Didn't mean she hadn't checked her phone every eight minutes just in case she'd missed a notification. Charlie sure must be struggling if she hadn't reached out once after they'd established a pattern of texting throughout their days. Or worse, she wasn't. The silence was loud as hell.

Across the room, Sasha danced with a girl from their dorm, who just might be the one from the vending machine. She'd mentioned running into her again and asking for her number. Well, that was very nice for Sasha. Taryn was feeling a little bit like joining the Love Bites club herself. She took a pull from her beer, opting to never drink trash can punch again.

"What's up?"

She turned at the sound of the male voice only to find herself looking up and into the eyes of Danny McHenry, otherwise known as Charlie's boyfriend. The beer went still on the way down from her lips. Other than a brief exchange at the library, they'd never had a true conversation. She'd forgotten he was one of the frat sponsors. He'd been there the night Charlie had walked a drunken Taryn home. "Not much. Hey."

"Taryn, right?"

She nodded.

"On your own tonight?" He seemed friendly enough. She wasn't sure if that was good or bad news.

"I'm with some friends." She gestured across the room to where Sasha and her girl were dancing like the world was ending, bless their happy little hearts. "What about you?" She offered him a smile. Charlie had said he wasn't a bad guy, so she'd follow her lead.

"Just checking in on the party." He surveyed the room a moment. "Perfect opportunity for you to kiss someone else's girlfriend. I hear you're good at that." Taryn blinked, nearly knocked over by the comment. "Hope you fucking enjoy yourself."

He didn't seem to want a response, and by the time she could have formulated one, he was gone. Okay, that had stung. "Fuck," she said, allowing her head to drop back. Charlie was MIA. The boyfriend hated her. And she was all alone with an aching heart. She stared across the room at the trash can punch, knowing a quick way to put an end to her overly active thoughts.

No way.

Instead, she decided to call it an early night and slide into bed and lose herself in a bingefest of procedurals from ten years ago while mainlining Sour Patch Kids until she passed out. She liked the plan and walked home with a dark cloud over her head, very aware of how alone she felt.

As she approached Alexander Hall, she blinked to clear her vision because sitting on the steps out front was a blonde who looked a little like Charlie, even though she'd yet to see her face. As Taryn approached, the blonde turned, and the blue eyes that sent her every time were staring back at her. They weren't sad like Taryn's either. They were soft, inviting, and—God—a breath of fresh air.

When Charlie saw Taryn, she offered a smile and a slight wave. Just the tiny gesture calmed the storm within Taryn.

"I know it's late, but I wanted to see you."

"You did?"

Charlie nodded. "Gray said you were out at a party, so I thought I'd wait awhile and see if you came home."

"You could have sent a text."

"Seemed impersonal at the time." Why was the world so much better, so much calmer when Charlie was near? At the same time, Taryn worried what Charlie would have to say in the next few moments. She dug her nails into her palms. The pain somehow propped her up. Maybe she'd say that Taryn would always be special to her, but she had no plans to walk away from Danny. Then what? They'd return to their friendship, wiping away any memory of that night in Charlie's apartment. She could ask where she stood, but prolonging the potential blow seemed safer. "Wanna walk?" Charlie asked.

"Yeah. I have time." *She had time?* A tamped-down response to how Taryn truly felt. She was apparently going with nonchalance. They shared a smile that Taryn still felt carried question marks. A smile could mean so many things. Her heart thudded, and they'd only been walking beneath the shadows of the campus trees for a minute at most. No one had said anything, and the tension only seemed to expand with each step before Taryn decided she couldn't take it anymore.

"How are you?" she asked.

"Well. It's been a strange week."

"You could say that again." Why were they not them right now? The anxiety of the past few days seemed to catch up with Taryn in an uncomfortable flurry she couldn't smother. "And I'm just going to let you off the hook. If you're here to smooth things over and pat me on the head, we can skip it." Charlie watched her, listening, but said nothing. "And you can ride off into the sunset with Danny, and I won't hold it against you. Deal? We'll be just fine."

"Hold on a second."

"We won't be fine? Then I don't know what you want from me. I'm a little on edge about all of this and equally apologetic about that."

Charlie paused their walk alongside the foreign language building that was responsible for so many of Taryn's late-night study sessions. Tonight it offered a halo of light that allowed Taryn to see Charlie's face as she frowned at her. "I think I'm gonna need you to slow down," Charlie said.

"Yeah. Fine. I can do that." But that was easier said than done. Her emotions swirled, and so did her nerves.

"Taryn." Charlie inclined her head to the side, a questioning look on her face. She had a tiny scar above her eye, barely noticeable, but Taryn adored it. She adored so much about Charlie, from the way she tucked her jeans into her boots to her vanilla and tangerine scent that drove Taryn wild. But hoping for something that was never going to happen was taking a lot out of her, and she just needed to let her heart off the hook, let it grieve, and find a way to accept things as they were. Damn that scar and the way it made her want things she had no business wanting.

"What?" she fired back with an edge she couldn't mask.

"I came to find you because I wanted to talk to you about the other night."

"Okay. Let's talk about it." Taryn shoved her hands into her pockets, distantly aware of the slight taste of beer on her lips. The party now seemed so very long ago.

"I want you to know that it mattered a lot to me."

This was already a breakup speech, and they'd never even been a couple. Taryn couldn't take it. "But it was a mistake we shouldn't repeat, given your current situation."

"I don't know about you, but I'd like to revisit it many times over. That's why I'm here."

Well, that certainly shut her up. Taryn played the words back not one, or two, but three times in her head to verify she'd heard correctly and understood their meaning.

"Taryn?"

"Sorry, I was caught off guard. I had assumed…"

"That I was here to tell you the opposite. Yeah, I gathered."

Taryn felt the edges of her mouth pull. This was good news, but something held her back. Almost as if she got too close, the amazing bubble might burst.

"Look at me."

Taryn did. That helped. Their connection had always been a powerful one, and this moment was not different. A full smile bloomed. "I like looking at you."

Charlie nodded. "Yeah, well, looking at you has been my undoing these past few weeks."

She could hardly imagine that scenario playing out but liked the idea very much. Charlie had been struggling with an attraction to her for weeks. She'd have to unpack that little enjoyable gem later. There were bigger matters. "What about you and Danny?"

"I told him everything, and we're not together anymore. I explained that I couldn't let this thing between us go unexplored."

"Oh." She pulled in glorious air and felt a burden lift. Charlie was giving them a chance. They were going to explore. She didn't have full confidence, but she did have feelings that had just been fully let out of the box she'd held them in so closely. "Well, now I'm nervous."

"Same. But I have a feeling that's temporary, don't you?"

"Yeah, because it's just you and me."

"I don't think there's anything *just* about us."

The comment sent a shiver across her skin. Charlie had a way of eliciting those. "You're right. There's not." For an extended moment, they simply watched each other as electricity crackled on low. "Now what?"

"I'm going to walk you home and hope I get to see you tomorrow. Can I?"

"Charlie, you're going to find that there aren't many things I would deny you. You tend to have a way with me."

"My way with you?" Charlie looked skyward, opened her mouth, and closed it, thinking better, perhaps, of the quip that was on the tip of her tongue.

Taryn laughed. "Decided not to go there?"

The pink rushed to Charlie's cheeks immediately. Adorable. "Not just yet. No."

Yet. Taryn exhaled slowly because the whole insinuation nearly sent her up in flames. Her heart kicked rapidly in her ribcage as she imagined taking things farther with Charlie, alone in a room with time on their hands.

"Come on," Charlie said. "I'll walk you to your door." Without a word, she threaded her fingers through Taryn's and met her eyes with a soft smile. Their hands intertwined that night had not been on Taryn's bingo card, but she would memorize the sweetness of this moment and play it back whenever she was alone. As they walked, a barrage of emotions hit and expanded in her chest.

"I've missed you," she said quietly to Charlie. "Three days was too much to be apart."

"Come here," Charlie whispered, impulsively pulling her beneath a shadowy tree just off their path. Taryn followed her under the branches. An invitation, and not one she'd ever turn down. Charlie's back was pressed against the trunk, and that brought on all kinds of thoughts. It took Taryn a moment to adjust to the darkened space, but when she did, she was hit with the one-two punch of Charlie's earnest gaze and her slightly parted lips, full and perfect. Charlie cradled Taryn's face and pulled her mouth down into a very much longed for kiss. Tentative at first, a soft press, before Charlie's lips began to move possessively, expertly. *Good God.* That's when the wheels came off the car, and Taryn went hazy. Her bones melted. Her blood ran hot. Charlie was her only anchor in a spinning world that was too good to be real. Yet it was. Tonight was her reality.

"What do you feel?" Taryn murmured when they came up for air. "I'm a jumble."

Charlie smiled against her lips. "When I kiss you, my body hums and my toes disappear. I can't feel them."

"I don't know what kind of review that is."

"Oh, you can trust me implicitly when I tell you it's a good one." She tilted her head and leaned in. "Kiss me again."

Taryn grinned and did just that. She caught Charlie's mouth with hers, and their lips clung in delicious fashion. Dammit, their hands were too well behaved for their own good. Taryn wanted to touch Charlie, push the boundaries of decency, and act on the impulses she'd only dreamt about. Patience, she told herself, to little result. As they kissed, an unfamiliar zing moved through her, from her fingertips to her shoulders to the roots of her hair. Every erogenous zone she had, even ones she hadn't been aware of, shot to life. When they pulled apart, Taryn's entire world was different. Their first kiss had been wonderful, but laced with uncertainty and fear. This kiss came with purpose, intention, and a promise of more to come. There had honestly not been a more invigorating moment in Taryn's life. "I could do that all day," she confessed softly. Somehow her hands had made it to the small of Charlie's back, the bark of the tree pressing against her fingers.

Charlie ran her thumb along Taryn's bottom lip as if memorizing it. "I definitely see where people could lose time."

Taryn knew one thing for certain. She would never regard this tree the same way again. She'd think of Charlie and her amazing mouth every single time she passed it. Bring on the walk to Spanish class because Taryn wanted to relive these tantalizing moments over and over again. Charlie in her arms, her warm lips moving over Taryn's. Maybe they'd even revisit it someday. The fact that they now had the potential of a *someday* was logic-annihilating, but she wasn't about to argue.

"When I see you tomorrow, will it be a date?" Taryn asked.

Charlie smiled. "Um, yeah. Is that okay?"

She jokingly looked unaffected. "I guess so or whatever."

Charlie gasped and kissed her again. "That shut you up."

"You will steal my words every time with those kind of moves."

"Pocketing that information for when I need it. Now come on, youngster, I need to get you home."

"Five years is literally nothing."

"You and I both know it's close to six."

"If you say so…"

Charlie squeezed her hand and walked her dutifully to the doors of Alexander Hall. "Delivered, safe and sound."

Taryn took a deep breath. She didn't want to say good night but assured herself in the knowledge that she had more to look forward to. "I'll see you tomorrow. Newsflash: you may hear from me much sooner."

"I better." Charlie kissed the back of her hand. It felt conservative after what they'd just done, but they were new, and a display in front of the building might be premature. Taryn understood. Charlie was also likely still coming to terms with her sexuality, and Taryn certainly didn't want to apply anything close to pressure. "Good night, Taryn."

"It really was," she said before slipping inside the glass doors and offering a final wave.

The manner in which the evening began and ended was startling. She'd not shared with Charlie that she'd had an unfortunate run-in with Danny. She'd have to do that at some point. She'd also not asked for too many details about the last three days. What she knew beyond a shadow of a doubt was that she and Charlie were on the path they were destined to be on. She had no clue what lay ahead for them, but she was more than eager to finally, at long last, find the hell out.

❖

What was this life, Charlie asked herself, as she checked her watch the day after she'd taken the terrifying leap. Her shift at the library had twenty-two minutes remaining before she planned to hurry home, change her clothes, grade a couple of essays to decrease her stack, and finally head to dinner with Taryn, who she couldn't wait to lay eyes on. Taryn, she'd found, made every day so much better. She calmed Charlie's storm with that soft, soulful gaze of hers. Just thinking about those eyes sent an enjoyable shiver.

"Where are you right now?" Emerson asked, leaning back against the counter. Caught again. This time, Charlie didn't mind as much. They were manning the main desk that afternoon. "Because it looks pretty good. Danny again?"

Charlie smiled politely, not quite ready to show her cards to the world. Yet it was probably important for her to share her relationship status with those that were close to both her and Danny. "I do need to tell you something."

"Juicy? Because you know I have to live through you. The single lane is trash these days."

"Well, depends on your definition, but Danny and I aren't together any longer."

Emerson blinked. "I'm sorry. I just hallucinated. I thought you said you and Danny broke up, which I know is not cosmically possible."

This would be difficult for someone like Emerson to digest. She turned off news broadcasts because she couldn't face hearing anything negative. Her writing was squeaky clean to a fault. Charlie was not surprised that hearing of her friends' breakup would be startling.

"Unfortunately, it's true. We're going our separate ways but most definitely going to remain friends. It was my choice."

The smile dissolved on Emerson's face. "Did he cheat on you?"

"No. He didn't. Danny's a good guy, just not right for me."

"What's he going to do with the ring?" Emerson immediately covered her mouth, realizing her error.

"What ring? What are you talking about?"

"I shouldn't have said anything. He swore me to secrecy. But he was planning to propose in a couple of weeks. On Christmas Day."

Charlie swallowed, and her stomach churned. "You know that for certain?"

Emerson nodded and paused to accept a stack of returned books.

"That's a lot to process," Charlie said when she returned.

"Everything is going to be okay," Emerson said, just as much to herself as to Charlie. "Transitions aren't easy, but you'll get through this section."

"Thanks, Em."

"How does his mom feel about all of this? I know they're your second family."

Charlie swallowed. "He asked that we not tell her quite yet." She felt the emotion bubble and press down on her. "I'm hopeful she'll understand." Underneath it all, she prayed her own mother would, too. "I don't want to hurt anyone, but it's my life and my happiness at stake."

Emerson turned from the tablet in front of her and stalked over to Charlie. "Don't take candy from your bowl and put it in someone else's. Then they have all the candy, and you have an empty bowl. Who wants that?"

It was a highly specific analogy, but Emerson always seemed to have one at the ready. Her writing was riddled with them. But this one did resonate. "I'm gonna remember that."

Emerson stared at her hard. "Hold on to the candy." Her intensity was daunting, prompting Charlie to nod obediently.

The whole thing made sense, she thought thirty minutes later while struggling to see the road. Her windshield wipers worked overtime to combat the rain. They'd talked about when to get engaged multiple times, and with such pressure from Monica, Danny likely wanted to make a big splash in front of his family. God, he had a ring and a firm plan to get down on one knee just before she blindsided him. She hated that part of all this, yet felt helpless to fix it.

The only saving grace on this dreary evening was that she got to see Taryn tonight for what would be their first official date. With Taryn still being fairly new to town, Charlie'd picked out a local restaurant she'd heard about, the North Star. It was far enough away from campus that they could unplug and enjoy a nice meal in an intimate atmosphere. She hoped Taryn would enjoy her choice and got a bump of happy energy just imagining her smile because it was honestly her everything lately. That smile kept her going.

She knocked on Taryn's door on the fourth floor at precisely the time they'd agreed upon, hating to be late but also never too early. She opened the door wearing black pants and a red sweater that hit at the waist and offered a purposeful glimpse of her left shoulder.

"Hi. You're here." They shared a grin, and Taryn hooked a thumb over her shoulder. "Let me just grab my bag real quick."

"Hey," Charlie said, catching the door so it didn't close between them. "I haven't been here since the drunk walk circa beginning of the semester."

Taryn closed one eye. "Can we never speak about that again?"

"We will always speak about it. It's a favorite memory of mine. Where's Caz?"

"Am I allowed to come out?" she heard a female voice say in a stage whisper.

"Yeah, weirdo. You are," Taryn said. "You live here."

"I didn't want to harsh the vibe you two had going with any kind of interloping." A wide-eyed brunette with a long ponytail emerged from the door to her right, smiling openly, her hands pressed together. She remembered her from the party.

"Interloping. Good word. I'm Charlie."

"Hi. Welcome to our pad. I've heard a great deal. Big fan. Caz."

"Likewise." She accepted Caz's firm and impressive handshake. She seemed like a fun person, and she remembered Taryn describing her as witty and warm, a favorite combination of hers.

Taryn rocked on her heels. "Everyone is acquainted and off to a great start. Shall we go?"

"Yes, we have reservations."

"And thoughtful, too," Caz said, walking back to her room. "This is going really well, Tare."

"Don't embarrass me, Caz."

"I got you," Caz called back to her.

They really were a cute duo with a fun give-and-take. In many ways, Charlie was envious. She had friends, but no one she had a true shorthand with, or inside jokes, or who knew her better than she knew herself. She'd always kept people one step away without even fully realizing she was doing it. Trusting people enough to let them close was still a tall order. She looked over at Taryn as they made their way to her car, feeling the tug to make this time different. She wanted to go into this thing open and vulnerable, which terrified her no end.

"You're quiet tonight," Taryn said as they drove. The sun had long left them as they moved through the quiet streets of town. Holiday lights twinkled brightly from the houses and businesses they passed, sprinkling the whole occasion with extra added magic. She had something to celebrate this year. She tried to concentrate on that.

"I am? I'm sorry." She sent Taryn a smile. "Just enjoying the drive with you. Truly." But there was more to the story that she'd left out. She'd been in her head since Emerson's newsflash at the library. Why hadn't she just said so?

"I'm enjoying it too, but are you sure that's all?"

Instead of hanging on to the information any longer, she decided to take her own advice and try to be open with Taryn. "I found out that Danny was planning to propose later this month. On Christmas."

"Ah. And you likely have a million different feelings after hearing that."

"A few." She placed a hand on Taryn's knee. "But regret isn't one of them, okay?"

"Okay," Taryn said, but it was clear that she felt off balance now. How could she not?

She tried to concentrate on Emerson's advice as well. Transitions were tricky. That's all this was. Once everyone settled in, everything would right itself.

"But do you know what I need more than anything right now?"

"What's that?" Taryn asked.

"To escape with you. I'm really looking forward to having a dinner away from campus and stress and all the expectations that hover. Just you and me."

Taryn exhaled slowly. "And I think that's all I needed to hear." She pointed at the road ahead of them. "Take me to this restaurant because now I can't wait." She cranked the music and Charlie laughed, feeling her spirits lift easily along with Taryn's.

When they arrived at North Star, Charlie was immediately taking in the details. As a writer, the little things mattered a great deal, and the specifics of a setting had always intrigued her. The room had approximately fifteen tables, of which about two-thirds were occupied. The soft sounds of clinking glassware and hushed laugher welcomed them along with quiet music.

"This is gorgeous," Taryn said as they were shown to a table in the corner, adorned with a white linen tablecloth and a small flickering candle.

And romantic, Charlie's brain supplied. As they sat, she allowed herself to bask in the shadows and light the flame cast on Taryn's face. She glowed in the soft chair across from Charlie as she surveyed the tall menu, like Belle in the castle.

"What are you laughing about over there?"

"I'm not laughing. I'm taking in my date."

"Your date," Taryn said. "Still getting used to that."

Charlie sipped her water. "Me, too. Some wine or a cocktail?"

"My question exactly," their server said, arriving just on time. Tall and blond with kind eyes. "I'm Justine, here to make sure your evening is everything you'd hoped."

Charlie already liked Justine and her warmth. "I'll have a glass of the house pinot, but then cut me off. I'm the driver."

"I'm not. I'll have the rum breeze."

"Now you're just showing off," Charlie said once they were alone. Taryn nodded solemnly, and Charlie laughed. This woman was thoughtful and funny. In her opinion, it was the absolute best combination. "This right here is what I've been looking forward to."

"I mean, it's okay," Taryn said and passed Charlie a sly grin she wanted to kiss off her face. That was the thing about kissing Taryn. Once she'd done it, she just wanted to keep doing it more. Even in the most inopportune moments. Class discussions. Traffic lights. In the middle of teaching her class. The desire really didn't discriminate. It was a new and somewhat perplexing experience. Had she ever once fantasized like that about anyone else? She didn't even have to search for the answer.

Charlie began to butter her warm bread. "I'll see what I can do to make it better."

Taryn's eyes went wide, and she sat slowly back in her chair. *Jackpot*. Dating was actually more fun than Charlie'd ever realized. After a quick scan of the menu, Justine returned, and Charlie ordered the scallop risotto and Taryn chose the roasted chicken.

"Is the restaurant family owned?" Charlie asked Justine.

"It is. Rosemary and Eva are the owners, and everyone adores them. Been together for forty-two years and were married just as soon as they were allowed." She craned her neck to the left, searching. "Rosemary is around here somewhere, probably in the kitchen making sure the food is just how she likes it. She just might swing by and check on you." Justine touched the table. "Back shortly with your food."

Charlie went still. Rosemary and Eva were a lesbian couple. It was an incredibly common occurrence in this day and age, but it hadn't been back in theirs. Yet they'd held on to each other anyway. Something about sitting in their restaurant with Taryn felt like a giant arrow sign, telling her that she was finally living the life she was meant to live. And it felt so damn good that tears sprang into her eyes.

"Hey," Taryn said quietly, leaning in. "Everything okay?"

"It really is," Charlie said, dabbing the corners of her eyes with her napkin. "I'm a sap every once in a while."

Taryn seemed to register that these were happy tears and reached across the table and took her hand. "I happen to like occasional saps. And I like you. This feels like a win-win."

The food arrived and the cocktails were at half full, which loosened them up nicely. "When do you head home?" Charlie asked. The fall semester would end in just over a week, and with them being so new, they'd yet to discuss what the month apart would entail.

"End of next week, I take my last final. I'll probably get on the road the next morning."

"Back to Dyer."

"Mm-hmm. Want to come visit? What about Christmas?"

Charlie's forkful of amazing risotto was placed on pause. "Really?"

The reality was that Charlie didn't have a family anymore beyond the one she'd made with Danny's. She'd planned to linger at Hillspoint until closer to Christmas, writing and preparing for the move to New York in May. She was originally supposed to join Danny in Indianapolis for Christmas and New Year's. Now, she had nowhere to be.

"Are you kidding? I'd love it." She proceeded to eat, dropping her brows in thought. "But I can't imagine your parents would want you bringing someone home."

"They would love every second of it. Same house. Same friendly people. They'd make you cocoa with a peppermint stick and ply you with Hallmark movies."

"That's not real."

"It is." Taryn cut a bite of chicken. "It's a two-person operation in Dyer, and you should come witness the wonders. They also dress up and go caroling, likely taking you with them if that's your jam. Do you sing? I realize I don't even know. Personally, I prefer to take photos and cheer them on."

"You've offered some really impressive selling points. I do like to sing." She hesitated because it sounded so wonderful that she nearly turned to tears a second time, which seemed gratuitous. "Why don't I think about it?"

"Because you're not sure you want to come or because you don't want to intrude?"

"Definitely the latter. You all are a family and probably don't want an outsider at such a special time of year."

Taryn grinned and chewed her food. "Then it's settled because you're forgetting my parents and their overly social agenda. You're coming to Dyer. The great homecoming. We can take a photo of you next to your old lifeguard stand. Swimsuits are encouraged, but I have selfish reasons to vote yes."

"Taryn." Charlie laughed and shook her head, so not used to blushing at comments like that one. Yet this was the new normal.

"Yes?" she asked innocently, blinking her eyes slowly.

"Why are you so adorable?" Charlie asked with a tilt of her head.

Taryn furrowed her brow. "It's my life sentence."

"I can't with you."

"Yes, you can."

Charlie let the wineglass linger and peered at Taryn over the top of it. "Yes, I can." A healthy drink from her glass followed. She placed it in front of her just as an older woman approached their table in a white coat with glasses on her head and brown hair with soft curls.

"How was your dinner tonight?" she asked with kind eyes and a quiet voice as if to purposefully not disturb the ambiance at their table nor the other diners.

"It was the best meal I've had in years," Taryn said. Her plate had been mostly cleaned, and it had been fun to watch her taste and enjoy the food. As with everything, she'd seemed to give a lot of thought to each bite.

"Are you Rosemary?" Charlie asked. It was forward, but she simply had to know.

The woman pulled her face back in exaggerated surprise before breaking out into a smile. "I am. And who do I have the pleasure of meeting?"

"I'm Charlotte Adler and this is Taryn Ross. We're so happy to meet you."

"Likewise. Are you celebrating anything special tonight?"

Charlie hesitated, trepidation firing. She looked over at Taryn who nodded her encouragement, and suddenly she felt strong and at home. The truth was she was proud of Taryn, and there was no reason not to share, other than this was all new for her. "We're on a first date."

Rosemary took a moment, struck and seemingly touched. "It's an exciting night, then," she said quietly. "I'm going to send over a special dessert not found on our menu. I save it for the special people."

"That's so kind of you," Taryn said. "Thank you."

"My pleasure. Promise me you'll come back sometime. I'd love to check in, see how things are going." Rosemary placed a hand on her round hip, maternal and kind.

"We promise," Charlie said.

"And hopefully I can introduce you to Eva, my very own sweetheart of many years. She's responsible for half the menu." She touched her chest. "The other half is mine," she whispered, gesturing to Charlie's risotto. She gave her a pat on the shoulder. "That dessert should be out soon."

"This is the best date I've ever been on," Taryn said automatically as soon as they were alone.

"There's still dessert," Charlie told her. "It could go straight to hell."

"Good point. I will reserve my judgment but know that things are looking up." She squinted. "You're not planning to rob the place or anything, right?"

"I mean, not at this very second, but plans change."

Taryn considered this. "Still don't think it would change my ranking, and I went out with Bianca Mack, who was known around school to be a really good kisser."

"You kissed Bianca Mack?"

"I did. And this date, robbery and all, still wins."

"I'm jealous. I remember her well." She offered a playful smile. "She's missing out."

"Oh, that right there was really nice."

"But I do have an unfortunate confession."

"Tell me."

Charlie squinted. "I once kissed her older brother."

Taryn covered her mouth, nearly spitting her cocktail across the table.

Charlie quickly handed her a napkin, laughing. "I'm so sorry. I didn't mean to drop such a bombshell on this lovely, potentially criminal, dinner we're having."

Taryn successfully swallowed and let the laughter out. She sat back in her chair and just let it hit, which was unusual because Taryn's reactions to most anything were conservative in nature. "I had no idea I was so funny." Taryn fanned herself attempting to regain her voice. This might be the first time Charlie had seen her full-on laugh without control, which only prompted her to join in.

"You kissed her brother," Taryn hissed. "For real?"

Charlie nodded, her eyes tearing. "Two stars. Cannot recommend."

That only seemed to make Taryn laugh harder. They likely would have kept going if Justine hadn't appeared with deconstructed strawberry shortcake with two spoons. "You're gonna die for this one. We all do. And dinner was all taken care of."

Charlie's smile faded. "Rosemary doesn't have to do that."

"She insisted, and when Rosemary insists, it's best we all just get out of her way." Justine's eyes went wide to make her point.

"So noted," Taryn said, dabbing her eyes. "In that case, we will eat every last bite."

"Such a harsh sentence," Charlie said lifting her own spoon. The truth was that it was the best dessert she'd ever eaten in her life, and Rosemary likely knew that would be the case. She regarded Taryn. "How are we ever going to eat at another restaurant again?"

"Lesbians preparing fantastic food can't be beat. It just can't."

"No. We're ruined."

They stared at the last bite left on the plate. "What are we going to do about that?" Charlie asked and sat back.

"It's a tough one. But I have a win-win idea."

"I'm intrigued."

Taryn expertly scooped the cake, a strawberry sliver, and the last bit of vanilla ice cream onto the fork and glided it toward Charlie, who understood the mission. She accepted the bite and made happy eye contact with Taryn as the decadent flavors melted over her. "That one was my favorite," she said, dabbing her mouth.

"Oh, mine, too," Taryn said and grinned. "By far." They shared a smile and Taryn softened. "Seriously, though." She lifted a shoulder. Charlie was learning that when lighthearted exchanges moved into sincerity, Taryn was less comfortable. "This was really nice." Her gaze that generally carried self-assuredness brushed the table before she pulled it back to Charlie. It was a glimpse behind the curtain. "Thank you."

"You're welcome. I have a confession. This was exactly what I needed." She glanced toward the kitchen. "And I would happily pay the check, but it appears there won't be one."

"We made a splash."

Charlie laughed. "We did. Let's get outta here and make more."

Chapter Twelve

The walk to the car from the restaurant was quiet. The buzz from the cocktail was all but gone, and that was okay. Taryn was in a good mood and knew this was a night she'd always look back on in wonder, making her excited for whatever might be ahead for them. Life had a way of truly delivering on surprises. She squeezed her shoulders together against the cold. The sky was clear, showing off how many stars it claimed, making it easy for her to see her own breath as they moved, hands shoved into pockets. She'd scarcely thought of much else for days. It was true that listening to Charlie talk, laughing with her, exploring a new place like this was amazing, but the elevated tension that came with not knowing when they'd get to touch, kiss, and explore was never far away in her mind. There was this constant physical draw that Taryn was finding harder and harder to ignore.

As Charlie pressed the ignition, bringing the car's engine to life, her hand went still on the gearshift. She turned to Taryn, pressing her cheek to the seat. Taryn's stomach tightened because though they were still early, she was already learning Charlie's looks. This one, eyes laced with hints of desire, was her absolute favorite.

"What if we just stopped the world for a moment?"

Taryn nodded, unable to fully come up with interesting words to speak while also being lost in those eyes. Her heart rate increased, her stomach went tight, and an infusion of warmth rushed from her shoulders to her fingertips and downward. *Waiting. Waiting. Waiting.*

The seconds that ticked by as they watched each other only seemed to drizzle gasoline on the fire that licked and danced between them. Charlie made the move before she could, placing a hand on Taryn's cheek and pressing her mouth firmly to Taryn's. It felt like a claim, like a burst of action that could not be held back a moment longer, and God, did Taryn identify.

Lips began to move. Arms reached. There was a quiet desperation now that they took what they wanted. Charlie's skin was warm as Taryn slipped her hands beneath the back of her sweater, a startling contrast to the crisp air pressed to the car windows. A roaring sprang up in Taryn's ears as they kissed, signaling the overwhelming need she wrestled with. It rushed rapidly south, blazing a trail of heat. This was beyond good, and Taryn warred between wanting to savor every second and driving them forward, forward, forward. Slanting her mouth over Charlie's for better access, she took everything Charlie offered, desiring more still. She longed to know what it was like to have Charlie beneath her, whispering her name, parting her legs, skin on skin. What an addictive dance they were.

"Too much," Charlie whispered, going in for another kiss, her tongue exploring Taryn's mouth. Her voice was different, and there was something mind-bogglingly sexy about that, the knowledge that Taryn had turned her on and sent her to somewhere affected and new. It fueled her determination.

The hands that had been at the small of Charlie's back began to wander, ambitious and without Taryn's total intention. Somehow she'd gained the upper hand and found herself leaning over the center console. She placed her palms flat against Charlie's ribcage, sliding them up more and more until her thumbs ran into the underside of Charlie's breasts, which just about short-circuited the remaining portion of Taryn's brain, power. Charlie nodded, her hands in Taryn's hair holding her in place.

That's when the laughter floated in the air, which was puzzling. As much as Taryn tried to ignore the now loud combination of overlapping voices, it oriented her and she remembered their surroundings.

"Dammit, I think they're parked next to us," Charlie said with wide eyes.

Taryn mimicked her expression and they sat up, righting themselves and adjusting their clothing like two fourteen-year-olds caught behind the movie theater. Laughter came next because the situation was harmless enough that they could see the humor and make fun of themselves.

"I think they stole our moment," Taryn said, as the intruding group of diners drove away.

"Temporarily," Charlie said, but there was a shy undercurrent to the way she carried herself that meant the spell had been broken.

That was okay. They were early in this thing and still maneuvering the important details. Sex was certainly one of them. "We should probably get back."

"*Fiiiine*," Taryn said, drawing out the word like a petulant teenager. "Let's return to our regular boring lives when this parking lot was actually the nicest place I've visited in years." She folded her arms to demonstrate her feigned dismay.

"Don't be cute when I'm trying to do the responsible thing."

Taryn unfolded her arms automatically. "But only because you called me cute."

Charlie reached over and touched her chin affectionately before firing up the ignition and whisking them back to the Hillspoint bubble. They lingered and chatted and shared a brief kiss in front of Alexander, their first public show of affection that left Taryn feeling like the luckiest girl ever. True, the area had been mostly deserted, but she wasn't going to be choosy. She spent the rest of the night studying for the final she had in two days, in between drifting back to the memory of their evening together. When she finally closed her textbook, just shy of two a.m., she found a message waiting for her on her phone.

Off to bed. I will think about our night till sleep comes. And those thumbs. Night, Taryn.

Like a princess in a cartoon, Taryn's jaw dropped, she crushed the phone to her chest, and she fell back onto her bed, starry-eyed and smiley. When she'd arrived at Hillspoint that first day, she'd never once imagined that she'd run into her childhood crush and then fall down the rabbit hole of an actual burgeoning romance with her. Yet, somehow, here she sat. What was this life and how did she make sure she lived in it forever?

❖

"'Tis the season to be flunked out, fa-la-la-la, la-la-la. Send us straight to a nice pour house, fa-la-la-la-la, la-la-la."

Charlie smiled at the band of fraternity brothers standing in a line, wearing overly large mutton chops, known for their less-than-traditional caroling year after year. It was a Hillspoint tradition that she enjoyed—this year even more than others. Probably because everything just felt lighter. Charlie had a spring in her step, feeling more alive, hopeful, and like a truer version of herself than she had in years. And she knew why. She'd likely been doing it wrong all this time, forcing herself into relationships that looked good on paper rather than allowing herself to feel. Growing up with a man like her father taught her not to hope for too much and to shove down dreams and desires so there would be no chance for disappointment. If Taryn hadn't stepped back into her life, how would she ever have corrected her path? She imagined herself married to Danny and mildly content, wondering why nothing ever seemed to click into place for her the way it did other people.

"Do you think people can be completely oblivious to their own sexuality?" Charlie asked Anders, the librarian's assistant who never seemed to smile. He turned 180 degrees, now facing her, eyebrows low, mouth in a frown. He'd attempted one of those winter spray tans that hadn't gone in his favor.

He stared at her hard. "Who talked to you?"

She tilted her head. "What? No, I'm not talking about you, Anders. I've not heard any kind of scandal associated with your dating history."

"Oh." He visibly relaxed. "Well, then we're just speaking in the general sense?"

"We are. Very general."

"Well"—he turned to face her fully—"studies have shown that people discover their true sexualities at all sorts of different junctures in life, some being more fluid than others, of course. There are a lot of factors to take into consideration—exposure, life experience, religious expectations, personal bias."

"Right," she said, chewing on the information. "I imagine a certain person could trigger an awakening."

"They damn well can," he said softly, gazing past Charlie at the wall, lost in a sea of his own thoughts and what looked to be spicy memories.

She folded her arms and nodded. "We're really getting to know each other today, Anders."

"What?"

She grinned and gave his arm a rub. "Nothing. You stay right where you are because that looks really nice. I'll run the system update on this station for you." She slid between him and the computer. The least she could do for the guy.

"I appreciate that," he mumbled as the evening marched on, the library full of overcrowded tables, study groups exchanging notes and typing on shared Google Docs. There was a buzz in the air born of no sleep and overcrowded brains. Everyone was rushing to winter break and hurdling one exam at a time to get there. Luckily for Charlie, nearly all of her finals consisted of projects and papers she'd diligently prepared for in advance.

And as she left the library that evening, she paused on the steps because soft snowflakes had begun to fall. Backlit by the moon, they shimmered and swayed as they drifted to the ground with a grace that caught her right in the throat. Just then she heard the sound of a click, almost like a shutter, pulling her attention to life. There she saw Taryn seated on a bench, camera in her lap.

"Isn't it beautiful?" Taryn asked with a soft smile. "I have a feeling that's going to be a really breathtaking shot."

Charlie turned, a grin already tugging because this was the most fantastic surprise. "What is going on here? Have you emerged from the doldrums of your cram session? I wasn't expecting to see you for a few days." Taryn had been drowning, having not prepared for exams in as timely a manner as Charlie had. One way they were different.

"I'm out of jail on account of good behavior. I worked through lunch and dinner so that I might get to come say hi."

Charlie squinted in protector mode. She'd put on her black peacoat, navy newsboy cap, blue and white scarf, and matching gloves to exit the library in the frigid temps. Taryn, conversely, wore a light jacket and nothing else. Her dark hair was swept to one side and rested on her shoulder. Her neck was visible, stunningly attractive, and likely very cold. Yet another way they were different. "Where are your scarf and gloves?"

Taryn shrugged. "I like the cold, and this jacket is enough. Wanna sit?"

Charlie nodded and descended the remaining steps until she slid onto the bench next to Taryn. "Hi."

"Hi," Taryn said with a soft smile, her eyes never leaving Charlie's. "My day just improved. Tell me about yours. It's been hours since I've heard a single detail."

"Hours? Wow." Charlie took Taryn's bare hands in her gloved ones, attempting to keep them warm. "I did have a rather exciting morning."

"Already better than my History of Eastern Europe reading. What happened?"

Charlie sat a little taller, excited to share. "Remember the contact Monica set me up with at Broadland Rhodes? June DiCarlo?"

"The executive from the really fancy publishing house. Yes."

"She called this morning and wants to set up a time for me to come to New York for a meeting, which I think is code for interview. I talked to Monica afterward, and according to her, if June likes me, I'm golden. She said to get my writing résumé together and include the couple of awards my short stories have pulled in."

"Stop it. You've won awards?"

"Come over someday and I'll show you. All three of them." She added a laugh because Danny and Lawson had so many more.

"You could literally offer me uncooked broccoli from the kitchen floor and I'd be there."

"You offend my culinary ability."

"I forgot! You're like Julia something, the one with the accent."

"Child. And thank you. That's the nicest thing you've ever said to me."

"Way hotter than her, though. By a mile. Do you ever cook in just an apron?"

"Not yet."

"Such a good answer."

"Oh!" Charlie sat forward and turned. "And June also wants me to submit something I'm proud of, and I was considering the short story about the little boy. What do you think? I wasn't sure I should fully lead with my manuscript. She probably wouldn't want something so long. Plus, it feels like we should work up to *the book*, ya know?" The thoughts poured out of her like a faucet, a testament to how Taryn was a safe place where she could just *share* without fear of judgment or comparison.

"I love that story and think that's exactly what you should submit. June is going to eat it up."

Charlie took a deep, nervous breath. The idea of an actual career in publishing with Broadland Rhodes while also writing with the intent to publish with them one day was the ultimate dream come true. "If I have the opportunity to work near June DeCarlo in any capacity…" She trailed off because the concept was too staggering for her brain. "The connections I'd make alone would be invaluable." Not to mention, all the knowledge she'd acquire about an industry she'd always dreamed to be a part of. Plus, June knew she had writing aspirations, and Monica was confident she'd shepherd them along, offer advice, maybe even a critique. Who knew?

"So in a few months you're going to be an aspiring novelist and a publishing industry rock star, living in New York City of all places."

Taryn turned. "I'm not sure you should be hanging out on benches with people who wait until the last minute to study about Europe."

She nodded. "Guess I'll go." As she stood, Taryn grabbed her hand and pulled her back down, this time much closer, pressed up against Taryn. Their gazes locked. "On second thought, I'll stay. It's nice here." Snowflakes dotted Taryn's dark hair, and when one fell onto her nose, Charlie couldn't resist. She leaned in and kissed it softly away.

"You're amazing," Taryn said quietly.

"Well, I like you. A lot. And you came to the library to surprise me. Want to walk to the Bump and Grind and have a boring black coffee?"

"You are temping me right now, but I only carved out a few minutes to lay eyes on you when you got off work."

Charlie looked behind them at the darkened lawn that was partially covered in snow now. "It's a fifteen-minute walk from Alexander over here."

"Worth the round trip for these five minutes. Best of my day."

She felt incredibly special. Taryn had done that. In many ways, it was difficult to let herself buy in after years of her father keeping her humble and under his thumb, and the last few trying to keep up with Danny's many accomplishments. But Taryn looked at her like she was the smartest, most important person in the world, and a little bit of that was starting to sink in.

"Will you kiss me before you have to go?" Charlie asked quietly.

"Always." Taryn nodded and brushed her lips over Charlie's, lingering as if she wanted the moment to extend into forever. Charlie went liquid beneath her touch, memorizing the smell of Taryn's shampoo and the faint press of her fingertips on Charlie's cheek. *Everything.*

"I was going to see if I could catch up and ask you what time grades are due, but you seem occupied."

Charlie turned to her right to see Emerson standing a few feet away, and her mood entirely shifted. Charlie straightened and her brain panicked. She stood and shoved her hands into her pockets feeling guilty, like she'd been seen stealing at the Walmart. *Why?* What was that about? She'd have to figure it out later.

"Emerson, hey. Why don't we walk together and talk about it?"

"Are you sure?" Emerson looked from Charlie to Taryn with a puzzled look. "I don't want to pull you away." She gave Charlie's arm a squeeze. "I had no idea you were seeing somebody."

"Oh. Um, this is Taryn. We're just getting to know each other." It sounded like a downplay, and the way the smile slid off Taryn's face sliced at Charlie. She hated herself for it, but she'd have to fix it later because she'd just gone into some sort of weird preservation mode. She wasn't homophobic. She wasn't ashamed of Taryn or herself. Yet there was something about this new area of her life that she was guarding like the keys to the kingdom.

"Yeah. We're super casual," Taryn said flatly. The light in her eyes that had been there just moments ago had fled. She rocked up on her toes, hands going into her pockets. "I better get back. You two have a good night."

"I'm Emerson, by the way," she called after Taryn.

"Really happy to meet you." However, her gaze was square on Charlie when she said it. Finally, she turned and, with a last dejected look, headed off across the lawn.

"Charlie," Emerson said quietly once they were alone. "I think it's a really good thing."

She pulled her focus from Taryn in the distance and back to Emerson. "You do?"

Emerson slid her arm through Charlie's. "And if you're worried what kind of gossip you might spark in the department because of your history with Danny, don't. People talk about new and interesting things for about five minutes before they move on. You hear me? Five minutes."

Suddenly, Charlie carried regret for all those times she'd written off Emerson as a surface-level friend who existed only in the cheerful column. How shortsighted of her. Because in this moment, she'd needed helpful words, and Emerson knew just the ones to say. Not only that, she seemed to mean them.

She turned and met Emerson's heartfelt green eyes. "You're a good person, Emerson. I mean that. I'm glad you're my friend."

"Really?" The comment seemed to resonate, and Emerson softened. "Thank you. I don't have a ton of friends, Charlie, but I've always considered you a good one. I hope you know that."

And before she knew what she was doing, Charlie pulled Emerson into a tight hug, aware of the tears that pooled in her eyes, aware of the snow falling more heavily all around them, and aware of the chiseling away of self-doubt that was happening in real time. There were people in the world who cheered for others, who lifted them up and made life a better place, and Charlie vowed silently to pay more attention to those people and mirror their light.

"Well, you're stuck with me," Charlie said, releasing her. "And I was going to swing by the Bump and Grind. Wanna come with me?" They'd been work friends and school friends but hadn't socialized a ton together outside of those umbrellas. Time to change all that.

"I'm in!" Emerson said. "I love that place. That have the hottest barista named Brian who wears these supremely tight T-shirts. You have to see." She paused. "But maybe you'd prefer his coworker Lara. I'm so sorry to presume."

"You know what? Let's head over there, and I'll tell you all about it."

CHAPTER THIRTEEN

Taryn sat with her friends at a high-top table at Toby's, nursing large schooners of dressed Dos Equis and celebrating the first half of exams in their rearview mirrors. Soon they'd all pack up and say good-bye for a month before returning to do it all over again.

"So on a scale of one to ten, what's the report?" Sasha asked. Behind them a group of guys threw darts and occasionally erupted in a round of raucous cheering, causing them to raise their voices.

"Ten. No doubt," Taryn said. She stared into her beer. Her enthusiasm was still there, but the run-in with Charlie's friend had taken a bit of wind from her sails. No, that was an understatement. All she'd thought of for the past forty-eight hours was the look on Charlie's face when she realized someone she knew had been watching. Her whole demeanor had shifted.

"If it's a ten, why do you say it with so little conviction? Damn, Tare, you need some caffeine or maybe a little action with your girl-friend."

"She's not my girlfriend. We've not had that talk."

"Is that why there's a little raincloud following you everywhere you go, like Eeyore on very little sleep?"

"Maybe." She shrugged, and the tiny beer buzz she had going dragged the words right out of her. "We had a moment where it was clear she didn't want her friends to know about us."

Caz and Sasha exchanged a look. "You or me?" Caz asked.

"You then me," Sasha said quietly. They put their hands in a pile and broke like a seven-year-old's soccer team.

"Is it possible, Counselor, that Charlie is still quite new to her journey of self-discovery as it relates to her sexuality?" She stared at Taryn, brow furrowed, awaiting her response.

"Yes, undoubtedly."

"Me?" Sasha asked, rising her hand.

"Tag in," Caz said.

"Are we lawyers?" Sasha whispered.

"If you want," Caz said. "Feel it out."

"Is it or is it not true, Ms. Ross," Sasha literally yelled, making even the rowdy dart throwers turn around, "that no one tapped their foot impatiently while you found your way to officially coming out?"

"First of all, I'm not a hostile witness, so slow that passionate delivery." Taryn, still processing, took a moment to consider the question. "Secondly, yes. I took my time literally over a few years."

"And should we not afford Charlie a small amount of grace for not arriving on the scene with the perfectly minted tools to maneuver her own journey?"

Why hadn't she framed it like that for herself? Taryn sighed, feeling like an ass. How had her friends seen something so simply while she'd fumbled around, lost in her own emotions. "Fuck. I'm being a selfish asshole. She texted me three times today, and because I was licking my wounds, I sent back short blow-off responses each time."

"Okay, well, that's already in the past," Caz stated over the roar from the group throwing darts. "You can't undo it. The question is, what are you going to do now?"

Taryn downed the rest of her beer and checked her watch. It was only eight p.m., and Charlie would likely be getting home soon from some sort of departmental Christmas gathering. "I'm going to fix it and grow the hell up. I can be a supportive partner and need her to see that we're not in a rush."

"Case dismissed!" Sasha shouted and lifted her schooner.

There were only so many times Charlie could nod her head knowingly and laugh at the anecdotes from one of the men in the writing department. "No, that must have been such an honor. Really? Impressive." She tossed in an obligatory laugh as one of the tenured professors continued to gloat about his year. The fact was, as a woman, she was in the definite minority and found herself glossed over, brushed aside, or expected to fall all over herself at how great they were.

Even Danny.

Across the room, she watched as her now ex held court as the entire graduate department listened to him talk about all the literary agents who wanted to take him on once he was ready to shop his work around. The last name McHenry brought forth a lot of opportunities, and she wasn't one to complain. Monica had made the connection with June DiCarlo, and she'd be forever grateful for that open door.

"Your mother was special to me, Charlie, and I will always look out for you," Monica once told her, pulling her into a warm hug. Charlie felt the emotion well at the memory, recognizing how lucky she was to have had someone like Monica step into that maternal role when her mother passed away. Monica checked in on Charlie, took her in on holidays, hugged her tight, and made her feel like she was forever in her corner. She exhaled as Danny accepted a refill of champagne and made his way toward her. She took a deep breath and prepared herself.

"Happy holidays," he said, running a hand over the thin beard and mustache he'd added since their breakup. "I wanted to talk about the Christmas break."

"Okay, we can do that."

"I know you've spent the last few years with my family, and if you still want to join us, it's definitely something that we can talk about."

"I just think it might be a little awkward, given where we are now."

"Speaking of which, Mom got into town today to help me pack and drive back. She mentioned getting together with you, something about handing off some of your mother's books."

"Sounds good. I'd love that. Have you told her?"

He studied his glass. "She's already naming our children, Charlie."

That part tore at her. She remembered the two moms making plans to babysit together. "So what's the plan? We can't keep leading her on. She should know the truth."

He hesitated. "I think I kept waiting for you to say you'd made a mistake." There was a sadness in his eyes that hadn't been there the last time they'd talked.

Charlie softened, because none of this with Danny was easy. "As hard as it is to say, I don't think I did make one. I'm still figuring out who I am, Danny, and part of that is learning who I fit with. We're not a match."

He straightened. "I hear you. I don't have to like it, but I can understand." He met her gaze. "I'll talk to her when I get home tonight. Tell her everything."

"Thank you." Charlie honestly didn't know how Monica would

take the news. She was protective of Danny, but she loved Charlie, too. Surely, she'd understand, even if shouldering disappointment. Suddenly, all kinds of doubt descended. "And if there's anything I can do to make sure everyone's okay, please let me know. I'll definitely give her a call tomorrow to check in. Maybe we can even go for coffee when she brings the books." It was wishful thinking, but Charlie felt a strong call to hold on to her relationship with Monica. Danny, too. They were her family, and she hoped they felt the same way.

"Yep." He nodded, killed the rest of his glass, and lifted it to her. It seemed he was done with the conversation. "Anyway, Merry Christmas."

She deflated. "To you, too."

By the time Charlie made it home, her feet hurt from the high-heeled boots, and the red sweaterdress she'd selected was itchier than it was fashionable, and Taryn was out with friends and hadn't so much as checked in, which meant her feelings were still hurt and all Charlie wanted in the whole damn world was to crawl into bed and escape.

That's when Charlie saw her, and the vibrations went quiet. Her stresses were placed on pause. Unless, of course, she was hallucinating. "Taryn?"

"Hey, you," Taryn said, standing from her spot on the stairs in front of Charlie's apartment. "I hope you have the magic key that will take us inside. Provided it's okay I'm here."

Without a word, she moved straight into Taryn's arms, grateful when Taryn caught her and wrapped her arms around Charlie wordlessly. For a minute, they stood just like that, holding each other and hovering happily in the feel of it. She breathed in Taryn, her hair, her smell, the press of her cheek. It had only been a couple of days on the calendar, but the time apart had taken a toll.

"I'm sorry I've been an ass lately," Taryn said quietly into her hair.

"I'm sorry I acted like a frightened child when Emerson showed up the other day."

"Well, I'm sorry that I probably smell like a snack mix and beer."

"I'm sorry that my sweater is itchy." Charlie lifted her face, propped her chin up on Taryn's collarbone, and looked her in the eye.

"We're an apologetic pair," Taryn said.

"I want to get in bed and be a vegetable. Want to be a vegetable?"

"If veggie status is on the table, then yes, I want it."

Charlie laughed not out of just amusement but relief. They were going to be okay. She was. Taryn was. She let them into the apartment, flipped on some lights, grabbed a bottle of wine and two long-stemmed glasses. With them dangling upside down over her shoulder, Charlie inclined her head for Taryn to follow. She'd never been in Charlie's bedroom, and the newness of her presence there carried a certain hum of forbidden tension. This was new territory.

Charlie opened the bottle and began to pour the red wine for them. "Action or rom-com?"

Taryn's eyes went wide. "Why do I feel like this is a test I'm about to fail?" she asked, shrugging out of her jacket. She accepted her glass, eyes on the screen that hung on the far wall. "Rom-com."

"Is that what you would choose for yourself?"

A pause. "No."

Charlie passed her a look.

"I'd be down for an action movie, but only if you're interested in one, too."

"Better." Charlie climbed on the bed. "Let's always be real with each other, okay? Hard for me too, sometimes, but let's shoot for that."

"A new pact. Done"

Charlie arranged the many pillows she had on her bed so they had a comfy little nook to watch the film that Taryn had found and selected for them on the menu. Just as they were settled and about to hit play, Charlie sat up. "What are we doing?"

Taryn quirked a brow.

"We don't have popcorn with butter." She widened her eyes and stared at Taryn for a beat. "What kind of heathens are we?"

"Awful, awful people," Taryn said, then made a spitting sound. "Blech."

"Be right back."

Taryn grinned as Charlie scampered from the room. She quickly microwaved a bag of popcorn and promptly topped it with fresh Parmesan, her favorite addition.

"Popcorn and wine," Taryn stated when she returned with the silver bowl.

"That sounds like commentary. I'll have you know that it's an excellent combination. There's Parmesan on that popcorn, and the wine's *Italian*. Bam. Perfectly paired."

"If you say so," Taryn said.

Charlie gasped. "The skepticism lacing your voice!"

"You're attractive when you're outraged."

"I will be forced to tackle you. This is serious popcorn business," Charlie informed her. "You've been warned."

"That you're defending the honor of a strange snack combination? Sure. Yeah. I hear you."

"Strange?" Charlie leapt, and Taryn caught her, but she wasn't fast enough to stop Charlie from getting a couple of fingers into her ribs for the tickle punishment she deserved. Taryn shrieked and squirmed.

"Say you're sorry."

"Never!" Taryn yelled, reversing their positions until she was on top. The smile fell right off Charlie's face when she saw the image of Taryn looking down at her. The room went still, and Taryn slid off to the side, part of her body still covering Charlie's.

"You know what?" Taryn asked. "Maybe it's not such a bad combination after all," Taryn murmured, holding eye contact. She seemed drunk on the moment and lost in their eye contact. Charlie was, too. She reached up and cradled Taryn's cheek with one hand. They didn't need words, she realized, as Taryn leaned in to it. Charlie smiled and shifted out from underneath, until they were lying side by side, facing each other. The top of her forehead was pressed to Taryn's.

"I'm glad you've seen the error of your popcorn ways."

"What's popcorn?" Taryn asked.

Charlie's laughter broke the spell, and they both seemed to breathe again. "Maybe we should watch that movie?"

"Yes. That's all I'm thinking about. A movie. Desperately want to watch people interact on a screen while you're nearby," Taryn deadpanned and then tossed in a smile. It was such a classic Taryn response that Charlie translated expertly. She had sexier things on her mind, and to be honest, so did Charlie. The only obstacle was that she was entirely too nervous and in her own head to go there. She'd been sexually active since seventeen, and after the first time, she'd never been intimidated by sex. Yet the concept of her and Taryn did just that. What if she was bad at sex with a woman? What if she missed important signals or fumbled or was a disappointment? She wasn't sure how well she'd handle that horrific outcome.

Charlie grinned. "Hey. Don't underestimate the power of The Rock to deliver a really convincing performance." She tried for levity because that made all of this less intimidating. But as they settled into the film, sharing the popcorn and sipping the wine, Charlie couldn't keep her attention on much besides the fact that Taryn was next to her, and their thighs were touching while they watched a movie in her bed of all places. *She's in my bed.* Charlie blinked, trying to follow the scene in which a helicopter was flying too low, but she lost the thread because Taryn shifted as she reached for the popcorn, and that pressed her in even closer. Charlie's body flared, sending heat and a wash of sensation…everywhere. She stole a glance at Taryn's profile, so perfect and sexy and gorgeous. What was she waiting for? What logical person would watch a *movie* in this moment?

Taryn clearly felt her gaze, turned, and met her eyes. She must have recognized what she saw in them, too, because she quietly took the popcorn bowl and set it aside. She brushed a strand of hair off Charlie's forehead and looked at her, really looked at her. It made Charlie's stomach muscles tighten as if she and Taryn were climbing the most terrifying hill on a roller coaster, not at all certain what was on the other side. Yet she wanted Taryn. She'd never felt more sure of anything.

"Come here," Charlie said, silencing the film and sliding down the pillow. Taryn nodded and slid on top, their thighs staggered. The sheer weight of Taryn pressing down on her was heaven. "Take this off," she said quietly. Taryn sat up and pulled her shirt over her head, revealing the soft skin of her stomach and a sky-blue bra. Charlie could hear her own heartbeat in her ears as her hands itched to hold, touch, explore.

"This, too?" Taryn asked.

Charlie sat up, which put Taryn in her lap. "No. I want to." Her hands shook slightly when she reached around to unhook Taryn's bra. She let her gaze drop to her breasts, round and perfect. And when she let her fingertips circle a nipple, Taryn hitched in a breath. "You're beautiful," Charlie breathed. She dipped her head and placed an open-mouthed kiss on the top of one and kissed her way down to the nipple, pulling it into her mouth to a small cry from Taryn. She paused a moment, making sure she hadn't hurt her, until it became clear that Taryn enjoyed the attention. The knowledge sent a shot of something potent right between Charlie's legs, making her yearn, fueling her passion and determination. She continued to explore her breasts with her mouth as Taryn began to slowly rock against her. Charlie was drunk on desire, foreign and unfamiliar. Maybe that was why she didn't protest when Taryn took back control, laying her down and kissing her neck. This was so new, so different. She felt out of control and in heaven in the same breath.

"Is this okay?" Taryn asked, fingertips on the hem of Charlie's shirt. While she wanted to say *God, yes*, all she was capable of doing was nodding as her shirt was removed, then her bra. Taryn kissed under her jaw, trailing her way down Charlie's neck to her collarbone, sending shivers and pinpricks of pleasure as she went. Charlie wasn't sure she was going to survive this, and they'd barely done anything.

❖

Taryn wasn't sure what would happen when she sat in front of Charlie's apartment waiting for her to come home. But this wasn't it. Her head swam, her body ached, and she knew unequivocally that she would remember this night for the rest of her life.

With her breasts now pressed to Charlie's, she kissed her long and deep. Gone was her logic, her overthinking and premeditation.

"I want to kiss every inch of you," Taryn said in Charlie's ear. She pressed her hips snugly against Charlie's center, desperate to get rid of the last of the fabric between them.

"Oh, not enough time for that," Charlie said, digging her nails into Taryn's shoulder blades. The implication was she wouldn't last that long. They were a hurricane when they came together, unstoppable and strong.

"Still want to."

"This is so much."

Charlie's hips pressed upward against Taryn, searching for release. She was warm and wet and Taryn's senses were on overload, an intoxicating sensation she wanted to live in forever. The ache between Taryn's legs grew by the second, and now she understood what Charlie meant. Slow wouldn't be part of the equation tonight. *There'll be more times*, she told herself. Palming one of Charlie's breasts, she lavished attention on the other, pulling a nipple into her mouth and sucking, gone on the satisfaction it brought her. Charlie hissed in a breath and slid her fingers into Taryn's hair, holding her in place. She had sensitive breasts, and Taryn thrilled in that intimate information.

Charlie managed a hand between them and was tugging on Taryn's jeans, and before she had a chance to react, they were unbuttoned and her zipper pulled down. "Can I touch you?"

"Yes." Taryn closed her eyes and nodded, acutely aware of each small movement and the pinpricks of feeling that came over her when the slightest bit of pressure was applied. Her jeans were only to her knees when Charlie slipped her hand between Taryn's legs, stroking her softly through her underwear. It was too much. She wanted to hold on and knew she wouldn't last with that kind of attention. Reluctantly she moved out of Charlie's touch. "Give me just a minute," she said and attempted to steady her breathing.

"Hard to get," Charlie said, her darkened eyes making Taryn want to do decadent things to her. First, the little matter of clothing. She removed the rest of hers while Charlie propped herself up on her elbows watching. She swore quietly and pulled Taryn to her. She kissed her with fire and determination, shrugging out of her own remaining clothes with an assist from Taryn, who took a moment to just behold. Memorize. Admire. Charlie was soft and beautiful with curves that made her look like she'd been painted by one of the greats. Taryn could scarcely believe this moment was real but knew exactly what she wanted to do. Yes, she was new at this and definitely inexperienced, but that couldn't stop her. She ran her palms from Charlie's breasts down to her stomach and over her hips, memorizing every inch, allowing her fingertips to linger and explore each soft section of skin. Charlie murmured her approval, and Taryn made those sounds her guide. Finally, she parted Charlie's legs and tasted her, kissed her, and then ran her tongue in circles, prompting Charlie to moan and arch into her. "Taryn."

She couldn't answer.

Charlie's fingers were tangled in Taryn's hair, and as Taryn continued to explore with her tongue, tracing languid patterns, they found their rhythm. Relying purely on instinct, she did her best to pay attention to cues. When Charlie's hips began to pick up speed and the wonderful little noises got louder, she slid her fingers inside slowly at first, amazed at the warmth that enveloped her, and then more firmly, matching their dance. She was overcome with the strength of their connection, the emotion every bit as potent as the satisfaction. She slid her arm behind Charlie's back and held her as she brought her closer and closer to the brink with each thrust.

Charlie called out as she broke, her hips rising off the bed, her skin shimmering, and her eyes closed. "Oh God," she whispered, her hand grasping the fabric of the pillow next to her. Taryn held her close, still intimately joined, until the orgasm receded and Charlie's breathing evened out. She withdrew her hand but remained where she was, stunned and happy.

"Taryn?"

"Yes?" Taryn asked. She still hadn't moved or crawled back up the bed. She was in awe of the experience she'd just had and wanted to hold on to it a moment longer.

"It's lonely up here."

"Sorry," she said, smiling up at Charlie, the most beautiful creature she'd ever seen. Her hair was to one side of her on the pillow, and her gaze was trained on Taryn as if she was the most important person in the world, which was, of course, how she felt about Charlie. "I think I was trying to capture how I'm feeling like I would a photograph. Only you can't see what's in here," she said, touching her chest. "Impossible."

"I can't tell you how much I love how your mind works."

"It's not fully back yet." Charlie stroked Taryn's hair softly, before letting her fingertips trail up and down Taryn's bare back. Taryn had almost forgotten she was naked, but the delicious shiver reminded her.

Charlie slid down until she lay alongside Taryn and urged her onto her side. With Charlie's gaze roaming her body, Taryn felt the warmth touch her cheeks. With one finger, Charlie circled her nipple. Taryn swallowed as a wash of desire hit, not to touch but to be touched. Charlie eased her knee between Taryn's thighs and lifted. She was already so sensitive it was nearly too much and wonderful at the same time. As she attempted to recover, Charlie slid on top and settled her hips in between Taryn's legs and began to rock. It was only moments before the pressure began to build to astronomical levels. Charlie had barely touched her, and Taryn was climbing and climbing, higher and higher, until she saw light behind her eyes and shattered. She heard herself calling, but Charlie didn't stop. She was inside her, creating a fullness Taryn had never known. When her thumb pressed down, a second orgasm tore through her like a speeding train. Pleasure rained down, and Taryn held on to Charlie, lost in the beautiful, satisfying oblivion.

"Did you just…?"

"Twice," Taryn said, eyes still closed as the final shockwaves moved through her until she could think in full sentences again. She lifted her head and laughed. "So that happened. Does everyone get this memorable a first time?" She rested her cheek on her arm above her and Charlie mirrored her.

"Our first time, you mean?"

"And mine."

Charlie's eyes went wide. "With anyone? Even guys?"

"Anyone," Taryn said, now a tad self-conscious.

"How are you that good at this, then?"

The self-conscious part flew right out the window and she laughed. "Can I get that in writing? I might want to frame it. I'm serious. Where's some paper?"

Charlie laughed. "I'm confused. Aren't you supposed to be awkward and clumsy? It's not fair."

"You weren't."

Charlie matched her grin. "Yeah, we should find that paper."

Taryn stole a kiss because she couldn't go another second without one. "I will spray-paint it in your kitchen if you want."

Charlie looked thoughtful. "Not a bad idea. My guests will know who they're dealing with."

"You know what? Never mind," Taryn said quickly, pulling Charlie to her.

"Hi," Charlie said, her voice quiet. "I really enjoyed tonight. Right now. All of it."

"It was okay," Taryn said back and then offered a smile. "Or the best night of my life."

"I like option B better. Hoping and praying it's B."

"Ding, ding, ding." She pressed her forehead to Charlie's. "Should I stay? Should I go? Would you like space? Tell me how this works. I'm new here. First day on the job."

Charlie didn't hesitate. "Please, stay. I would be lonely if you left."

"Decided." Happiness gathered in Taryn's chest. "It's a sleepover, I suppose."

Charlie raised an eyebrow. "You don't even need pajamas for this one."

"Good thing because I don't have any."

They slipped beneath the crisp, cool sheets and tried to watch the film, but wound up talking over it much of the time, not really able to fixate on anything but each other. Taryn updated Charlie on her finals, and Charlie told Taryn all about the different neighborhoods she'd been researching in New York and which ones seemed the most affordable.

"I don't know what my exact salary might be, but Monica has given me a good indication of what I can expect. The trendy neighborhoods are out. But instead of living in Chelsea, maybe I'm Chelsea-adjacent. I might need a roommate or eight."

"You're gonna love it no matter what neighborhood you land in." Taryn stared at the ceiling, their fingers playing, intertwining and then loosening, over and over again as they talked. "I don't want to imagine a semester without you."

Charlie paused. "Just temporary. And here's a thought. You don't have to do much with it other than mull it over. Okay? Just hear me out."

"I'm listening."

"New York is great for the arts."

Taryn went still, hoping Charlie was headed where she seemed to be, but she didn't want to jinx it by getting ahead of the words. "It definitely is. It's the place for them."

"And I'm not talking about anyone specific, but if one wanted to pursue photography as a career, maybe it's not a bad place."

"I hear they have a few reputable graduate programs for random individuals without names," Taryn said, propping her head up on her hand. "Wait. I'm actually interested in grad school. Coincidence?"

"It really is!" Charlie proclaimed.

"Weird. Should I look into them?" Taryn said it so casually it was ridiculous. Could Charlie not see the excitement vibrating off her, like a poodle about to be fed?

Charlie slid closer, as if preparing a pitch. "I'm just gonna say it. Come to New York with me after you graduate."

She exhaled. There they were. The coveted words she'd longed to hear. "I'd love to, but what if things are different between us by then? You might get there and realize there's a world beyond this. Beyond me." It was unthinkable, but Taryn tended to lead with fear, expecting something to always go wrong. Something she was working on.

"I don't think that there's better than this, than you, than *us*, anywhere in the world, but what if we made it a goal? We don't have to talk in absolutes."

"Goals are healthy, right?" Taryn said, hovering just shy of Charlie's lips before closing the distance, angling her head, and kissing Charlie long and deep. The kiss carried the happiness that moved through every inch of her. Their night had been amazing, they were making actual plans for the future, and Taryn couldn't come up with a complaint in the world—other than the fact that she was heading home in two days and would have to say good-bye to Charlie.

"I think this means you definitely need to spend Christmas with me."

"Tonight was the definitive sign?"

"Tonight was everything."

Charlie snuggled her face against Taryn's neck and let out a deep satisfying breath. "It really was."

Chapter Fourteen

Sleep came easily that night. And though Charlie had always been a solo sleeper, preferring her space, sleeping with Taryn was different. They'd drifted off tangled up in each other, and at several points in the night Charlie woke to find them in different positions—Charlie's head on Taryn's shoulder or Charlie as the big spoon behind Taryn's back—but always touching in some way. In fact, Charlie couldn't imagine them not. It had led to one of the most perfect night's rest she could remember. If this was any indication of what their future might be like, Charlie was eager, excited, and full of an immense amount of gratitude. This felt right in every sense of the word.

She hadn't set an alarm that next morning because she didn't have anywhere to be until her final critique session with her short fiction class at eleven a.m. They'd be evaluating each others' resubmissions before hanging up their boxing gloves until the spring semester. Plus, she was in no rush to start her day when she had Taryn next to her in bed. That's why it was so jarring to hear the sound of her apartment door opening. She raised her head and blinked, attempting to orient herself. Sunlight was streaming in through the window, and Taryn, still asleep, was naked and pressed against her side, warm and wonderful.

Then who was in her apartment?

She quickly snuck out of bed, grabbed a long T-shirt, and made her way into the living room. There in the kitchen stood Monica, writing a note at her kitchen counter. She looked up when Charlie entered.

"Were you asleep? I'm so sorry for busting in on you." She placed a hand over her heart. "I had these books of your mom's to drop off, and they're so precious that I didn't want to leave them on the doorstep in case someone took them, so Danny let me use his key. Please forgive me."

That's right. Danny still had a key. She took a deep breath and forced a smile, attempting to bury her terror. Taryn was on the other side of that door, and this was not the moment for Monica to find out about them. "Oh, right. Danny mentioned that you had brought the books with you on your visit."

"And here I am." Monica held her arms open and Charlie dutifully moved into them, surprised and terrified. "So good to see you, sweetheart. Do you want to grab lunch a little later?"

"I wish I could. I have a critique session at eleven."

"That's right, Danny said that he—"

"Hey, where'd you go? Are you coming back to bed?" Taryn called in the pouty voice that Charlie would have loved in any other instance. She went still, unsure what move to make. Monica looked to her in question, brows drawn. Before either of them could say another word, Taryn emerged wearing Charlie's robe. "Charlie? Oh." Taryn paused. "I'm sorry. I'll just—" And she quickly slipped back into the bedroom.

"I bought you that robe for Christmas," Monica said, as if piecing together a puzzle. Her features changed in the next moment, and she stood a little straighter. The bottom dropped out from Charlie's stomach, and she felt like she was plummeting down a mine shaft into darkness. Her heart hammered and her brain raced, her logic not yet back online. But she knew one thing, this was not ideal. Monica eyed her. "I see that I've come at a bad time." Her voice was clipped and devoid of warmth.

"Just unexpected is all." Suddenly, Charlie was acutely aware of her own lack of clothing. "If you'll excuse me for just one moment."

"Of course," Monica said. "I'll make a pot of coffee…for us *all*."

"What just happened?" Taryn asked, arms crossed in front of her when Charlie entered.

She attempted to keep her voice measured and calm. A tall order. "Monica had a collection of books that belonged to my mother and is here to drop them off."

"And I just ruined everything, didn't I?" Taryn asked, looking horrified.

The panic had not subsided yet, but Charlie did what she could to slow down her breathing. "Definitely not an ideal morning," were the only words she could manage.

"I'm sure this is not how you wanted her to find out. Maybe she'll think I'm just a friend sleeping over."

Charlie closed her eyes, rejecting the notion. "She's Monica. Too smart for that. From the look on her face, I can tell you she knows exactly what we are to each other."

"Right. Okay." Taryn looked around like the solution might be sitting somewhere in the room. She was just as out of sorts as Charlie. "What would you like me to do?"

"Stay here." She took a beat. "And maybe get dressed."

Charlie hated having to say those words and the lack of warmth beneath them.

This was their first wake-up together. It didn't seem right or fair that after such a wonderful night, their sweet morning after had been snatched away. Instead of focusing on Taryn and making sure she was okay, happy, and taken care of, Charlie's objective was damage control. And Monica certainly hadn't seemed too happy about what she'd walked into.

When Charlie emerged from her bedroom in jeans and a red sweater, she found Monica in her kitchen making herself a cup of coffee. She turned as Charlie entered the room.

"Monica. I'm sorry about all this. It wasn't how I intended for you to find out."

Instead of answering, Monica took all the time in the world to blow on her coffee. "That was clear," she said finally. Monica never left the house without a full face of makeup and a perfect curated outfit, and today was no different. She peered at Charlie, her expertly lined eyes moving over her as if searching for clues, information. "Do you want to explain?"

"My friend Taryn stayed over last night." Even Charlie winced at the use of the word *friend*. Nothing felt right about it.

"Do you sleep in the same bed with all your friends?" Monica set her cup on the coffee table and took a seat on the couch. "Let's be grown-ups, Charlotte."

"Did Danny talk to you about him and me?"

"He said you'd pressed pause on the relationship. I had planned, when I saw you this morning, to find out if you were okay and to ask if you'd come to a decision about the holidays. They are looming, after all. I think I just received my answer."

Words and their arrangement, which had always been Charlie's strong suit, failed her. How did she explain that she was in the process of getting to know her true self and understanding who she was in a whole new sense? That she was experiencing a shockingly high level of happiness she hadn't known was an option? But no. She couldn't say any of that. Not when it came at the expense of Monica's son.

"Who is she, if you don't mind my asking?" Monica asked, taking a seat on the sofa and crossing her legs.

"A family friend I used to know from back in Dyer. We reconnected when she transferred to Hillspoint."

"I see. And is this"—she took a moment to select the word—"a relationship or merely an evening together? Think carefully."

This one was hard. She knew the answer without question but found it difficult to confess to Monica of all people. Instead of eye contact, she focused on Monica's dark pink nail polish and the round/square manicured edges of her nails. "I have true feelings for Taryn."

The silence was overwhelming.

"I hear you, and as always, I want the best for you, Charlotte. But I'm very much afraid that you've gotten caught up in something that could easily ruin your life." She snapped her fingers in demonstration.

"I promise, that's not the case," Charlie said, defenses flaring. Nothing about her feelings for Taryn felt like a mistake. They were the most honest thing Charlie had ever known. She just wasn't sure how to go about making Monica believe her. It would take time, she realized. Charlie would have to be patient, and she could. They were family, after all.

"Oh, sweetheart. I'm afraid you've gone and lost your head over something shiny. It happens to all of us," Monica said with a sympathetic wince. "Come here." She stood and held her arms open for Charlie, who moved into them automatically because this was Monica, who mattered. She clearly wasn't ready to hear Charlie in this moment, but she would understand when time passed, and Charlie hadn't wavered.

"I promise you that's not what this is," Charlie said as Monica released her. "I do care about Danny and hope that we will always be friends. You all are my family, and I would hate to lose you just because the romance portion of our relationship has come to an end."

Monica nodded, but the kindness behind her eyes dried up. "I told your mother I would always be here for you, and I will." She picked up her mug, took another sip, and moved to place it in the sink. "The whole thing is a great shame. Are you a lesbian now, Charlie?" She'd said it as if the words left an unpleasant taste in her mouth.

Monica was on the board of multiple organizations that supported LGBT rights and was liberal across most any social issue. Yet that support seemed hugely absent in their conversation. "I'm figuring it all out in real time."

Monica offered a slight shrug. "Then I suppose I'll check in on you when you know more. You're of course still invited for the holidays, should you choose to be there. We'd love to have you. Arlene will be making her famous brisket, which I remember was your favorite." She kissed Charlie's cheek and placed a hand on each of her shoulders. "I sincerely hope you know what you're doing and that you're right about this. Regret is an awful thing."

Charlie nodded. "I'm right."

"Famous last words." Monica offered what could only be described as a sad smile. "Good-bye, Charlie. We'll talk soon, okay?" She didn't wait for a response, closing the door behind her with a soft click.

Charlie exhaled slowly and gripped the back of the nearby chair to ground her. She was shaking, she only just realized, and felt like she might cry. Taryn emerged from the bedroom in the clothes she'd worn the night before, and Charlie didn't hesitate. She moved straight to her, pulled her in, and kissed her. In that moment, she needed that kiss not just for her, but for Taryn. To show her how important she was, to express it in the most vital way she knew how. Their morning had been turned upside down, but they didn't have to be. She wouldn't let that happen. Taryn kissed her back with just as much urgency, which in the end left them breathless and reconnected.

"I was coming out here to ask if you were okay," Taryn said, likely bewildered by the ambush.

Charlie ran her thumb across Taryn's bottom lip. "I'm going to be. That was so not how I wanted you to wake up this morning."

"The fact that you're even thinking about *me* right now says a whole lot." A soft smile appeared and Charlie felt it all over.

"I love your smile. You're gorgeous in the morning, you know that?"

Taryn touched her hair absently as if checking in on its status. She'd tamed it since Charlie saw her last, but there was still a wild quality that she liked a great deal. "I've not heard that before, but then again, no true overnights like this one." A small blush blossomed.

"I'm honored," Charlie said softly. "I'm going to pour you boring coffee."

"Good. The more boring, the better." Taryn took a seat on the couch. "I hope it's okay to say that I heard most of the conversation."

"It is." She paused, mug in hand. "It wasn't a great exchange. I don't think she wanted to hear what I had to say, and I'm not sure what to do about that." She hesitated but then pushed forward. "It left me off center."

"But you stood your ground, and I can't tell you how that made me feel."

She turned around, back against the counter. "Everything I said is the truth. All of it. These aren't passing feelings." She touched her chest. "I'm sure of that. You don't have to be. But I am."

Taryn was up and moving quickly until she stood in front of Charlie, downright in her space. "I know as plainly as I know it's a morning in winter that we're real." She exhaled. "I'm a relatively fearful person but not about this, okay? I refuse to be." She projected confidence and vulnerability, which was the perfect combination for the moment. It said she knew what she wanted and was open to the intimacy of their relationship. "And I love hearing that you're sure because I am, too." Taryn slipped her hands under Charlie's sweater to rest on the skin of her waist. She loved the little liberties Taryn took with her. The touches, the advances, the kissing. She'd never had a relationship where she craved the other person's touch with such intensity. Part of her wanted to crawl back in bed with Taryn, take their clothes off piece by piece, and just forget the world and everyone in it.

"Why does everything seem so much easier when I'm this close to you?" Charlie asked.

"I don't know, but it's the same for me." Taryn kissed her softly.

"I could really get used to feeling this way."

"I don't think I ever will," Taryn said, shaking her head. "I never in a million years thought I'd see you again, and I sure as hell never thought I'd be with you like last night." She let her head drop back and looked at the ceiling. "Which, can I say, was life altering."

Charlie took the opportunity to place a soft kiss on the column of Taryn's now exposed neck and felt Taryn tighten her grip on her waist. "I love the cues you gave me." Another kiss. "The way your fingers dug into my skin when you got close. So incredibly sexy. I can't stop thinking about it." She kissed Taryn's collarbone.

Taryn returned to looking at her, her eyes wide. "Are you trying to turn me on?"

"Maybe. It's a nice distraction from the trainwreck of a morning."

"We could make it better," Taryn said, stepping in and pressing Charlie more firmly to the counter. Her thumbs slid up Charlie's ribcage to the bottoms of her breasts. A spark of anticipation erupted across her skin. She felt herself go damp. Her shirt was pushed up. Taryn's hands moved to her breasts, at first over her bra, until she pulled the cups down, exposing them. *God.* Charlie gasped, her eyes slamming shut and then open again because she didn't want to miss a detail. "I don't have much time before class."

"Noted," Taryn said, pushing against her breasts, releasing them, rubbing a nipple between her thumb and forefinger, a move that made Charlie fully wet. She had no idea that was possible. She was aching and ready. Moments later, her jeans were undone and partially down her thighs. They were actually doing this. The presence of Taryn's hand in her underwear while she stood in her actual kitchen nearly sent her over the edge immediately. She pushed against it, fitting her hips into the rhythm Taryn set. Then she was inside Charlie, as the intensity rose to near painful heights. Just when she thought she couldn't take it another second, the pressure broke, and she was a shooting star hanging on to Taryn as the tidal wave of sensation engulfed her, wonderful and complete.

"Best thing ever," Taryn said quietly in her ear as she floated back to Earth. She pulled Taryn's hips up against her thigh and lifted it, to hear a murmur of appreciation from Taryn. She was just as aroused as Charlie had been, and late or not, she needed to do something about that. No choice.

"On the couch," Charlie said, reassembling herself into her clothing.

"No, you need to get ready to leave," Taryn said, but her eyes were hooded and had taken on a hazy quality.

"To the couch," Charlie said, kissing her jaw. "I'll make time."

Taryn took a seat and Charlie knelt in front of her, pulling Taryn's mouth to hers and kissing her, deep and long. All the while, her hands worked the button and zipper of Taryn's jeans, and when they came up for air, she tugged them right off. Taryn held her gaze as Charlie removed the last bit of clothing between them and settled her face between Taryn's thighs. She kissed the soft skin of one thigh and then the other, kissing her way to their apex. When her tongue touched Taryn intimately for the first time, she was greeted with a quiet murmur and adjustment on the couch. The circles she began to draw pulled a moan, and the repetitive swipes sent Taryn's breathing ragged and quick.

"What are you doing to me?" Taryn breathed, which was the perfect signpost for Charlie, who was following her instinct and making it up as she went. Drunk on power and desire, she continued to tease, to give a little and then take away until Taryn tossed her face to the side, rested her cheek on the couch, and said, "Please."

How could she resist? With the tip of her tongue, she altered her placement, moving in tiny circles where Taryn needed her most. It was seconds before Taryn cried out louder than she had the night before, arching her back and going still beneath Charlie's mouth, and it was the most satisfying thing in the world.

No. The morning hadn't started on the best note, but it had definitely ended on it.

Chapter Fifteen

Christmastime was meant to be spent with the people you cared most about, which made this separation that much harder. Taryn hadn't seen Charlie in six whole days and felt every single excruciating one of them. Charlie had declined the somewhat icy invitation to the McHenrys' Christmas and agreed to spend the holidays at Taryn's place in Dyer. She'd remained at Hillspoint until the morning of the twenty-fourth and should be arriving at some point within the next thirty minutes. Taryn exhaled slowly and tried to remember what to do with her hands.

The house smelled heavenly. Her mother had been baking for the past three days and even had her hot mulled wine simmering on the stove, full of fruit, spices, and everything wonderful. Taryn hadn't let herself indulge quite yet, wanting to wait for Charlie. That evening, her extended family would come over, dishes in hand for mingling, songs, and all-around Christmas cheer.

"You nervous?" her father asked, coming up behind her, hands on her shoulders.

"Not about you and Mom seeing Charlie again. But just in general, you know."

"You're quite serious about her, aren't you? I can tell by the way you're unable to settle." He had a gleam in his eye that Taryn allowed herself to enjoy.

"I'm very serious about her, Dad. I think I've been serious about her since the moment we met. It's only the capacity that's changed."

"Fate is a hurricane."

Taryn turned. "What does that mean?" She frowned, trying to make sense of it.

"A hurricane sweeps in and rearranges your patio furniture. But when it's your life, it's the people who are rearranged and what they mean to you."

"I see. Fate decided my babysitter might be the perfect girlfriend for me."

He laughed. "Exactly."

"Why am I missing all the good conversation?" her mother called from the kitchen. "I'm a confectionary prisoner!"

"Because you refuse to come in here and relax with us!" he yelled back.

"I want to make sure the cinnamon pecans are ready for Charlie!" she bellowed.

"Charlie doesn't mind waiting a few extra minutes for pecans!"

Taryn laughed. "I've missed you two and your hollering sessions." She picked up her camera, aimed her lens, and took a shot of her mother in the kitchen through the window created by the counter and the overhanging cabinet. The shape of the foreground would hopefully create an interesting entry point.

"Well, I hope Charlie's okay with how lively it can be around here," her dad said. She'd noticed he was stronger on his right side than he had been when she'd left for school.

"Charlie *has* met you both before." A pause. "But maybe cut the volume in half when you think of it."

"Impossible!" her mother yelled, followed by a warm, full laugh. It was good to be home.

The doorbell sounded and they all froze. "Willie Nelson in Luckenbach, she's here!" Her mother scurried around the corner into the living room and left them in the dust on the way to the front door. "I'm doing it. Me. Me. Me."

Taryn laughed and placed her nervous hands on her hips, dropped them to her sides, and put them back again. Her girlfriend was about to spend Christmas with them. Everything in her glowed like a warm candle in a window. Deep breath and a brace. She heard her voice before she saw her. Charlie greeted her mother with an, "Oh my goodness, hi." Taryn's heart melted. Her bones were liquid, but she refrained from rushing in and stealing this moment from her mother, who had been so excited to host Charlie for these few days.

"Charlotte Ross, you look more beautiful than the last time I saw you. So sophisticated, too."

"Oh, that's the nicest compliment."

"Give me the biggest hug." A moment later. "I hope you're hungry."

"I could definitely eat."

"There's wine, too," her mom said. "All kinds. A beer if you'd rather. We're informal here."

And then there she was, practically ushered in by a choir of angels in Taryn's ears.

Charlie's hair was partially pulled up with the rest down around her shoulders. She wore a green and white Fair Isle sweater, jeans, and brown boots with little fur borders on top. Her blue eyes sparkled, and everything in Taryn sang at the sight of her.

When their eyes connected, Charlie didn't hesitate. She moved straight to Taryn and pulled her in to a hug, rocking a little as she held on. "Hi, you," she said quietly in Taryn's ear.

"Hi." She was smiling ear to ear, on happiness overload. "Six days is longer than I thought."

"Tell me about it," Charlie said. Finally, she released Taryn and turned to her father. "I'm so sorry to pass over you like that. I just saw this one and had to say hello."

"No, no," he said, beaming. "You did the exact right thing." He grinned at Charlie and accepted her hug but couldn't seem to help stealing glimpses at Taryn, needing to witness her happiness, which was the sweetest thing. "Can I help with your bag?"

"Oh no. It's light. I can manage."

"Martie and I got this guest room all ready for you," he said. "But far be it from us to tell you where to sleep." He looked straight at the ground. This was new territory for everyone.

"You have your own space if you want it," her mom said from the entryway, looking on. "It's chart your own course around here. That's what I say. Everyone is an adult, right, Tad?"

"Time flies, but yes." He looked around for a way out. Shuffled his feet. "We should break into that hot mulled stuff now, right?"

"Immediately." Taryn laughed at their floundering attempts to be cool, when they so didn't have to be.

"On it!" her mom said. "Charlie, do you like warm cinnamon pecans? I thought I might put some out, if anyone was interested." The feigned casualness of the offer amused Taryn.

"I adore them," Charlie said.

"Whoop!" was the response that came from her mom, already buzzing around in the kitchen. They had a couple of hours until the rest of the guests for the Christmas Eve gathering would arrive, and her dad was already seeking out the mulled wine, mug in hand. Carols played softly from the Bluetooth speaker near the fully decorated nine-foot tree.

"While they worry about food and wine, I'm gonna help you with your bag," Taryn said. "That way I can remind you where everything is."

"Good idea," Charlie said, meeting her eyes. The electricity that sizzled and popped when they looked at each other was back and powerful. Taryn could live right here in this space forever.

Once they were alone in the guest room, which was conveniently next door to Taryn's own bedroom, she closed the door and turned the lock. This time it was Taryn who moved to Charlie, pressing their foreheads together. "I don't know how we're gonna manage with you in New York when I can barely make it a week."

"Shut up and kiss me already," Charlie said, tilting her head and moving in.

Taryn eagerly met her halfway and sank into the warmth and wonder of Charlie's mouth. Their lips clung and moved and intoxicated Taryn. The soft skin beneath her fingertips when she cradled Charlie's face made her sated and happy. "Thank God you're here."

"I'm really happy I made the decision to come. It would have been a lonely Christmas if we'd been texting the whole time without actually seeing each other. Plus, this place is so incredibly homey." Charlie smiled and intertwined their fingers. "Your parents are just as sweet as I remembered them."

"Just as loud?"

"That, too, but in the best sense."

"Kiss me one more time before we have to behave in front of other people."

Charlie went up on her tiptoes and slid her fingers into Taryn's hair, holding her by the back of the head. It was a move Taryn found infinitely sexy, along with pretty much everything else Charlie ever did. Their kiss was deep and long, meant to last them until they'd be alone again. Taryn's toes curled in wonderful satisfaction. When they rejoined her parents, she spent most of the time watching Charlie as she gestured, ate, and laughed with the rest of the room. When the house filled up with extended family and neighbors, Charlie was a superstar. She charmed most everyone she talked to, several of whom remembered her from back in the day. By the end of the evening, she was front and center singing carols around the piano as her mother played for the group. The best part? She held Taryn's hand through a good portion of the evening. They weren't just two people kissing and making eyes behind the scenes. They were an actual couple spending Christmas with her parents in plain view of the people she loved. Charlie didn't seem the least bit nervous about that fact either, and that made Taryn feel like absolutely anything was possible.

It was close to midnight when the final guests said good night and the weary original foursome picked up plates, cups, and empty snack trays.

"They cleaned us out," her mother said happily. "I hope that means they liked my cheeseball. It was a new recipe, and I gotta say, I was worried it wouldn't live up to last year. People still talk about the wonder of that ball."

"You killed it," Taryn said, giving her mom a squeeze as she passed.

"The cheeseball might have been my favorite of the night. Though there were so many amazing dishes," Charlie said.

"You're a sweet girl, Charlie Adler. I've always thought so," her mother said with a wink.

As the light in the room grew dim after each lamp and switch was turned off, it was time to sleep. With a great big hug from each parent for both Taryn and Charlie, they all said their Merry Christmases and snuck off to bed.

Taryn waited all of eight minutes before slipping into Charlie's room. She found her in a cute pj set, standing in front of the attached bathroom's mirror. "I wondered if I would see you."

"It's Christmas. I couldn't stay away." She met Charlie's eyes in the mirror, her arms around her waist. "Is this okay?"

Charlie nodded. "It's perfect." She turned in Taryn's arms and then glanced down at her clothing. Navy pj's with green piping and the letter *T* monogramed on the corner. "You have your initial on your shirt and it's adorable."

"I don't want you to forget who I am in the night," she said.

"Trust me when I say that wouldn't be a problem. It's also sweet that you plan to keep those on."

Taryn's eyes went wide.

"What?" Charlie covered her mouth. "Is it bad that I'm going there with your parents under the same roof?"

"It's Christmas Eve and you're here. There's no way we're not sharing a bed. If extracurricular things happen to occur"—Taryn shrugged—"then we were merely victims of our own ridiculous chemistry."

Charlie went up on her toes and wrapped her arms around Taryn's neck. "It's not our fault."

"Innocents corrupted by proximity."

As they slipped beneath the sheets that night, the moon illuminated the swaying of snowflakes on their way to the ground. They spent the first part of the evening talking quietly, wrapped up in each other until Taryn's hands inevitably made their way beneath Charlie's shirt, and Charlie's lips found Taryn's neck, and they were off and on fire.

"Fa-la-la-la-la," Taryn sang quietly half an hour later.

Charlie laughed and pulled Taryn's outside arm around her waist so they could drift off together. Just as sleep was seconds from claiming her, she heard Charlie murmur, "That's one way to deck the halls."

Taryn felt her shoulders start to shake. More laughter.

She had a feeling their life was going to be full of it.

❖

Charlie had no idea how her time in Dyer with the Ross family had gone by so quickly. In many ways, it felt like she'd arrived on their doorstep just hours ago, ready for the Christmas Eve party, rather than the week it had been. In other ways, she felt like she'd been a part of their family for years, which was a testament to how warm and welcoming they'd been. The four of them had played Codenames and spades around the kitchen table. They'd tried two new restaurants that had opened recently in town, and on New Year's they'd celebrated with a fancy dinner at the golf club where the Rosses were members.

The next day, Charlie would be heading back to Hillspoint ahead of Taryn to prepare for her final semester and attend various departmental meetings for the two classes she would teach. It was hard to believe that, in just a handful of months, she'd be off in the world, likely living in another city, and trying to find a way to pay the bills. Her heart still hoped that all would work out with Broadland Rhodes and she'd actually be living her dream life in New York. Her interview was scheduled for February, which meant she'd know soon enough.

She glanced back at the warm bed where Taryn still slept with the sheet to her waist and her bare back facing Charlie. She smiled at the expanse of dark hair across the pillow behind Taryn. She didn't think she'd ever get tired of watching her sleep, while at the same time always impatient for the moment she'd wake up. Taryn, she'd come to find, liked her sleep and could stretch the hours into midmorning before ever lifting her head. Charlie, more of an early riser, slipped out of the guest room in search of coffee. Martie was seated at the kitchen table with a hot mugful of the good stuff along with a lemon poppyseed muffin she'd baked fresh the day before. The whole place still smelled wonderful.

"Good morning, Charlie." Her smile was sweet. "What can I make for you?"

Charlie pulled her shoulders to her ears. "Oh, nothing at all. I'll just pour myself some coffee and join you for a muffin if that would be all right."

"That would be wonderful. Tad and Taryn are never up this early, so it's a treat to have some company." She'd used a knife to cut her muffin in two, which made it much more manageable. Charlie smiled because she was learning a lot from Martie Ross this week. She couldn't remember being hugged as many times as she had been since arriving. It had done something remarkable to her soul.

The sun was just coming up, casting a warm glow over the backyard and the melting snow. She sat down next to Martie and stared out at it. "This is a beautiful spot this time of morning. Do you sit here every day?"

"I do. There's something about the quiet of the early hours before the rest of the world wakes and the hustle and bustle starts. It helps me find my peace and organize my thoughts." She took a sip from her Mom Fuel mug, thoughtful. "When we were worried about Tad and his prognosis, this was the spot where I would gather my courage to face the day ahead." She smiled but her gaze fell promptly to her plate, emphasizing the weight of the memory.

Charlie covered Martie's hand with her own. "I'm so sorry that you all had to go through such an ordeal. He seems to be so much better."

"He has good days and bad days. But overall, I'm thrilled with his progress." She turned to Charlie. "I was sad to hear that you lost your mother. Before Taryn told me, I had no idea we'd lost her so young. She was a true light, and I see that reflected in you."

Charlie swallowed the painful lump that always seemed to arrive when the subject of her mom's passing crept in. "Thank you. I miss her every day. She was always..." She paused to find the words because talking with Martie brought forth the emotion on full blast. She had a hunch it was because Martie made her feel comfortable and supported enough to allow it. "My bright spot. My dad wasn't the greatest, but I had my mom, you know? And she had me." Martie's eyes were soft as she listened. "I still haven't gotten used to a world where I don't have her."

"You have me," Martie said, leaning in and meeting her gaze. "I'm not Deirdre. Definitely not as glamorous and probably not as funny. But if you and Taryn are as real as I think you are, I'll be your mom, Charlotte."

Tears sprang into Charlie's eyes at the overwhelmingly sweet sentiment. The fact of the matter was that Martie and Tad had treated her like she belonged from the moment she walked in the door.

"Thank you," were the only two words her voice had the strength to manage. Her hands shook when she stood to accept the embrace Martie offered. She let herself be squeezed and loved and taken care of. It felt like water where there'd been a desert for so long.

"Oh, now I'm getting teary, too," Martie said.

Charlie laughed. "Contagious, I'm afraid."

"What's contagious?" They turned to see Taryn in the living room coming toward them, looking like the cutest sleepiest person ever. She touched her bed hair and squinted. "Did you guys have muffins without me?"

"I'll get you a muffin, baby," Charlie said. She took her hand, led her to the couch, kissed her temple, and sat her down. "You just take your time waking up."

Martie pointed at Charlie as she passed. "That one's a keeper."

Taryn smiled and nodded. "I couldn't agree more."

The day was a nice one. She and Taryn took a drive together and ended up at the playground at the edge of Taryn's neighborhood before coming home. As they sat side by side on a bench, children playing on the playscape nearby, Taryn turned to her.

"I don't want you to leave."

Charlie attempted a smile but it never quite blossomed. Her heart hung heavy. "I'm trying not to think about it." She turned to Taryn, met her gaze, and held on. "This has been the best week, and I mean that."

"Charlie, you should know that I'm falling for you so hard." Taryn looked up at the sky, cloudy today and overcast.

"You're not alone," Charlie said, sliding her arm around Taryn's.

"Really?" Taryn asked, turning to look at her. She searched her eyes as if needing that confirmation.

"I'm gone on you, Taryn." She offered a soft smile. "And I may not get everything right all the time. But please know that I'm trying. It's new to let someone in like this."

"Just know that you deserve happiness, Charlie."

And there it was. Evidence that Taryn saw deeper into Charlie than even she realized. Because Charlie often got in her own way when it came to accepting love. After years of being made to feel like she was a burden and a duty, it was hard to believe she was worthy of someone's sincere affection. What she'd found with Taryn, she had to remind herself, didn't have to be earned. It was the purest thing she'd ever known.

"Just keep telling me that, okay? It helps."

"Eighteen times a day if that's what you need." She kissed Charlie's forehead and then placed a lingering kiss on her lips, making Charlie feel like she'd stepped onto the screen of a movie where this beautiful, thoughtful woman was hers, and they were happy with nothing at all in their way. She just kept waiting for the other shoe to drop, but maybe it never would. How wonderful would that be? Was it possible she was that blessed?

CHAPTER SIXTEEN

It was good to be back.

Taryn's first spring semester at Hillspoint was underway, and she was more than motivated. She loved her classes and the elevated privileges that came with advancement within the photography department. Her friends had tackled her with hugs and whisked her off for drinks and a catch-up session. But best of all, she'd been reunited with Charlie, who had been the definition of a sight for sore eyes. They'd spent the first couple of days back smiling and staring and acting like people obsessed with each other.

"Do you want to get boring and dessert coffee and people watch?" Charlie had asked that first afternoon.

"Immediately I do," Taryn said, dashing for her jacket. She'd spent the rest of the evening at the Bump and Grind, talking to Charlie about their new schedules and stealing glances of her profile as she watched customers come and go.

Once classes officially kicked off, the chaos took over. They had to find their focus, and that meant less time together, which Taryn felt all over. Though they'd talk every hour, there were days when it just wasn't possible to get together. Charlie's classes, teaching, and work at the library commitments had her busy most every second of the day, which meant Taryn had to rely on memories and daydreams to get her through.

That night, they'd planned on spending the evening together after a whirlwind week. She'd been looking forward to this date of theirs for days, counting the seconds. Unfortunately, Taryn was going to have to occupy herself while at the apartment because Charlie hadn't made the progress on her short story that she'd been hoping for, which meant she needed the time to write. "I'm just going to make popcorn and sit in a corner and watch the talent work," Taryn proclaimed.

"I wish it was going to be more exciting for you." Charlie rested her chin in her hand. "At least we're in the same room, though. I like having you here."

An hour later, and Taryn was craving attention. "Wanna take a break soon?" She blinked her eyes slowly.

"No, baby, I can't be taken in by those big brown eyes and your ridiculous body right now. I'm smack in the middle of this thing."

"Why not?" Taryn asked with her best pout. Charlie was a sucker for pouting, and she used it to her advantage.

"Because I have a five-thousand-word story due tomorrow. And because I've spent every available moment drooling over you and smiling as you talk and watching you taste food, I'm sitting on only two thousand."

Taryn straightened, feeling the need to help and not distract from Charlie's goals. "We need a plan."

"Exactly my thinking."

"I could stay back at my place and give you the whole night to work." It was the mature thing to do, even though she craved Charlie in every way possible. They hadn't had enough time lately, and suddenly it felt like the most precious commodity. Taryn was wildly aware of the calendar and Charlie's impending graduation date, which meant every moment mattered.

Charlie deflated. Her blue eyes flickered with sadness. "Any other ideas?"

Taryn gave it some thought. "Well. There's always a reward system."

"I like the sound of that." She tapped her cheek. "How's this? For every thousand words I write, I get ten full uninterrupted minutes with you."

Taryn made a point of looking thoughtful. "Hmm. I don't know. What are we going to do in those ten minutes? How would we possibly fill them?"

Charlie closed her eyes, her gorgeous lips parting slightly. Taryn wanted to suck on the bottom one but refrained from saying so. "I can't really guess," Charlie said with nonchalance. She shrugged. "I guess we'll figure that out once we get there."

"If I'm the reward, I say you get to decide. In the meantime, I'm going to sort through my digitals and organize them by theme and then color because that's who I'm becoming."

"You're already making this sexy." Charlie's eyes darkened, and Taryn felt it all over. *Nope. Don't get ahead of yourself.*

Taryn took a step back. "Then you better get that first thousand words. I'll be waiting." The reality was every inch of her was already longing to kiss, touch, and stare at Charlie up-close and personal. The next fifteen minutes crept by with only the quiet sound of Charlie ticktacking away on her keyboard. The tension in the room was heavy, and Taryn felt it pressing down on her skin. It felt warm in the apartment, but she had a feeling she'd done that to herself.

Another twenty minutes passed. "I'm almost there. Three hundred more words."

"I'm just gonna take this off," Taryn said, losing her T-shirt, leaving her in black joggers and a black sports bra.

Charlie went still. "What are you trying to do to me right now?"

"Motivate you."

"I've never wanted to write three hundred words so badly in my life." She went back to her laptop and, just a few minutes later, shut it abruptly.

"Shall we start the clock?" Taryn asked from her spot on the couch. Charlie didn't answer. Instead she walked straight to Taryn, removed the laptop from her lap, and crawled into it instead, straddling Taryn. Her hair had all been shifted to one shoulder, leaving the column of her neck exposed on one side. Without a word, she caught Taryn's mouth with hers and kissed her deeply. Her hands were immediately at Charlie's waist and then around it, pulling her closer. They'd surely already lost a minute or two. With her tongue in Charlie's mouth as Charlie cupped her face, Taryn slipped her hands beneath Charlie's sweater to find, to her delight, that she wasn't wearing a bra. "God, I love these," Taryn said against her mouth. She palmed both breasts to a murmur of pleasure from the gorgeous woman in her lap. "I have to see you," Taryn said, pulling her lips back and offering a wicked grin. Charlie sat back with a smile as Taryn lifted her sweater to reveal her round, perfect breasts. Wordlessly she pulled a nipple into her mouth and let her teeth skate its ridges. Charlie's fingers went into her hair and gripped, holding her in place.

"If anyone can make me come from this alone, it's you. Good fucking God."

The next thing Taryn knew she was flat on her back on that couch, topped by Charlie, who kissed her like an expert offering a master class. She placed Taryn's hands above her head and held them there as she kissed her lips, her neck, her collarbone just in time for the alarm she'd set on her phone to sound its garish, unfair signal.

"Ignore it. It's awful," Taryn said.

Charlie nodded and tugged on the strap of Taryn's sports bra. Guilt began to infuse her senses. She wanted to shove it away but knew full well it was Charlie who would pay tomorrow if they got carried away.

"We have to stop."

Charlie popped her head up, a strand of hair in her face. She blew it away. "Do we, though?"

"Yes. You have an essay thingy to write." She hated herself for applying logic.

"A short story."

"Or that. My brain isn't working because your body's on mine and we are fire and gasoline."

Charlie began to kiss her neck, ignoring the suggestion. "You're definitely fire. God, I could devour you right now. Why are you so hot, Taryn? You have to stop being this way."

"Charlotte Adler."

"Okay, that just makes me hotter for you." More kissing of her neck. The weight of Charlie's body on hers was heavenly. She soaked up the moment, knowing it would be over shortly. That is, until Charlie wrote another damn thousand words. "We don't have to stop. We just have to pause until you hit your next goal."

Charlie sighed, paused, and buried her face against Taryn's neck. "I guess that's something."

"Go, go, go. Write fast. Give it everything you have and then get your ass back over here."

Charlie laughed. "I suddenly have a cheerleader in my corner." She pushed herself off Taryn into a seated position.

"You write a thousand words, and I'll be anything you want me to be." She stole a kiss and lingered, the payoff too good.

"Ms. Ross, I think you have yourself a deal, and I have my motivation."

The night continued much that way. The ticktack of the keyboard followed by a torturous groping session on the couch that never quite took them to home plate. They needed more time. Taryn's hands and mouth needed space to work. She wanted to touch and be touched, and she wanted it soon.

"How many more words?" Taryn asked, as Charlie stood and adjusted her pants that were now askew thanks to Taryn, a badge she wore proudly.

"A thousand or so," she said, recapturing air. "The *last* thousand. They are going to be either amazing because you are ridiculously inspiring, or half-assed because I want to get back to the ridiculously inspiring girl on my couch with the body I'm addicted to. What have you done to me?"

Taryn grinned. "I can do more. I want to. I'm thinking with my mouth. Perhaps over—"

"No more of that," Charlie said, hand outstretched. "Do you want me to be able to think straight or not?" She pulled her hand back.

"Tough, tough question. Does your story really need an ending?"

"Do you want the woman to find out that the child she once adopted was the one who tried to kill her or not?"

"I mean, that's a hard one." She reluctantly gave in. "I guess she should probably know, but it feels rather secondary to the really good thing we have going over here, if I'm being honest. I want your weight on me. I want to kiss you."

"Not another word." Charlie returned to her laptop at the table across the room. A moment later, she peeked around the screen. "Are you as incredibly turned-on as I am right now?"

"Uncomfortably," Taryn answered without hesitation. "Write the damn ending."

"Oh, I kind of enjoy when you tell me what to do."

The seconds seemed to crawl by, and she decided Charlie was the slowest writer on the planet. Taryn adjusted her position on the couch, uncrossing her legs, hoping the new arrangement would lessen the aching between them. It didn't. The sound of the keyboard continued to mock her. She simultaneously understood that each word written got her closer to a naked Charlie beneath her fingertips, beneath her lips. It meant release from the pent-up tension coursing through every inch of her body. She could almost hear the little sounds Charlie made right before she came, feel Charlie's heated skin pressed to hers and the weight of Charlie's body pressing down on her. God, she loved to be pressed.

Just then, the light over her head went off, leaving the room dimly lit by a small lamp on an end table across the room. The result was cozy and romantic. At last. Anticipation licked its way around her body. She turned to Charlie just in time to see her walking toward Taryn as she pulled her sweater over her head, leaving her with a generous view. God bless sweaters and the manner in which they came off. Charlie slid her jeans down her legs and stepped out of them. The technique impressed.

"You're done?" Taryn breathed. Charlie stood in front of her in just panties, and there was no sexier image in life.

"The end," Charlie said quietly with a tilt of her head. Taryn loved her quiet voice. The manner in which she strung thoughts together. The way she looked when she did so. Everything.

"Best words ever." She waited for Charlie to reach her, surprised when she did and then passed her by. The crook of Charlie's finger beckoned Taryn, and she grinned. "Bedroom it is. I really like the bedroom."

But she was hijacked in the darkened hallway and pressed up against the wall and kissed into the sweetness of next week. Charlie's hands were on her bare waist below the sports bra, the softness of Charlie's breasts pressed into Taryn's.

"God, you're worth waiting for," Charlie murmured into her mouth, owning her.

"And you're really good at sweaters."

Charlie chuckled. "I don't know what that means, but I don't care." She dropped to her knees and pulled Taryn's joggers to her ankles, which prompted her to step out of them. Grasping her hips, Charlie kissed the small rectangle of fabric between her legs as Taryn hissed in a breath. When she increased the pressure of the kiss, Taryn placed her palms flat on the wall for support.

"Don't get comfortable," Charlie said, resting back on her heels. "My bedroom. Now. I'm going to kiss every inch of your body."

Taryn, whose words had been stripped from her just moments ago and hadn't returned, went hot like molten lava. Her bones were liquid and she was fire. She nodded obediently and allowed herself to be pulled through the door to Charlie's room. The overhead was off, but the white twinkly lights Charlie had strung across the perimeter of her ceiling cast their luminance gently over the room like a halo.

"Come here," Taryn murmured, pulling Charlie to her.

She went up on her toes and slid her arms around Taryn's neck where their gazes connected just before their lips did. Kissing Charlie in a dizzying storm, Taryn was in heaven. Time was no longer a thing, nor was reason. She walked Charlie to the bed and waited, knowing full well what she'd do. She loved that she was learning her moves.

With a grin, she turned them, gave Taryn a little shove onto the bed, and followed her down.

"Such a top," she said.

"Please. You love it."

"More than you know," Taryn said. "Just know it's temporary."

That did it. Charlie crushed her mouth to Taryn's and pushed her tongue inside. Moments later, she sat up, a show Taryn wouldn't miss for anything. Charlie smiled and shook her head. "Such a boob girl. Is this what you wanted?"

"Yes, please." Her hands were on them, pushing, releasing, kneading. She loved Charlie's breasts and could spend hours with them alone.

Charlie nodded in appreciation, and when Taryn sat up, ultimately placing Charlie in her lap, Charlie slid her fingers into Taryn's hair, gave it a tug, and pulled Taryn's head back, exposing and kissing her neck. "Fuck," Taryn breathed. She closed her eyes and let the pinpricks of pleasure wash over her, leading to a much larger need she wouldn't be able to ignore for long. She was wet and on the very edge, but Charlie had announced her plans in the hallway and nothing about them sounded fast. That might be a problem.

"I'm gonna need you to take me soon," Taryn whispered.

Charlie looked up and grinned. "Excuse me?"

Taryn cradled her face and kissed her thoroughly, taking what she needed. "I'm not gonna last. Too much short-story foreplay."

"I should have written more," Charlie said with a wicked grin. "How's this?" Charlie asked, stroking her softly, which equated to slow and torturous. It was something, though. It was everything.

"Yes." Taryn's eyes slammed shut as a shot of something potent and powerful moved through her. She pressed herself against Charlie's hand, only to have it pulled away. "Mean."

"Hot," Charlie countered.

The tension was unreal, the ache so very intense. Taryn was over the bikinis she wore, and Charlie must have been, too, because they were adeptly removed from her body moments later.

"What are you doing to me?" Taryn said, half question, half rasp.

Charlie leaned her back and settled her hips between Taryn's legs. "I don't know what you're referring to," she said, as she went up on her forearms and began to rock against Taryn, softly at first and then with more intention. She slid her fingers inside, and she slowly took Taryn higher and higher with each well-placed thrust.

"I'm so yours right now," she murmured, hand flat against the wall.

"Look at me," Charlie said, and Taryn did. It was those fathomless blue eyes that she was lost in when the ground fell out from beneath her and she was flying, overcome with trembling pleasure.

"Too good," Taryn said, limp, eyes closed, hovering on a blissful cloud of satisfaction. But that didn't mean her desire for Charlie had abated one bit. It was only a few moments before she sat up and ran her fingertip from Charlie's neck to her bare shoulder. "Turn around," she whispered.

Charlie complied and leaned against Taryn. With one hand around Charlie's waist, she slid her other into her underwear and began to explore, to stroke. The tiny gasps and murmurs guided her until the undulation of Charlie's hips had her pressing her fingers firmly to a cry from Charlie.

Taryn had been waiting for this moment all night and reveled in the feeling of Charlie tensing in her arms, in the sounds she made as pleasure tore through her. She kissed the side of Charlie's neck softly as her hand brought her back down with soft, gentle touches.

With a final exhale, Charlie turned and kissed Taryn's lips over her shoulder. "I should write on a deadline more often."

❖

Taryn had crunched the numbers, and if she picked up a class both this semester and next and did one of the summer semesters in addition, she could graduate a semester early and join Charlie in New York months in advance of when she'd originally anticipated.

"Is that something you're honestly considering?" Charlie asked from across the high-top at Toby's. It was the first week of classes, and Taryn had already checked the calendar. There was still time to make the change in her schedule. "I would be thrilled if you were able to make that happen, but I also don't want you to overwhelm yourself."

"I'm pretty positive I'm doing it," Taryn said. "I just wanted to make sure you were okay with me showing up a little early."

"More than okay," Charlie said, raising her pint glass. "To speeding up the hard part."

"To speed," Taryn said, touching her glass to Charlie's.

"What are we cheering to?" Sasha asked from the pool table adjacent to their table. "Is it love? Because I'm always a celebrator, even if my heart has been recently stomped on and crushed like a bug beneath a soccer cleat."

"Did the snack machine girl not work out?" Charlie asked Taryn quietly, not moving a muscle.

"She left Sasha for the captain of the girls' soccer team," she answered. "It's a bit of a tense topic around Alexander, and cleats have been banned on the fourth floor for the time being."

"Fuck cleats!" Sasha yelled and returned to her game of pool.

"Words to live by," Charlie said, raising her glass. "You're cute," she said to Taryn.

"I didn't even do anything," Taryn said.

"Exactly." She checked her watch. "But I need to go."

"No."

"Yes," Charlie said, kissing the back of her hand. "I have all of those prewrites to grade and respond to in the morning, and I want to get in an hour of writing. Any more of these drinks and I won't be able to string words together."

The time they'd spent together in Dyer had done wonders for their relationship. Charlie was more confident than ever. She held Taryn's hand in public, introduced her to friends they'd run into, and one afternoon surprised her in the library with a to-go coffee from the Bump and Grind.

"You didn't have to do this," Taryn said, touched that Charlie had clearly gone out of her way after Taryn had texted that she was having trouble staying awake.

"Well, I was the reason you're on so little sleep. Plus, if you can't surprise your girlfriend with coffee every once in a while, what is the point of anything?"

They both paused because they'd heard it at the same time. *Girlfriend.* The first use of the word, even though that was clearly what they'd become.

"I'm your girlfriend," Taryn said and sipped her coffee. She felt ten feet tall, capable of not only acing this entire semester but probably the rest of her life, too. As Charlie Adler's girlfriend, she was unstoppable.

"You are," Charlie said, running her hand down the back of Taryn's head. It was a gesture Charlie favored, and Taryn was growing to love. "Now I better get to work and not steal glances at you with your concentration face on."

"Do you like my concentration face?" Taryn asked, attempting to demonstrate in hyperbolic fashion.

"Very much. But that's not it." Charlie pointed at the Spanish textbook in front of Taryn. "Study those words. That subject is your weak spot."

"I'm wounded you think I have one."

Charlie backed away, shrugging. "Maybe I can help you heal."

Taryn's brain stammered. She flashed on all sorts of fun scenarios. That was the thing with Charlie. They'd unlocked a world all their own where the sky felt like the limit. Their sex life, which had already started off with a bang, only continued to blossom as they grew more and more comfortable with each other. They'd tried several new positions and locations, learning more about themselves and what they liked. Who knew Taryn would enjoy the pillow so much? A surprise. Yet the view with Charlie on top was too good to ever pass up.

Taryn stayed at Charlie's place several nights a week, only staying at Alexander so the two of them could stay on top of their studies and obligations. In no surprise to anyone, they were wildly distracted when together. Along the way, she'd casually started taking photos of Charlie, attempting to capture each and every part of her, and she had so many layers.

"Are you taking my photo again?" Charlie asked, turning the rosemary chicken in the pan full of sauce she would soon ladle over it as it cooked. "I have a messy ponytail. That can't be a good shot."

"You look gorgeous, and I need cooking Charlie for the case study. Plus, I'm using you to experiment with dragging my shutter a bit. It's an ambient light thing."

"I don't know what that means, but I'm here to assist." She blew Taryn a kiss as she clicked away. Cooking Charlie just might rank high on her list of shots. There was a joy in the air when Charlie went to work on a dish, almost as if she abandoned her stresses and immersed herself in something she loved. It showed in the photos, loud and clear. She had Ashley to thank for some of her technique in capturing it.

If you take the shot half a second before the smile reaches someone's lips, you've captured the realization of happiness, Ashley once told her. It was invaluable advice.

As they enjoyed their time together, soaking up the newness of what they had, the future loomed and there were details to sort through.

"I can't sleep," Charlie whispered one night.

Taryn, holding her, kissed the top of her head. "Do you have something on your mind?"

"What if New York doesn't work out? What if June DiCarlo meets me and passes? Monica's been distant, and I don't feel comfortable going to her for last-minute tips."

"You're going to go there and be yourself. She's going to see how talented you are, how competent, and be thrilled with you."

"I feel like I've invested so much in this plan that I don't know what I'm going to do if it falls through. How am I going to look myself in the mirror? Even more, how am I going to pay my bills?"

"What's the plan B?" Taryn asked calmly. Sometimes understanding all the options helped quiet her own fears—maybe it would work for Charlie.

"After I'm done rocking in a corner? I could look into teaching while I query my book, but without a foot in the door, it's going to be bleak." She slid up the bed so they were facing each other on the pillow. "I'm terrified, Taryn. And I'm only confessing this because it's you, but I've never been more scared about anything in my life. I want this so badly. I feel like I don't ask the universe for a lot, but I'm asking it for this."

"It's going to be okay, Charlie. I promise."

"I hope so." Charlie took a deep breath. "I wish I could just relax, but this is simply too important."

They'd had a reoccurrence of the conversation several times, making Taryn acutely aware of how important this meeting in New York was. With only a week until Charlie's interview, she did what she could to keep Charlie distracted and out of her own head. Once as she watched Charlie behind the circulation desk, her brows down, looking like the weight of the world sat on her chest, she fired off a text.

Meet me in the far back corner. Dusty books.

It's giving mysterious, Charlie wrote back.

It's giving a lot of things. Taryn grinned and typed. *Come find out.*

She took off from her seat and made it there first. Charlie, who knew what she was doing, waited a couple of moments before casually making her way to the back of the library, where very few students ever spent much time. "What is going on back here?" she asked. But there was a curious-amused expression on her face, which meant Taryn's plan had worked.

"I wanted you to myself for just a few stolen moments."

"And what do you want to do with me?" she asked, blue eyes dancing.

"I'm happy you asked," Taryn said, crashing her lips to Charlie's. Apparently, library kissing was extra sexy because the sparks that flew when their mouths began to move weren't any ordinary variety. The kiss was slow and deep, and then hot and fast, before settling into a rhythm that made Taryn regret they were in a public venue and Charlie's place of work.

"If I didn't work here…" Charlie said in Taryn's ear, nipping a lobe.

"Who needs a job?" Taryn asked. "Let's live on the street and be happy."

Charlie pulled her lips away and found Taryn's eyes. There was an earnest quality behind hers. "I'm already happy. I want you to know that."

Everything in Taryn softened and spread out. "I'm happy, too."

"I'll be even happier when I can act on all the things I want to do to you right now."

Taryn smiled. "How long until you get off?"

Charlie raised an eyebrow.

"Off *work*," Taryn amended, the blush on its way, she could feel it. "But I like where you're going with that."

"Three hours."

Taryn kissed her soundly. "Think about me until then?"

Charlie touched Taryn's lips with her thumb reverently. "I will think of nothing else."

CHAPTER SEVENTEEN

Charlie stared at the street sign ahead to orient herself as a sea of yellow cabs flew through the intersection, one of the cabbies leaning on their horn for reasons she was unclear on. Across the street, a line of people in business attire had formed in front of an Indian food cart that made her remember she hadn't exactly had lunch. She double-checked the address to make sure she'd located the right building in Midtown East and, with her heart in her throat, headed for the elevator bank.

She'd received a text from Monica reminding her to ask questions, be specific about her goals, and not to be shy about showing off what she was capable of. While there wasn't a ton of affection in their occasional communication, she was grateful for Monica's support, and it was clear she did still care. Their relationship would come back around. She knew it. Charlie was willing to be patient.

"Charlie?"

She looked up from her spot in the lobby to find the one and only June DiCarlo smiling at her in a sleek skirt and jacket combo. She had blond hair that fell just past her chin and smart-looking black glasses. *Literary glasses*. Simply being between the walls of Broadland Rhodes made Charlie want to stop everything and write.

"Hi, June. It's so nice to meet you."

"Likewise. Why don't you come on back." She followed June into her office, which was comfortable, yet stylish. The picture window behind her desk looked out onto Lexington Avenue from the twelfth floor. A lovely view.

June settled in behind the desk and smiled. "Monica is a good friend, and she says you're like a daughter to her."

"My mother passed some years back, and the two of them were very close."

"Well, she speaks very highly of you, and you know how the world feels about Monica McHenry." June spoke at a very fast pace and had the most direct eye contact Charlie had ever seen.

"She's a force," Charlie said. Not a lie.

"Here's the thing. Your résumé and your commitment to education tell me you're serious. Are you a hard worker?"

"I am."

"And if I set you up with a developmental editor, in addition to your potential position with the company, are you going to be able to take their notes?"

"Revising is my favorite part of the process."

"Good to know." June sat back. "This is a fast-paced environment. The work isn't glamorous. Sometimes I need someone to act as a liaison between departments. At other points, I might need someone to stand in for me at meetings. I also might desperately need a cappuccino from downstairs."

Charlie smiled. "I can liaise, stand in, and fetch coffee with the best of them. I want to learn, grow, and form a solid foundation for my career."

June nodded. "Good answer." A flashed smile. "I go with my gut and don't feel the need to waste time with a lot of introspective get-to-know-you questions. In fact, I hate them. Let's give it a shot and see how it goes. If you're awful, you're fired." She flashed a smile that said she was only half kidding.

That was it? She'd been in the office for all of five minutes. "I would love that."

"The hours aren't easy, but you could learn a lot here, Charlie. I'll have my staff send over the paperwork to get you a start date shortly after your graduation, which I have written down here somewhere." She glanced down at her notes and then abandoned the mission. "Give Monica my best. She owes me an extra dirty martini because I bought the last three."

"I'll tell her."

After the whirlwind meeting that felt more like a drive-by than anything, Charlie was back outside with her phone to her ear. Taryn was easily her first call, and she answered on the second ring.

"Is it over? How did it go?"

Charlie gulped air, too excited to drag out the news. "She's bringing me on board. I'm officially working for Broadland Rhodes in less than three months. June's setting me up with a developmental editor for my manuscript. It's happening, Tare."

"I would kiss your face off," Taryn said. "This is the most amazing news, and now I can sit down because I've been walking in circles waiting to hear. Congratulations, Charlie. We're going to have to celebrate the second you're home. Hurry."

"Taryn?"

"Yes?"

Charlie placed a hand on her head and grinned, feeling brave, vulnerable, and—above all else—truthful. "I love you. I just wanted to say that."

The line was quiet for a moment and then, "I love you, too, Charlie. With all I have. Get home already."

❖

It was a big night. The photography department was holding its annual reception celebrating the work of their most promising students, a Hillspoint tradition every spring semester. While Taryn hadn't expected to be included, she was over the moon to learn she'd have two of her photographs featured alongside those of her classmates. While she wished more than anything that Charlie could be there with her to experience the exciting evening, which was turning out to be a much bigger deal than she'd realized, unfortunately, she wasn't yet back from New York. Instead, Taryn planned to memorize every detail, just as Charlie had instructed her to, and share it with her later, maybe over coffee at the Bump and Grind. In the meantime, she stood near her photographs, as instructed, answering questions and smiling brightly at donors who came by.

"I love the protest photo," Ashley said as she passed. "You're doing great things."

"Thank you," Taryn said, appreciative of the guidance Ashley had provided. She'd miss her around the department once she graduated.

During a small lull, Taryn snuck away to secure a cup of the fruit punch in the corner of the reception space. When she turned, she found herself face-to-face with a woman who seemed familiar for a reason Taryn couldn't pinpoint. She smiled at her as she turned to go, figuring she was likely an instructor she'd seen around.

Before she could get very far, the woman held up a hand. "Taryn. Good to see you. Enjoying your evening?"

"I am. Thank you." She was surprised the woman knew her name and now wondered more than ever where she recognized her from.

"Do you remember me? I'm Monica McHenry."

"Oh." Danny's mother. *Fuck.* The one from Charlie's apartment. "Hello." This was unexpected.

"I've heard a lot about you," Monica said. Taryn wasn't sure what to say, so she didn't. "Your work is striking. You show great potential."

Butterflies swarmed, and Taryn blinked, trying to orient herself to the moment, to officially meeting Monica, an important person in Charlie's life. While out of the blue, she welcomed the opportunity to make a good impression. Maybe Monica was one of the department's VIP donors. Roger had mentioned that there would be a few in attendance.

"Thank you so much. It's really wonderful to meet you. Charlie speaks so highly of you and your family."

Monica touched her chest. "That girl is a love, isn't she?"

"She's amazing."

"I'm glad you agree. I want us to have a conversation that I'm hopeful will prove beneficial to all of us."

"All right. Sure. We can do that." Taryn, fruit punch in hand, looked around for a quiet spot, but Monica was already leading the way to a lounge off the reception hall. She clearly knew her way around.

Once they settled at a table and chairs, Monica regarded her with soft eyes. "Charlie has a bright future ahead of her. I'm sure you do, too."

Taryn wasn't sure where this was going, but she hoped it was Monica's way of bridging the gap that had sprung up between her and Charlie. She knew they were still in contact, but according to Charlie, it hadn't been the same, which was unfortunate. "I think we're still waiting to find out about me, but she definitely does. She had a great meeting with your contact in New York and will be back tomorrow."

"You said *we're* waiting to find out? Does that mean you and Charlotte? *We*?"

"I think I just meant the collective."

Monica flashed a smile that appeared way too fast to be sincere. "But you two are a *we*, correct? That's what I've heard anyway."

She had no reason to lead with anything except the truth. "Yes. We're together."

Monica winced. "It's a bad idea for her, don't you think?"

"I think when two people are happy together, it's never a bad idea." Taryn felt like she'd waded into shark-infested waters but wasn't quite sure why.

"Unless it destroys someone's entire life." Monica leaned forward. "Charlie was on a very favorable path, headed toward an engagement, a future family, and a promising career as a novelist. Then you appeared."

"I don't want to take anything away from Charlie, but I think—"

"Don't, though. Fix it instead."

"I don't know what you mean." Taryn hated that she was allowing this woman to intimidate her, and she was. It was all she could do not to crumple. Where was all that strength she'd been working on when she needed it?

"From what I hear, Charlotte's presented herself in a very impressive manner in New York. She's excited for the opportunity, a door that will lead to so many great things in the literary community. Broadland Rhodes is a fortress to someone on the ground floor, but I escorted her in. I can just as easily escort her right out again."

Taryn frowned, attempting to follow the thread. Surely she'd misunderstood. She remained still. "Are you saying you would do that?"

"I'm asking you to step away and I won't have to. It's time for Charlie to get back to her life. Playtime is over." She touched Taryn's wrist. "I say that with respect. This is nothing personal, but I won't have my family disrupted. You're treading on a lot of history, my dear."

"What if Charlie doesn't want me to go anywhere?" Her voice sounded small and meek.

"She's lost right now. She's a woman about to step into the real world for the first time, and she's panicking. I think we've all been there. Do her the biggest favor of your life and get out of the way so she can remember who she is again." Monica lifted a shoulder. "Or don't, and I'll rescind my recommendation. Broadland Rhodes is hoping to sign me for another three-book deal and is willing to do just about whatever I ask."

Taryn couldn't believe what she was hearing. She wasn't sure whether to laugh or cry. It was ludicrous and awful all at the same time.

"Do the right thing, Tina."

"My name is Taryn."

"An easy mistake." It wasn't. It was meant to show her how

replaceable she was. Monica gestured to the reception hall behind them. "Your professors speak highly of you. You have a promising future if you play your cards right. Give me a call someday if you'd like me to make a connection for you."

"No. That won't be necessary," she said evenly. Never in a million years would she want help from this woman, who professed to love and care about others, when in fact, she used her power to manipulate and get what she wanted.

"Suit yourself." She turned to go and paused. "But I implore you to think about what I said and do the best possible thing for *Charlie*. If you feel for her what you seem to, you'll want her to have everything she's dreaming of right now. Don't take it all away from her."

And then she was gone, taking with her Taryn's sense of stability, clarity, and trust that the world was a good place. She went through the rest of the reception like an automaton. She smiled in the right spots and complimented the work on display. She nodded and feigned gratitude when many told her how much they enjoyed her photographs. But underneath it all, Taryn was numb.

She didn't walk straight home but instead took a circuitous path through campus. She passed through the grouping of trees where she and Charlie had once watched the copper glow. She found a bench near the foreign language building where she could still see them kissing against a nearby tree beneath the cover of darkness. Everything in her screamed to go straight to Charlie and tell her everything Monica had threatened. But to what end? Charlie would run angry to Monica, only to have the arrangement pulled out from beneath her. Or worse, she'd get the fire in her eyes she often did, and let the opportunity go. Or would she choose the job over Taryn? The fact of the matter was she didn't like any of those options, making this whole thing wildly unfair. Yet here it sat on her shoulders.

So, she walked and walked, hands in her pockets, heart aching and mind racing, a wreck. Maybe the best solution was a temporary evil. Maybe she stepped away long enough for Charlie to find her footing in New York, establish herself in that world. If Taryn was patient, and Charlie was forgiving, they would find their way back to each other, right? They were meant to be together. Taryn was more sure of that than the sun coming up, but maybe timing was key and the only way around Charlie not losing everything she'd been working toward.

With several miles under her belt, and her feet aching, her heart had gone from counting the moments until Charlie was home to dreading the interaction ahead, whatever that might be. Her plan was to sleep on it and see if the morning brought any clarity.

Love did conquer all, right? She had to believe that she and Charlie would be okay, no matter what happened in the short term. The alternative was too impossible to consider.

CHAPTER EIGHTEEN

Charlie's feet hadn't touched the ground since her meeting with June DiCarlo, who she realized she was going to have to start calling June at some point. She'd treated herself to that fantastic food cart to commemorate the moment, enjoying chicken tikka masala in front of the building, and wondered if this might become a daily ritual for her when she returned full-time.

The next day, on the plane home, she pored through the helpful information June's office had sent over about apartments, MetroCards, and favorite spots to eat. It really was a comprehensive welcome package, and she couldn't wait to share it with Taryn. They would, after all, eventually be living there together, and Taryn should have a say in the kind of place Charlie picked out.

They'd made arrangements to get together after Taryn's afternoon class on the morning Charlie arrived home. She checked the clock, realizing Taryn was half an hour late. Not like her. Charlie sent a text and waited, antsy and getting concerned. Maybe it was just that she missed Taryn, and a couple of days apart made her itch to see her beautiful face again. Patience be damned.

Finally, a knock on the door followed by it opening revealed Taryn with her hair pulled back in a ponytail and a smile on her face when her gaze landed on Charlie. "You're home," she said softly, but the familiar energy was missing.

"I am. Hi," Charlie said, kissing her lips softly. She didn't receive much back. Odd. It was possible Taryn had experienced a stressful few days. Her smile also didn't reach her eyes, which seemed tired. "I hate being apart. Have I mentioned that?"

"You don't have to. I missed you, too."

Charlie dipped her head to examine Taryn head-on. "Hey, are you okay? Did you sleep last night?"

"Not a ton. No."

"All right." Charlie paused, waiting for Taryn to say more, but she didn't. "Everything okay?"

"Mm-hmm," Taryn said, sliding her hands into the back pockets of her jeans. "Still coming down from your high? I'm so thrilled for you. I know this job offer was weighing on you."

Charlie took a deep breath and let it wash over her. "I don't think I can put into words how happy I am and how relieved. I know I told you how worried I was, but that wasn't even the half of it. I feel like I can breathe and enjoy the semester now, knowing my life is sorted out and I have a firm plan."

Taryn squeezed her hand, tears filling her eyes. "This is your dream and it's actually happening. Think about that."

"Right?" Charlie put her arms around Taryn's neck and hugged her. "It's surreal. Things like this don't usually happen for me. I need to send Monica a giant bouquet for arranging the meeting. Whether she's still upset about Danny and me or not, she made this happen."

"Definitely do that," Taryn said, releasing her. She swallowed and seemed to be piecing words together. The vibe was off, and Charlie didn't quite understand why. "But I need to be honest and say that this is a lot for me."

"Okay. Say more." Her heart rate picked up, and her palms went clammy. She shifted her weight. "You're scaring me a little."

Taryn's gaze fell to the floor. Why wasn't she looking at Charlie? She always made direct eye contact, even at hard moments. "I think while you were gone, it all just became very real for me. I'm still in school, and this whole being-in-a-relationship thing is big."

"Right. I get that. Are you overwhelmed, having doubts? About us?" Her brain couldn't seem to wrap itself around the conversation they were having. There had been zero clues. No indication that anything was amiss between them. This didn't add up.

"I think I might be."

"You literally said you loved me on the phone less than two days ago. That felt like an amazing step forward, not back." It felt like the floor was crumbling beneath her feet. "I'm confused but trying to understand."

Taryn hadn't moved a muscle. "I wasn't expecting you to say it, and when you did…"

"You automatically said it back." She nodded once. "Wow. This feels…like a truck just came out of nowhere and is heading straight for me." She walked the length of the room and back again.

"I'm not saying that I don't want to be with you down the road, but maybe we're at different points in our journey. I might need to catch up first." She touched her hair, her face crumpling. "I don't even know what I'm saying. I'm so sorry about all of this."

It was Charlie's instinct to pull Taryn immediately into her arms and fix whatever had her sad, but it also felt like she no longer had permission. Taryn wasn't lamenting school or photography or her friends, she was uncomfortable with *them*. She was stepping away from Charlie, and did she have any other choice than to let her? She was losing another person she loved. It felt like she'd taken a jab to her face and hadn't yet regained clear vision.

Somehow she had to get through this in one piece. She swallowed her sadness as best she could, hoping to hold it back until the second Taryn was gone. "I think what you're saying is that this isn't what you want."

Panic zigzagged across Taryn's features, which was confusing. "I just need time. I should take the semester and get my head on straight, and once you're settled and happy, we can maybe see where we're at?"

"Yeah. Yes." Her heart cracked and then shattered. "We'll do that. See where we're at." She looked back at her kitchen table where she had all the information from her trip spread out and ready to share with Taryn. She simply blinked at it as she tried to reel in her plans for the two of them. How silly they seemed now, how far away. "Swing by the library soon so we can catch up." It was a strange thing to say, but Charlie was doing whatever she could to tread water and hold on to a scrap of normalcy.

"Definitely. It's still me. I'll be around a lot." It might have been a lie, but she chose to believe it in this moment. Taryn looked over her shoulder at the door she'd barely come through before leveling Charlie's world. "I better let you get back to whatever you were in the midst of."

This was it. She closed her eyes briefly and opened them. "Okay. Take care of yourself."

"Charlie. This isn't necessarily forever."

"Hmm. Yeah." She forced a smile that she held carefully in place until the door to her apartment was closed. The wobbly sob that tore from her throat sounded foreign. She walked blindly to her bedroom and closed the door, attempting to escape the world, afraid to trust the ground beneath her feet. She slipped beneath the quilt on her bed and wrapped it around herself as tears spilled onto her pillow. She'd allowed herself to believe that the happiness she'd always longed for was actually attainable. She'd slowly let down her guard to Taryn, to her parents, to planning a true future for them, only to have that trust trampled on in a horrific blindside. In this moment, she felt more alone than she ever had in her life. She missed her mother desperately and longed for her reassuring words, a shoulder to cry on.

She skipped her classes that day and stayed right where she was, sorting through details over and over again for any kind of clue. Only there had been nothing, which was the more terrifying conclusion. It wasn't fair. It wasn't okay. One thing was for sure, she would never, ever let herself be hurt by someone again.

Tulips, daffodils, and cherry blossoms had emerged around campus, signaling spring had shifted into full bloom. The warmer weather had most everyone in short sleeves, and the campus seemed busier, with more students opting to lounge outside or toss the Frisbee around. Taryn had spent the past two weeks in hell, second-guessing the decision she'd made and running through all the ways she could have handled the situation differently. Regret was an awful thing that followed her around like bricks on her back. The day she'd stepped away from Charlie, a god-awful humming took up residence in her ears, nausea clawed her stomach, and a cold sweat took over her body, signs that every part of her fought against the very thing she'd done. She didn't welcome spring. She didn't enjoy its bright colors, not when her own world had gone dim.

Didn't matter. She'd gone and ripped both of their hearts out, and the idea of Charlie running off to New York and finding a whole new life without Taryn was the equivalent of a thousand little cuts. She wasn't eating, she barely slept, and her grades had taken a nosedive since Monica had stepped into the picture.

"I don't like the idea of letting evil win," Caz said as they walked across the quad to the intramural fields to support the Alexander girls' soccer team. Taryn brought her camera with her, in love with the gorgeous day and the chance to shoot an action-packed game filled with competitive players.

"I don't either," Taryn said flatly. "It's eating my soul knowing that that woman drove a wedge between Charlie and me, and I let her. But at the time, it felt like I was in a maze with no real way out without robbing Charlie of what she'd been dreaming of for years."

Caz stopped walking. Her cavalier, fun personality had been bottled up in the name of Taryn's world falling apart. In its place was a serious version of her, capable of not only comforting Taryn but supplying her with excellent insight. "I think you need to consider telling Charlie the truth. It's the right thing to do. Underneath it all, I think that you know that."

"And have her lose everything?"

"Isn't that her decision to make and not yours? This isn't even about the romantic relationship. It's about Charlie having all the information before she makes a life-altering decision about this job. She'd be indebted to this awful woman forever, and that's not your call."

Caz had a point. Taryn blinked, seeing it from a new perspective. Monica was playing God, and now, perhaps, Taryn was. Was that fair to Charlie? "You might be right. I can fully admit that I'm out of my depth and drowning here. But I'm not sure what move to make, given where I am. I've sent a couple of check-in texts. Charlie answered one with as few words as possible and has ignored the others ever since."

"Tare, she's hurting. This came out of nowhere for her."

"Us both." She dropped her head back and stared up at the sky, praying for the sea of blue to swallow her up so she didn't have to go another day in this alternate reality that never should have been. What an absolute nightmare. "My only hope is that down the road she'll give me another chance. I've prayed for that every day since the last time I saw her. I can't get the look on her face out of my head. I'm such an asshole."

Caz didn't hesitate. "My advice is don't wait for that second-chance moment. Tell Charlie everything and let the chips fall where they may."

More and more, Taryn was beginning to believe that Caz was right. She needed to inform Charlie about her conversation with Monica and hope that she understood why Taryn did what she did. "I'm not a controlling person, but somehow I felt the need to control this?"

Caz shook her head. "That needs a reframing. You love her and wanted to make sure she was happy. As misguided as the decision might have been—no offense—you were sacrificing yourself for her.

It's noble in a way." She clapped Taryn on the back. "Now we just might need to tweak your technique."

"I have so much to learn."

"Don't we all."

"And I might be an asshole."

"Nah, not at all."

The conversation had kicked something loose, and Taryn knew what she had to do. There was a TKE brother in her narrative photography class who let her know that their weekly meetings, complete with advisors present, happened every Thursday afternoon. Armed with that information, she waited on the sidewalk in front of the house until Danny made his way up the walk at ten minutes before the hour.

He eyed Taryn as she approached and regarded her with a weary sigh. "Something I can do for you, Taryn?"

It was the kind of moment she'd shy away from normally—she was averse to conflict and facing the hard moments. Yet she refused to give herself too much credit for bravery when it should have been Charlie she chased down. And she would, once she found the words and the courage to face her in person. "I need a few minutes of your time."

"Can't do it. I have a meeting."

"I know. And that's why I'm here. It's that important." She shifted her weight and closed her eyes. "It's about Charlie. Please?"

That held his attention, and he softened. He still cared about her, that much was apparent. "All right. I can give you five."

Taryn nodded. And with a deep breath, she imparted the entire story of the showcase, Monica's surprising attendance, and the ultimatum she'd leveled at Taryn. If Danny was surprised, he didn't show it. If anything, the news seemed to hang on him, heavy and uncomfortable.

He stared at the sidewalk and then shifted his gaze back to Taryn. "And you're telling me this because…"

"Charlie needs to know before she heads to New York in a few weeks."

"Shouldn't you be the one to tell her?"

"I don't think she wants to hear from me." It was an excuse and Taryn damn well knew it. Standing in front of Charlie and admitting the truth was too daunting to tackle just yet. Fear had her in a stranglehold, but that didn't mean Charlie should be kept in the dark a moment longer. That had been a mistake. "Please just tell her."

Chapter Nineteen

Charlie's ten a.m. capstone course, designed to be the finale in her creative writing journey, was her one saving grace these days. Feeling let down, brokenhearted, and alone, she generally just went through the motions these days. Most everything in her life made her mad or sad, or—worse—reminded her of Taryn and all she'd lost.

Capstone was different. It allowed her to draw into herself and create worlds where she could escape from her own bleak reality. It pulled together everything she'd learned in the last three years and made her feel ready to take on the world. When things felt extra hopeless, she tried to focus on two things as a salve: her work as a creative release, and leaving Hillspoint University far, far behind. She didn't know the unique details of what her future held in New York, but it was a new start she desperately needed. Until then, she'd hang on and close out her time as a student with as much strength as she could gather.

"Hey. You okay?" Danny asked quietly during a lull in their class discussion. He sat across from her at the conference table, his brows drawn down and concern written all over his face. He knew her well enough to pick up on her cues. They'd kept up a polite friendship that never went much deeper than class procedures and casual hellos. She was grateful they'd been able to sidestep any unfortunate dramatic displays. They were adults and handling themselves that way. Today, Danny seemed to tear down the polite barrier and reach through.

"Me? I'm fine. Just need to catch up on sleep," she said quietly, not wanting to draw the attention of their classmates. She gestured to the dark circles that had crept up under her eyes recently. She wasn't looking her best but also had trouble caring, keeping her energy focused on survival and not beating herself up too terribly for trusting.

"You don't seem fine."

She bristled. Her walls were up these days because she'd learned a valuable lesson. She kept the world and everyone in it at arm's length, and that included Danny. "Can you just take me at my word?" She was too exhausted to fake it convincingly.

"We need to talk after class," he said, as the lecture resumed. She could only imagine what he had to say and honestly didn't want to listen.

"No, we don't," she mouthed back. She didn't even shoot for a civil exchange. She was done with pretense and seeking out harmony with others. What had it gotten her in the end?

He let the conversation die, but when their class dismissed, she found him waiting at the base of the steps of the Saunders Building, one foot propped up on the bottom stair.

"Danny, no. I can't and don't want to. I have my shift at the library and then forty-two papers to grade by ten a.m. tomorrow. My soul is tired. Do you hear me? And I don't have it in me for one of our talks."

"You're gonna want to hear this."

She exhaled, loud enough that he'd hear it. There was no getting out of this. "Hear what?"

"What if I told you I knew *why*?" His eyes were earnest and he didn't seem his normal confident self.

She shrugged. "You know why what?"

"Why Taryn ended things with you."

Her breath caught. It was the question she'd stayed up nights pondering, and he now dangled it on a hook like bait. While she wanted desperately not to care, to keep herself behind the emotional fortress she'd carefully constructed, everything in her rose to attention. "Okay. And why is that?"

"Can we sit?" He gestured with his head to the half wall nearby, and she led the way. "Here goes." He slapped his knee and gave his head one shake. "My mother means well, but she can be a bull in a china shop when she gets her mind set on something."

That part was true. Monica was a go-getter to an actual fault. She'd once snatched up her mom's crush when they were younger, nearly ending their friendship. "What does Monica have to do with *Taryn*?"

"She was a little too interested in the status of your relationship when I had lunch with her recently. She pressed and pressed for details." Charlie frowned at him, curious as to where this was all going.

Charlie nodded. "She wants you and me back together."

"Too much." He sighed. "After two martinis, I still couldn't get it out of her."

Charlie frowned, unsure where this was going.

"Then a couple days ago, I find Taryn waiting for me at the TKE house on the day of their weekly chapter meeting. She was nervous and sad, looking like a lost puppy dog. Anyway, she clued me in on a few things."

"What did she say?" Her heart thudded, realizing she was about to get an answer or two.

"Mom confronted Taryn while you were gone and told her she'd use her influence to pull the Broadland Rhodes opportunity if Taryn didn't back off."

"No." A pause. "Monica wouldn't do that. Would she?"

Her stared at her ruefully. "It's fucked up, but yeah. I'm afraid she would." He ran his hand through his hair and shook his head. "And did."

"And you're saying Taryn just said *okay, sure* and gave in?"

Danny shrugged as if it was beyond him as well.

"I don't even know what to say right now." Just when Charlie thought this whole thing couldn't get any more shocking…Monica had shaken the tree, and Taryn had leapt right out of it. Was it really that easy to just walk away from her? Apparently so. She was reeling. Emotions fired in every which way like an out-of-control shootout at a saloon. She squeezed her hands to keep herself calm, but her thoughts took off at a tear.

"I get the feeling Taryn was a little outmatched." Danny seemed intent on helping Charlie through this moment, which was appreciated but unnecessary. "You know how my mom can be. She takes over in a blaze."

"She does. But this is over the line." Charlie shook her head, going back through every moment with a new understanding. It was like watching a movie back after you were made aware of the twist. While the new information offered clarity, it didn't make her feel even one shred better, more like a pawn moved around a board without a single say-so in the matter. Insulting. Degrading.

"I used to think my mom always meant well," Danny said. "Even if her methods weren't the best. She got to where she is in her career for a reason. But after this one, I'm not sure what to think." He stood. "I'm really sorry, Char. I thought you should know."

She nodded numbly. "Thank you," she said, her words delayed as her thoughts took over.

"I'll give you your space, but reach out if there's anything I can do."

"I will."

Charlie sat right where she was, not caring that she might be late for work, not caring who saw her processing each of these very powerful feelings that took their turn with her one after the other until she felt dizzy and sick. In the end, anger won out, now champion of the day. She stood, checked her watch, and stalked her way across the quad, ready to put it to use. Someone had Spanish class in ten minutes, and she planned to be there.

❖

There were moments in life when the details rose to the surface. When each of the five senses overachieved, making that particular point in time roar. Taryn experienced exactly that when she approached the foreign language building and found Charlie standing in front. The wind picked up, lifting Taryn's hair and blowing it off her forehead. The faint smell of bacon from the dining hall next door wafted through the air. She could remember the exact moment she was close enough to Charlie for her features to snap into focus. Her blue eyes blazed, and a strand of hair was tucked behind her ear on the right side in an angelic contrast to her demeanor. There were students to her right laughing too loudly at something ridiculous. Charlie's face, creased with anger, and the way she'd folded her arms across her chest would be burned into Taryn's memory forever.

"Hey," Taryn said, as she approached. She looked at the building and back to Charlie. "Taking up Spanish?" Her stomach rippled with nervous energy.

"You're a coward." Charlie's eyes were ice. She slid her hands into her back pockets and watched Taryn in stillness. The word stung because it was the one thing Taryn never wanted to be yet knew she was.

"Okay." Taryn inhaled. "What's going on? Should we talk?"

Charlie turned and pointedly walked away from the gathering of students, securing privacy for whatever exchange they were about to have. Taryn dutifully followed, class abandoned. She was terrified of the Charlie in front of her now, yet still so in love that every part of

Taryn sang out to be in her presence again. It didn't seem fair that she was this gorgeous in anger.

When they settled, Charlie simply stared at her. Impenetrable. She'd armored herself, and Taryn felt the waves of self-protection radiating from her.

"Talk to me," Taryn said. "Please?"

"You let her get to you. Monica. How could you do that?"

Taryn nodded, understanding, her spirits plummeting in shame. Danny had informed Charlie, which meant Charlie knew everything, and Taryn hadn't been the one to tell her. She'd known it was coming, but it was still awful. Why had she hesitated to simply pick up her phone? All she could do now is do her best to explain. "I couldn't stand the thought of you losing out on New York. On the job. It was your dream, Charlie, what you wanted more than anything. You said so all the time."

Charlie blinked and shook her head. "I didn't want anything as much as I wanted you and me." She held her gaze. "Which seems foolish of me, because you walked away so very easily, Taryn."

"There was nothing *easy* about it. I promise you that." Her shoulders sagged. "I don't eat anymore. I don't enjoy anything. I miss you more than words can communicate, and I know it's my own fault." Underneath it all, she understood the damage she'd done. It took a lot for Charlie to trust and believe herself worthy of love, and Taryn had gone and shaken that trust to its core, snatched it away.

"Did you love me?" Charlie asked. Taryn remembered the phone call and the wonderful moment when they'd said the words to each other. She almost couldn't stomach the fact that she'd taken them back.

"Not did. *Do*. I've been deeply in love with you for a long time, and that's not going to change."

Charlie nodded, her eyes brimming with tears. The anger had faded and vulnerability snuck through. The woman in front of her now was sad and broken. Taryn had never hated anything more.

"I'm so sorry. I have so many regrets, Charlie, but not coming to you immediately after the reception is by far the biggest. If there's a chance to undo what I've done, I'd take it. In an instant."

Charlie wiped the tears the moment they spilled over. "That's the thing about an instant. Most anything can change on a dime, right? We established that, once upon a time. And you and I have changed, Taryn. I gotta go."

It wasn't an answer, but Taryn had to respect Charlie's words and their implication. She stood right there in that spot watching after the woman who was walking away with her whole heart, wanting more than anything to chase after her and make her remember all the good things about them. She wanted to apologize over and over, and to hold Charlie and let them both cry. But none of those things seemed to be what Charlie wanted, which meant Taryn would continue to feel and wait and hope for the day she'd have her chance. She just prayed there would be such a day. In the meantime, she refused to be the one thing Charlie now thought she was, a coward. She would harness what courage she could gather and go after what she wanted more than anything else in life, Charlotte Adler.

Chapter Twenty

Charlie was going to miss the quiet of the library when she finally turned in her badge. With just a few weeks left until that day, she soaked in her time behind the desk, interacting with students and reshelving books. Something about the weight of the hardcovers in her hand anchored her during a time she felt adrift. In fact, she noticed herself lingering beyond the hours of her shift, pitching in at the circular reference desk, which also kept her from sitting alone in her apartment where her emotions would swarm.

"You're extra quiet today," Emerson said, offering her a shoulder bump.

She smiled. "I noticed that, too. I apologize. Still not quite myself."

"I know," Emerson said simply. "And that's okay." She rested a hand on the return cart. "Any job leads?"

"One." After she'd turned down the Broadland Rhodes opportunity, refusing to be beholden to someone as manipulative as Monica showed herself to be, she'd scoured the internet for anything that would keep her in her field of study while she continued to develop her manuscript. "There's an instructor position at Littleton University, not far from Brooklyn. The course load is manageable, and I'd still have plenty of time to write."

"And it's still New York."

Charlie shrugged. "Dream-adjacent? Let's go with that."

The truth was she was excited by the idea. It wasn't the glamorous path she'd imagined, but she enjoyed the classroom and all the details seemed to align.

"You would rock that job. You're an inspiring instructor."

"Thank you. I have a final interview next week." She checked her watch. "And I've been here an extra two hours." She sighed. "I should head home."

"The books will miss you. Me, too."

She reached for Emerson, pulled her into a tight hug because she felt like it. Their friendship had become an unexpected bright spot that she refused to take for granted.

"Be safe out there. It's dark."

Charlie shrugged. "Not too far a walk to my place. Plus, it's nice out. I'm going to enjoy it." The library, to her detriment, was kept exceptionally cool, which meant emerging into the warmth of the spring air was like a welcome embrace. She descended the stairs with a small smile, pausing only when she saw a familiar face sitting on the bench nearby. For a split second, her heart soared seeing Taryn waiting there, transported back in time to when she'd wait for Charlie, scoop her up, and they'd head off to dinner or home or anywhere they could just be *them*. It wasn't long before reality came crashing through. Her instinct was to keep walking, but Taryn was too quick.

"Hi."

"Hi," Charlie said, eyeing Taryn. She'd cut her hair by about three inches. It looked good on her, more mature in a way. She'd never say so. "What are you doing here?"

"I'm here for you. I was hoping we could catch up. Can I maybe walk you home?"

"I don't think that's a great plan. But thank you." She walked away then, heart in her throat. She hadn't seen Taryn since their intense discussion in front of the foreign language building. She wanted to say that all that happened had erased her feelings, but they'd just roared to life the second Taryn looked her in the eyes.

Taryn was there the next night, too. Her eyes were hopeful, and she stood as Charlie approached. "Taryn, you should be out living your life. What are you doing at the library at ten o'clock?"

"I'm showing up in a way I should have shown up weeks ago. And I'm going to keep showing up because that's what you do for people you love."

Charlie shook her head, and her warring emotions went to battle until her brain overruled all. *No, don't get caught up again.* It didn't matter how beautiful Taryn looked, how sweet she was, or how much Charlie ached for her. This was a dangerous scenario for a heart that had been absolutely crushed. "Good night, Taryn."

"Good night."

She opened the door two mornings later to a delivery driver holding a to-go cup. "Dessert coffee for Charlie?"

She nodded and accepted the hot coffee knowing exactly who had sent it, and there, scrawled across the cup were the words: *I hope your day is amazing. –T.*

It didn't end there. A bouquet of wildflowers arrived, unruly and wonderful in their arrangement. She left them on her kitchen counter instead of throwing them out. The beautiful chaos reminded Charlie of the two of them, and the way they'd come together in such a beautiful fashion but ended in an out-of-control jumble. It began to resonate with her that Taryn was thinking about her each of the days that she was thinking about Taryn. They were living parallel struggles, two people hurting at the same time. She believed fully that Taryn missed her, but she believed even more fully that for self-preservation purposes, she had to shelve any thought of rebuilding what they had.

"Back again," she said when she found Taryn sitting on the bench the next week.

"Letting me walk you home isn't going to change anything."

Charlie shrugged. "I suppose that's true."

Taryn didn't hesitate when Charlie inclined her head the slightest bit, and Taryn fell into step beside her. "How was the library today?"

"Pretty desolate. Everyone wants to be outside."

"I've been taking long walks. It's kind of my new thing."

"It is?" How strange to not know these kinds of details about someone who had been her everything not so very long ago.

"Yeah. It helps me clear my head and plan my week."

"Like what kind of delivery is coming to my house next?"

"Those are improvised," Taryn said, touching her heart. The sincerity of her tone pulled Charlie. Gone were the jokes, deadpans, and quips. Today, Taryn was present and calm and stripped down. "Are you ready to graduate?" she asked, eyes on the ground as they walked.

"Yes and no. I'm ready for the next chapter, but I have a lot of history here. A lot of memories." They'd fallen in love here.

"I see us all over campus."

"Me, too," Charlie said.

They walked in silence the rest of the way, and when Charlie was delivered to her door, Taryn raised a hand. "Thank you for this. For letting me walk with you."

Charlie lifted her shoulders. "I got tired of seeing the sad girl on the bench."

"I'd say my plan worked, but that's not what this is. I love you, and I'm gonna keep showing up."

Their walks from the library became a regular occurrence, and though Charlie didn't want to examine it too closely, she was beginning to look forward to the six minutes she got with Taryn. They touched on their days and plans for the summer and, once in a while, checked in on how the other was feeling about things.

"Do you miss us?" Taryn asked one night when they landed on Charlie's doorstep.

"More than you'll know," Charlie said. "But that doesn't mean I'm going to invite you in."

"Nor do I deserve to be. But guess what?" Taryn grinned. The first time in a while. God, Charlie had missed that smile. It was honestly everything.

"You're gonna keep showing up."

"Nailed it. 'Night, Charlie."

"Good night, Taryn."

Charlie's days on campus were growing short, and realizing that there would be no more six-minute walks with Taryn tugged at her. She didn't have the courage to leap back in, but at the same time the idea of saying good-bye to Taryn forever was enough to keep her awake at night. She needed guidance, some sort of sign to direct her onto the right path. "Any help, Mom?" she whispered into her darkened bedroom at two a.m. "Let me know where I'm supposed to be in this world, okay? Send an arrow sign. I need you."

Though her mother couldn't be at her graduation, it seemed the rest of the world's population was. Charlie, in green cap and gown, sat with the rest of her classmates on one of the most monumental days of her life. She'd completed her MFA, and nothing, she could safely say, had ever been as educational…or painstaking.

"I'm too excited to breathe," Emerson said, squeezing Charlie's hand from the seat next to hers. Her face went serious. "No. Literally, I keep forgetting to."

"Em, stop that. Air is required if you want to make it to that stage."

"Finally here, fuckers," Lawson said. "Never thought we'd all make it out alive."

"Emerson hasn't yet," Charlie offered. "She's not breathing."

"Nothing's ever easy with you all," Danny said with a shake of his above-it-all head.

Quietly, Charlie reveled. As one speech moved into the next, it became more of a reality that she'd made it to the finish line of three very demanding years. Sadness settled, however, when she realized that she didn't have a cheering section of her own. No parents or grandparents to cheer when her name was called. And that was okay. It wasn't anything she hadn't prepared for, but the poignancy of the moment made it all the more noticeable.

And then it was their turn. Her row, full of her friends and classmates from the creative writing trenches, walked to the stage and waited as one by one their names were called. As Charlie stood on the second stair waiting to move forward, she scanned the crowd of thousands in the arena, intent on taking in the image and memorizing the moment. There were balloons, flowers, and signs in abundance. Families sitting close together poised to support their loved ones. In the distance, a white sign pulled her focus, a giant arrow sign pointing to its owner. She smiled and then froze. She ascended to the next stair as her mind registered what she was looking at. Taryn stood in front of her chair, holding up a sign that said *Proud Human* with a huge downward-pointing arrow sign beneath. She ascended the final stair to the stage as it all came together.

"You sent my arrow sign, Mama," she murmured. She looked out, and Taryn met her gaze and smiled. Taryn tossed a celebratory fist in the air, and so did the man next to her, who Charlie was now realizing was Mr. Ross…who was seated next to Mrs. Ross. Taryn's parents jumped and waved. They'd come there for her. *Her*. She wasn't alone after all.

"Charlotte Adler," the announcer said. She beamed and, with tears in her eyes, crossed the stage, knowing that there were people in the audience sending love and support. In fact, she felt it all over. She posed with her diploma for the official photographer, returned to her seat, and let every inch of her vibrate with happiness. For once, she didn't reel the positivity back in but let it wash over her in a warm glow. Her mom was with her today, and sending the clear-as-day sign she'd asked for. Literally.

"We did it," Emerson said.

"We sure did," Charlie answered. "I can hardly believe it's real."

CHAPTER TWENTY-ONE

The arena was a madhouse when the graduation ended, and Taryn didn't want to get in the way of Charlie's celebration with her classmates. She'd take her parents to dinner and spend a little time with them and hope to connect with Charlie later. She'd be leaving soon. Taryn had glimpsed the boxes stacked up in her kitchen just a few nights prior.

"I know you two aren't together, but do you think she was happy to have us here cheering for her?" her dad asked on their way to the car. "I wanted her to know she had her own cheering section up there."

"I have a feeling she was, Dad."

"Graduations always get me," her mom said. "I cry, I scream, I want to pursue my doctorate every damn time. It's a whole journey. I need a steak."

Taryn laughed. "I know a place not far from here."

They had a lively dinner together, and when Taryn had a spare moment from the boisterous conversation, she quietly sent a text to Charlie and prayed she'd hear back.

Congratulations, C. Like the sign says, incredibly proud of all you've done. Time to talk later?

To her surprise, she didn't have to wait long for an answer.

Yes. Come over later. Let's talk.

What? Seriously? A bolt of electricity shot through her. Taryn's eyes went wide. Talking could go a lot of different directions, and she needed to calm down and prepare herself in case Charlie patted her on the head and told her to go kick rocks. If that was the case, she would respect Charlie's wishes, wish her all the best, and become the best kicker of rocks there'd ever been. The thought made her want to crumple in a corner, but she'd keep that part to herself and get through whatever conversation they were primed to have.

When she arrived at the Sailor's Sound apartment complex after hugging her parents good-bye, Charlie's Rogue was parked in front, which meant she was inside. Taryn stood in the darkness, staring at the warm glow from behind the curtain-adorned window. This was terrifying. The stakes were high, and there was so much to lose. Taryn exhaled, attempting to slow her breathing, a relaxation exercise that had been serving her well. These were the last few moments before her and Charlie's future would in all likelihood be decided once and for all. She hoped against all hope for the second chance she'd prayed for and prepared her brain for the opposite.

She made her way up the walk and knocked twice, aware of the sound of her heart beating alongside the chirping crickets. Charlie answered with a polite smile that gave nothing away. Her hair was down, looking soft and like she'd just run her fingers through it, probably as she was walking to the door. "Hey, come on in."

Taryn did. "You have an MFA now." She rocked forward and back on her heels like an amateur. But that was okay. She was here and doing this. "Has it sunk in?"

"No," Charlie said with a smile. She glanced behind her. "Can I get you something to drink? Wine? It's Saturday after all."

"No, thank you." She honestly couldn't imagine consuming anything, in this moment that was laced with so much tension, she almost couldn't move. "Did you get a chance to celebrate?"

"Nothing fancy. We went to Toby's one last time." She leaned back against the counter. Her gray joggers and pink T-shirt meant she was in relaxing mode, in for the night. "Had a round of beers just like we used to do after a particularly hard class. I'm going to miss them all, eclectic little family that we are."

Taryn nodded. "End of an era."

"Do you know what I don't want it to be the end of?" She paused, the ends of her mouth turning down for a moment as emotion overwhelmed. "Us." Her blue eyes glistened with tears. Did that mean what Taryn thought it meant?

She blinked and played the admission back to be sure she was interpreting it correctly. "What are you saying? Could you please make it very clear because I don't want to leap to any conclusions if you just mean—"

Charlie's mouth on hers silenced the request. She heard herself murmur happily as their lips clung and then began to move, slowly at first and then with more determination. They were making up for lost time, breathing in the same air, memorizing each other, an exploration of what had been lost and what could be regained. Taryn's arms went around Charlie's waist, pulling her impossibly closer, never wanting to let go ever again.

"This right here," Charlie said, hand on Taryn's heart. "This is what I need. *You* are what I need." She found Taryn's eyes. "If we do this, you can't for a second let anything come between us. Do you hear me?"

"Not gonna happen. I swear to you." Charlie kissed her softly in silent promise. "You make me brave, and I will fight every damn chance I get for you, for us. That's not something you ever have to worry about again."

"I love you," Charlie said quietly. "I was so mad at you, but I never stopped loving you."

"I know," Taryn said, resting her forehead against Charlie's. "I was so proud of you today."

"I felt it." Charlie covered her mouth as if remembering something. "Your parents were there and adorable."

"They drove up this morning." Taryn placed her hand on her head. "They insisted. I couldn't keep them away."

Charlie laughed. "It was the sweetest. I need to give them a call and say thank you."

"Definitely." Taryn stole another kiss and threaded their fingers. "But maybe not tonight?"

Charlie's arms went automatically around Taryn's neck. "Why? Did you have other plans for us?"

Taryn kissed the underside of her jaw. "I just forget what your room looks like is all."

"Oh yeah? You want me to remind you?"

Another kiss. "Yes, please."

Charlie cupped her cheek, smiled, and led the way.

They made love by the light of the moon slanting in through Charlie's window, and Taryn didn't take a single kiss, touch, or sigh for granted. When the night shifted into early morning, they were still awake catching each other up, Charlie in Taryn's arms laughing at the story of Caz locking herself in the bathroom.

"You're going to have keep me up to date on all the shenanigans once I go."

"Brooklyn, right?"

Charlie nodded. "I'm going to teach."

"Those undergrads have no idea what's about to hit them."

Charlie slid more fully on top and looked down at Taryn. "But I have the whole summer to write and settle in. Do you think you'd want to visit?"

"What if I more than visited? I hear they have summer school in New York. I could pick up a few credits there just as easily as here."

Charlie's eyes went wide. "You want to come to New York for the summer?"

"I definitely want to."

"Do you know how much I would love that?"

"Then it's decided. We're spending the summer together." Taryn couldn't hold back the smile if she tried. And when she returned to Hillspoint, she'd have a semester left to graduation before she could join Charlie fully. Everything was coming together, and her heart, which had been limping along just hours before, soared with new happiness and possibilities.

"And there it is," Charlie said.

"There's what?"

"That smile. It does me in every time."

"God, I love you," Taryn said and kissed her again, excited for the adventures ahead, ready to live their lives hand in hand.

"You know, it may not always be easy," Charlie said. "We have careers to figure out. A new city to navigate."

"My parents to wrangle when they visit."

"That, too," Charlie said, laughing.

Taryn's smile faded. "But as long as we have each other, we can conquer anything. I fully believe that."

Charlie slid her hand beneath Taryn's jaw. "That may be one of my favorite things you've ever said."

"I'll remind you every day."

In the quiet of the new day, they drifted off to sleep safely in each other's arms, limbs tangled, hearts full. Happy, warm, and madly in love.

EPILOGUE

Three years later

As Taryn opened the door, the sun bathed the small apartment in a warm, golden glow. It was late afternoon and she'd been gone since the darkness of the early morning, carried into the city on the C train full of quiet strangers. Grad school was kicking her ass in the best way possible, but she'd learned to use her commute to get a portion of studying done, proud of her 4.0, and ready for more. She had leads on several summer internships in Manhattan. Two of them paid pretty decently, which would certainly help pay the rent on her and Charlie's one-bedroom apartment in Brooklyn. The place wasn't fancy, and the appliances took turns needing repair, but it was theirs and radiated warmth and love.

"It smells amazing in here," Taryn said, craning her neck to see Charlie in the tucked-away kitchen in the corner.

"Hey, gorgeous. It's because I'm making impromptu lasagna with a sauce recipe I found on the internet."

"Then I vote yes on internet sauce." Taryn dropped her camera bag on the couch as she made her way to Charlie. "In fact, I could kiss you right now."

"You better."

She grinned and cupped Charlie's face in her hands, and they shared a sweet, lingering kiss.

"How was your Contemporary Trends presentation?" Charlie asked, coming up for air. "I was thinking about you all day. Sending the good vibes."

She leaned back against the counter, watching Charlie butter the garlic bread. "I don't know why I get so nervous about those things, especially when I was entirely prepared, but it went better than I'd even planned. Tons of questions after. Lots of class discussion, especially on the influence of social media on storytelling. Milagros, the instructor, pulled me aside and thanked me."

"Baby. That is the best news. I knew you were going to kill it. Did I mention this is celebratory lasagna? Because it is. All for you."

"Celebratory lasagna?" Taryn let her mouth fall open. "I had no idea. My afternoon keeps improving." For Taryn, there was simply nothing better than coming home at the end of a long day to the woman that she loved. The meal was merely a bonus.

"How was the commute?"

"The sunset over the skyline was breathtaking. I was ready with my camera this time and think I got some good shots. Did I mention I'm loving the lens you got me for my birthday? Getting tons of play off it."

"Oh yeah? That sales guy said it was incredibly versatile." She ran her hand absently in circles on Taryn's thigh. "Show me the photos when they're ready."

"You're on. How was your day?"

"Class this morning went well. This particular group of students is so eager. I absolutely love it when a group like this comes together."

"Those are my favorite classes, too."

"Finished another chapter and had a very productive call with my agent. I'll tell you what she had to say over dinner. It's surprising."

"I hate to wait. I'm too impatient for that." Taryn pursed her lips.

"Don't give me the pouty face. You know I crumble," Charlie said, pointing at Taryn with her wooden spoon. "We'll talk over dinner."

Taryn surveyed the clock above the oven. "Do I have time to change?"

"Is six minutes doable?"

She kissed Charlie's cheek. "Sold."

"A glass of wine with dinner? I'm having one."

"Double sold."

She dashed off with a smile and found her favorite pair of black joggers and a comfy sky-blue tee that had been washed a hundred times and was soft as a baby. Nearby on the dresser, she spotted the photo book she'd made for Charlie, reminding her of the journey that brought them to this very moment in time. A delicious shiver moved through her, and she grinned, aware of how lucky she was. Their shared vision for home was quite simply anywhere they could be together, and the corner unit in Brooklyn with the window seat fit the bill nicely.

Charlie didn't have the fancy job at a major publishing company that she'd always imagined, and Taryn didn't have the connections or experience level to make it as a big-time photographer in New York. *Yet.* But they dreamed their dreams side by side. They supported and encouraged each other to reach for the stars by day before falling into bed together at night, exhausted and happy. Taryn couldn't imagine anything better.

The lasagna was close. "You hit this out of the park," she said, staring down at her plate in reverence. "I think I'm going to cook tomorrow. I want to get better."

"Oh, do you really think you cooking is a good idea for all involved?" Charlie laughed behind her napkin, probably remembering the time Taryn served dry and charred roast beef that came with a crunch.

"Let's just have the delivery apps fired up and ready to go as backup," she deadpanned.

Charlie laughed. "You're on."

"So, what did the agent say?"

"She called about the book." Charlie had been working quietly on her novel for quite some time. Having started it in grad school, she'd been revising, draft by draft, until the book became the beautiful work that it now was, about a girl's coming of age and the events that propelled her adult trajectory to extreme ends. Taryn found it to be a tearjerker for sure, and knew others would devour it the way she had.

"And?" Her heart rate began to pick up pace.

"She's had a couple of nibbles but no real bites. She thinks we should put shopping the book on hold for now."

Taryn deflated. "What? No, no, no. I think you just haven't found the right publisher just yet. Tell her that it needs to be someone—"

"She did present me with a book deal for the short story, however. A really nice one."

A pause. "Wait. What? An actual book deal?"

"Formally issued, just waiting on a few last-minute details to be negotiated and my signature."

Taryn blinked, processing. Her stomach had dropped out from beneath her. "For a short story?"

"The little boy and the fire. Remember that one? My agent shared it on a whim. They love everything about it including my writing style. I took a meeting this morning with one of the executives at Luner Meyers and—"

"Luner Meyers? Luner Meyers is huge!" She was standing up at this point. "They're the biggest there is!"

Charlie laughed, beaming. No, *basking* in the moment. "That's true. You don't have to stand up, but that was a pretty great reaction."

"Come here," Taryn said. Charlie stood, too, and Taryn pulled her into the biggest hug imaginable. Then a kiss. Then another hug. Then a kiss until they were laughing and jumping up and down together in their tiny but adorable kitchen. "Do you have any idea how proud of you I am?" Taryn touched her heart, which had swollen exponentially, aching with joy. "This is the best news I've ever heard, and I don't know what to do with myself. My hands are all weird and moving wherever they want." She shoved them rigidly to her sides like boards.

"Let's sit," Charlie said, handing Taryn her glass of wine. "Drink this. It will help you relax and enjoy."

"We're definitely going to enjoy." She took a sip and set the glass down. "And you're damn right it's celebratory lasagna." They laughed again.

Over dinner, Charlie filled Taryn in on all the details of the meeting and the offer in front of them. It happened to come with some big numbers, including an advance that would make Charlie a significant amount of money.

"You're going to be rich," Taryn said in awe. "You'll be too important to talk to me."

Charlie stole a quick kiss. "Never. You're too sexy to not talk to." Another kiss. "And I'm going to buy you so many charms for your little bracelet."

"You remember my bracelet? You know, I still have it tucked away somewhere."

"Of course I remember." She reached into her pocket, pulled out a small felt satchel, and presented it to Taryn, who stared at her in question.

"What in the world?"

"Something small I picked up. For you. Open it."

Taryn did and inside found the very four-leaf clover charm she'd pined for as a kid. "What? Are you kidding me right now?"

"Your mom said that you never did get the cash together to buy it. But I think it's more fitting that I buy it for you because you're my good luck, Tare. Everything in my life that shines can be traced right back to you and the moment you shook up my world." As she spoke, Charlie had taken the charm from Taryn's hands and strung through it a silver chain, also in the felt bag. "And whenever you wear this, I hope you'll remember what a blessing you are in my life and how deeply I love you."

"I love you, too. And I'm so very proud of you." Taryn's eyes filled. "You received the biggest news of your life today. I should be showering you with gifts, not the other way around."

"I disagree." After fastening the necklace, Charlie leaned down and kissed Taryn softly. "This makes me happy. You do."

Taryn marveled at the incredible woman she shared her life with. There were big things ahead for Charlie and, hopefully, for herself as well. The best part of all of it, however, was that they'd experience every second of it together.

"Do you understand how happy I am right now? My heart almost can't contain it all."

"I'm happy, too. And when you're done with that lasagna love affair, maybe we can fully enjoy our evening." Charlie's eyes dipped to the neckline of Taryn's shirt and darkened in the way they always did when she was turned-on.

"Lasagna who?" Taryn asked.

"Smooth."

She offered her best sly grin. "I got a lotta smooth moves. I'm hoping to impress you, soon-to-be-published author and all."

"Oh yeah?"

"It might take some time, though. Are you free?"

Charlie looked skyward in thought. "Pretty much for the rest of my life."

Taryn felt the grin hit her face and grow. "Best answer ever."

There weren't a ton of things in life that Taryn could say were permanent. Politics, fashion trends, buzzwords, technology, and the weather were all in constant transformation. But as sure as she was in the moon and stars, Taryn knew that she and Charlie would walk through this world together, gathering experiences and important moments to carry with them for always. She knew they'd fill a million photo books along the way, and she, for one, couldn't wait to watch them pile up. They'd also build a family one day, having already estimated two to three children, but decided they'd play that decision by ear. In the meantime, Taryn wanted to soak in every moment they had together, creating stories on paper and pixels and film.

"Today was everything," Taryn told Charlie later that night as she lay naked and gorgeous in Taryn's arms. She ran a hand absently up and down Charlie's back.

Charlie lifted her face. "I loved every minute of it." She placed a sweet kiss on Taryn's lips and studied her. "Let's do it again tomorrow. What do you think?"

Taryn arched a brow and pulled Charlie close. "If you're there, I'm there."

About the Author

Melissa Brayden (www.melissabrayden.com) is a multi-award-winning romance author, embracing the full-time writer's life in San Antonio, Texas, and enjoying every minute of it.

Melissa is married and working really hard at remembering to do the dishes. For personal enjoyment, she spends time with her Jack Russell terriers and checks out the NYC theater scene as often as possible. She considers herself a reluctant patron of spin class, but would much rather be sipping merlot and staring off into space. Bring her coffee, wine, or donuts and you'll have a friend for life.

Books Available From Bold Strokes Books

And Then There Was One by Michele Castleman. Plagued by strange memories and drowning in the guilt she tried to leave behind, Lyla Smith escapes her small Ohio town to work as a nanny and becomes trapped with an unknown killer. (978-1-63679-688-8)

Digging for Destiny by Jenna Jarvis. The war between nations forces Litz to make a choice. Her country, career, and family, or the chance of making a better world with the woman she can't forget. (978-1-63679-575-1)

Hot Hires by Nan Campbell, Alaina Erdell, and Jesse J. Thoma. In these three romance novellas, when business turns to pleasure, romance ignites. (978-1-63679-651-2)

McCall by Patricia Evans. Sam and Sara found love on the water, but can they build a future amid the ghosts of the past that surround them on dry land? (978-1-63679-769-4)

Promises to Protect by Jo Hemmingwood. Park ranger Maxine Ward's commitment to protect Tree City is put to the test when social worker Skylar Austen takes a special interest in the commune and in Max. (978-1-63679-626-0)

Sacred Ground by Missouri Vaun. Jordan Price, a conflicted demon hunter, falls for Grace Jameson, who has no idea she's been bitten by a vampire. (978-1-63679-485-3)

The Land of Death and Devil's Club by Bailey Bridgewater. Special Liaison to the FBI Louisa Linebach may have defied all odds by identifying the bodies of three missing men in the Kenai Peninsula, but she won't be satisfied until the man she's sure is responsible for their murders is behind bars. (978-1-63679-659-8)

When You Smile by Melissa Brayden. Taryn Ross never thought the babysitter she once crushed on would show up as a grad student at the same university she attends. (978-1-63679-671-0)

A Heart Divided by Angie Williams. Emmaline is the most beautiful woman Jack has ever seen, but being a veteran of the Confederate army that killed her husband isn't the only thing keeping them apart. (978-1-63679-537-9)

Adrift by Sam Ledel. Two women whose lives are anchored by guilt and obligation find romance amidst the tumultuous Prohibition movement in 1920s California. (978-1-63679-577-5)

Cabin Fever by Tagan Shepard. The longer Morgan and Shelby are stranded together, the more their feelings grow, but is it real, or just cabin fever? (978-1-63679-632-1)

Clean Kill by Anne Laughlin. When someone starts killing people she knows in the recovery world, former detective Nicky Sullivan must race to stop the killer and keep herself from being arrested for the crimes. (978-1-63679-634-5)

Only a Bridesmaid by Haley Donnell. A fake bridesmaid, a socially anxious bride, and an unexpected love—what could go wrong? (978-1-63679-642-0)

Primal Hunt by L.L. Raand. Anya, a young wolf warrior, finds herself paired with Rafe, one of the most powerful Vampires in the Americas, in an erotic union of blood and sex.(978-1-63679-561-4)

Snake Charming by Genevieve McCluer. Playgirl vampire Freddie is on the run and a chance encounter with lamia Phoebe makes them both realize that they may have found the love they'd given up on. (978-1-63679-628-4)

Spirits and Sirens by Kelly and Tana Fireside. When rumored ghost whisperer Elena Murphy and very skeptical assistant fire chief Allison Jones have to work together to solve a 70-year old mystery, sparks fly—will it be enough to melt the ice between them and let love ignite? (978-1-63679-607-9)

Aubrey McFadden Is Never Getting Married by Georgia Beers. Aubrey McFadden is never getting married, but she does have five weddings to attend, and she'll be avoiding Monica Wallace, the woman who ruined her happily ever after, at every single one. (978-1-63679-613-0)